OVERDRIVE

A NOVEL

DAVID HAIGHT

Beavers Pond Press Inc.

Edina, Minnesota

ISBN 10: 1-59298-114-3
ISBN 13: 978-1-59298-114-4

Library of Congress Catalog Number: 2005904644

Book design and typesetting: Mori Studio, Inc.
Cover design: Mori Studio, Inc.

Printed in the United States of America

First Printing: July 2005

08 07 06 05   6 5 4 3 2 1

Beaver's Pond Press, Inc.   7104 Ohms Lane, Suite 216
Edina, MN 55439
(952) 829-8818
www.BeaversPondPress.com

To order, visit *www.BookHouseFulfillment.com* or call
1-800-901-3480. Reseller and special sales discounts available.

At this point I can no longer avoid
actually answering the question
how one becomes what one is

—Friedrich Nietzsche *Ecce Homo*

ACKNOWLEDGEMENTS

For helping transform my manuscript into a publishable novel, I need to thank Adria Fernandez for her meticulous and quality work. I also need to thank Jennifer Manion for being the most intelligent, compassionate, and enthusiastic editor a writer could ever find. Thank you so much for everything you contributed. *Overdrive* wouldn't have been the same without you.

I should also like to thank everyone at Mori Studio not only for their great design work but for taking the time to match their work to the character of the novel. For this I am grateful. I'd also like to acknowledge Beaver's Pond Press.

I would like to give a special word of thanks to Kevin Crossley-Holland for being the first person to recognize my abilities as writer—I am forever grateful for the time you spent with me, and the things you taught me I still find invaluable; to Lawrence Sutin for challenging me, in my writing and my thinking, like no one ever has; and to Deborah Keenan for her endless compassion and support. I couldn't have become the writer I am without the belief the three of you showed in me.

To the immortals James Joyce, Brian Wilson, Frank Sinatra, and Charlie Chaplin, who have been my inspiration. And to Friedrich Nietzsche and Arthur Rimbaud—this book is published in the spirit of Zarathustra and the Season!

To my father, the most amazing man I have ever known.

I also need to give a special acknowledgement to my mother. If there's any one person who has made me who I am—it is you. Freud once wrote that "If a man has been his mother's undisputed darling he retains throughout his life the triumphant feeling, the confidence in success, which not seldom brings actual success along with it." I don't think I need to tell you that he was right.

And to my love, Ronnie. I have no words that could do you justice. You are perfect.

RAINBOWS

BY

DONALD LIPMAN

*I*t had been a terrible night. It was nearly impossible to wade through the small talk with people I barely knew. Several times the conversation, as smothering as the cigarette smoke that consumed the room, forced me into the bathroom just to sit alone. The worst was that I knew that my intolerance was not caused by these people or their conversation. Nothing had actually happened to make this a terrible night. It was what hadn't happened.

I had been falling in love with her for months. I was so ensnared by her that I immediately knew that love would be the natural conclusion for my budding feelings. Yet how did I know that? There had been no indication that she felt the same: no secret glances, no innuendo, no attempts to even sit by me. I, on the other hand, had done everything short of telling her how much I adored her. And I did even this! Leaving a club, destroyed by the attention she had been giving another man, hypnotized by her beauty, I picked up my coat, approached her as determined as I had ever been about anything and, as I said goodbye, whispered, "I've adored you for months!" If she heard me, I'll never know. I turned away, and dashed out the door before I could see her response. All I know is that it was never mentioned.

But on this night I was determined to make a friend of patience, hoping that it would lead me into her heart. I wanted none of that "patience for patience's sake" crap. I didn't want to learn to appreciate patience, or to learn something about myself. This girl was not a vehicle for self-exploration. Least of all did I want to become an object lesson for impatience. If I had to be patient it would be only because I wanted her. Yet all it had led me to was the memorization of I'm a Fool to Want You.

She was Cleopatra and I, a court jester. She wore a long white robe with a thick cardboard gold belt delicately encircling her waist like a hand around freshly picked flowers. She discarded her wig, which almost immediately became too hot too wear, leaving her long, thick, blond hair bobbing over her shoulders. In the pictures that I would later examine, I would place my thumb over my new friends: the bee, the porn star, the witch, and my girlfriend, the nurse, and say to the witch, "We look good together, don't we? Like a couple. I mean we'd be a cute couple, don't you think?"

The party eventually ended but no one wanted to leave. We had all exhausted everything that a one-bedroom apartment, a VCR, and a couple cases of beer could offer. Reminded that the porn star lived by a lake, we decided to take a walk. We felt the cool relief of dawn in the crisp, uncompromising air. It was an air that the beer, the cigarette smoke, and even the conversation couldn't dull.

To my surprise I found us walking ahead of everyone else—and at her prerogative. The long, steady strides that she set did not seem like those of a seasoned runner but the tangible representation of a direction: our direction. My fingers trembled as if they were speaking all the words I wanted to say. It didn't occur to me that I was the only one willing to walk at her pace.

The lake was calm but looked cold. The sun had come up some time ago when we were just over halfway around. I smiled. We had just spent the night together. It was semantics, but I took it and held onto it. To my joy we had outpaced the rest of our friends when she suggested we stop and take a break. "If you want. I could keep going."

"No, let's wait for everyone. I feel bad."

"Oh, okay," I said, my head falling.

We stood in silence. She stood, her back turned to me, watching our colorful friends slowly, slowly catching up to us. With each step I saw my chances at winning her diminishing.

"Why don't we roll up our pants and wade in the lake a little? It might be refreshing." It was so sadly a ridiculous proposition that I nearly told her that I was joking.

To my amazement, she thought it was a good idea. She slipped off her sandals and I my jester slippers, we pulled up our respective costumes to our knees, and waded into the ice-cold water.

We heard the voices of our approaching friends, which heralded the closing of our night together. I was in a panic to say something, but I was paralyzed. I just looked at her. She was so beautiful.

"Is that a rainbow?"

"Where?" I asked.

"Across the lake. Toward the horizon."

I looked up and indeed there was a rainbow, wide and faded like memories, soon to be overtaken by the forgetfulness of the breaking day. What caught my eye was the sky, how it seemed to part, to move out of the way, to create space for this apparition of beauty, and how the rainbow, so remarkable, seemed to turn its back on the indistinct sky. The rolls of my court jester pants slid from my knees into the water.

She looked at me blankly and said, "Isn't it strange how we can see it from here, but if we were to actually be there we'd find nothing?"

"Yeah."

"It makes them so mystical. Don't you think?"

It is always the case that when something cannot be possessed it becomes that much more desirable. I looked at her. We are surrounded by rainbows.

"I like your costume," she suddenly said.

I looked at her. Our friends were upon us.

GIRL

2

She had remained lying, unmoving, listening to his breathing. Although she was certain he had fallen into an immediate deep sleep, she couldn't find a compelling reason to pick herself up, to get out. Her things lay scattered around the room and at her side was this man, weighty but empty of substance. She simply remained motionless, staring into the still dark, listening to his breathing. It had that quality of a sleeping person: sonorous, as if he were trying to catch his breath. But she knew this wasn't correct. This desperateness was steady. She listened to him exhale once more. It was the sound of a man attempting to catch his breath who knew he never could. She leaned over him as he exhaled again. His breath was warm and ugly. Cigarettes! The desire for one entered her consciousness like a mute flash of dry lightning on the somber horizon.

Her eyes began to scan the floor nervously. Even in the night's obscurity, she could make out darknesses upon darkness, places where the uniformity of blackness was interrupted. She could sense the boundaries and mass the same way she might feel a stranger's eyes on her back. Not even the darkness was terminal. Within a few moments, she was sure that she had found everything she had formerly disregarded.

She uncovered herself cautiously, exposing her arms and torso (which was simple enough) followed by her legs (which was exceedingly difficult) and managed to slip from beneath the sheet without disturbing him. Not that she was concerned with his comfort. But she feared (dreaded) his awakening. He was an awful bore and not all that bright. She had concluded that his conversation, once so attractive, now had the effect of a hot breeze: neither refreshing nor desired again after experiencing it once. He was okay to look at though.

When she lifted the sheet, she had caught a brief glimpse of his naked body. He appeared shrunken to her eyes, a boy in a man's body. She was constantly surrounded by boys, boys pretending to be men. Failures. All failures. Having a sword does not make you a knight, she thought. She tried to laugh but could not call up the energy. Before getting up she glanced at him once more. Whatever it was that caused her to find him necessary was now gone. Throwing her legs over the side of the bed, she sat up, slightly hunched and tired but not exhausted. Then, without warning, he began to stir. She did not know what to do; her body seized in panic. But before she could even review her options, it was over. He did not wake, but merely stretched out in the bed, overtaking the emptiness she had left. His more comfortable position proved what she already knew: he did not expect or even want her to stay. His had been an insincere invitation.

Still, finding it difficult to leave, she attempted to finish her list of things to do that she had started as he began that tiresome build-up to his orgasm: pay car insurance, pick up Claudia's birthday card (making sure it expresses regret at having forgotten), get nails done. This is where she had stopped. Or, rather, where he had stopped, flopping clumsily beside her. She now added to her mental list: fill gas tank tomorrow morning. No use putting herself in any additional danger.

With this finished, she bent over, allowing her hand to search the floor. Within seconds her hand had deposited in her lap a number of her disregarded things. Like a pair of experienced eyes, her hands sorted and separated the items. Without any concern for order she put on her bra, quickly followed by her underwear and pants. After a few more moments of searching, she found and put on her shirt. When this was accomplished, she paused, tilting her head back toward the sleeper. His breathing continued uninterrupted. He was unaffected by her activity.

She found and lightly shook her purse to make sure her keys were in it (they were) and headed for the door. She opened it slowly, slipped through, and shut it behind her. She did not look back nor did she have an inclination to. Once in her car, she lit a cigarette and began driving. Although it wasn't a terribly long journey, it was one traveled by roads poorly lit or abandoned altogether. She passed no other cars and saw and thought of no one. The only sound she heard was the sound of the road passing beneath her. She looked straight ahead, unconcerned with the sky, the night, the trees, occasionally bringing the cigarette to her mouth but never letting it out of her hand.

Coming over a slight incline, she saw a red blinking radio tower. She was close to the trailer park where she lived; she was close to home. Ever since she was a little girl, this tower had appeared as something both fascinating and mysterious, communicating without language. It seemed to be drawing her near, its red lights blinking over and over like welcoming hands bidding her forward, its purpose shrouded in a mute serenity. Sitting in the backseat of her parents' car, or driving herself home now, she was incapable of taking her eyes off it. As the telephone poles, trees, and landscape passed her at various speeds, it stood perfectly still. What did it want? She would willingly pursue its beckoning, its character of unknowingness never a liability, her curiosity holding fear hostage. Yet when it approached, at that moment when contact seemed inevitable, the tower crept past, waving unremorsefully in the rearview mirror, offering itself to the next passing driver. It was one of those many instances in which something beckons, only to dismiss. Viewing it was only a prelude to its absence. She ashed out the window as she passed it. There was something about its denial of communion that she felt represented her many relationships. And yet every time she drove home, there it was. It was that temporariness that she found so haunting; it was so permanent. She thought of the man lying naked in his boy's bed. This was not different from any of the other times. She first refused the look of the tower, then peered restlessly into her rearview to watch it fade into the distance without ever disappearing.

She forgot about that man and immediately thought about Joe and all of the things he had said; all of the hurtful things that stuck to her like cotton on barbed wire. Why was it that the words always remained? They had a power that no physical experience could match. Her memories of living with him, of having sex with him, were as brief as a flashbulb's flash. Even now—she had moved to a different state, got a new job in a different field, and was finishing school at night in a different major. Her whole life seemed to be a quest to get away from those intangible afterimages. Worst of all was the fact that she was now twenty-five and she still hadn't let go of Joe. She cursed herself. Yanking a folded-up piece of paper out of her purse, she furiously rolled her window down and held it out. It struggled to loosen itself from her fingers. She knew she couldn't let it go. She had never met anyone with the imaginative powers that Joe had; powers that could mirror her back to herself. Since then she hadn't found fulfillment. Between college and becoming an adult she had gone from a strong woman to a pathetically weak, self-destructive woman. "Maybe I am necessarily incomplete," was the thought that always seemed to accompany her now. "So it doesn't matter what I let happen to my body." When she felt it had been long enough, she brought the paper back into the car, rolled the window back up, and placed it delicately back into her purse.

For a brief moment, she had no idea where she was. The surroundings were foreign, as if her car had been lifted in perfect smoothness from one trail of blackness and set on another. No matter how closely one paid attention to things, big things, they still seemed to slide by, to surprise and haunt. It was at first confusing, then quickly awful; her head began to spin and her thoughts ceased to make sense. Then, thought ceased all together. For a moment she thought she was going to lose consciousness. Her hands loosened from the wheel. But she wouldn't indulge. This would have been sinful. She pulled herself out of her self-induced confusion. Everything had a simple answer. Of this she was convinced. She looked around and proved herself correct. She had missed her exit.

As she continued driving, she confirmed another of her beliefs: serendipity was a bitch. She had never missed her exit before nor had she ever driven north of it. And now she knew why that she'd been lucky: there was not another exit for quite some time. The first sign told her eighteen miles. She sighed and lit another cigarette. Little things always seemed to cost her so much.

She considered just going through the ditch and turning around, but it was late and she was impatient with her mistakes. She even slowed down and began pulling over, but something prevented her. The lines on the road seemed to bolt in the opposite direction, warning the curious wanderer to avoid those unseen places in life. She sped up. She continued driving. Even after eighteen miles she ignored that first chance to exit. She watched without so much as a wink of acknowledgement as the sign and exit passed her by.

She allowed several more exits to pass. There was nothing about them that interested her. Nor did she have any desire to turn around for home. In fact, she never thought of home as home, at least not the way other people did, as a place of comfort or solace. For her, her trailer was a place where she slept and occasionally ate, a place where she stored her clothes, where her small black and white television sat on a small coffee table, and where her answering machine stared in constant mute friendship.

As she progressed, she noticed long stretches of fields to her right. She wasn't sure if they had just appeared, or if maybe she hadn't been paying attention before, but now they stood beside the road like rows of soldiers flat on their stomachs, flush with the ground. The wind was strong, pushing and pulling the long stalks of grass. She pulled over and got out.

The sound of crickets was deafening, pulsating like a flickering light that couldn't be seen and filling her ears like the buzz and snap of some horrible voice. The sound hissed at her without any regard for her reason for being there, for now it seemed there was a reason. For a moment, her pleasure diminished. She did not want to be saved. She turned to leave, to head for her tiny, messy place. She even kicked at the ground like she did when she was a little girl, scattering a mess of pebbles. Watching those pebbles disperse brought to mind something she had heard once. She'd been at a party, and someone was talking about Buddhism. She was quite bored, but something struck her as at least partially interesting, though she would never have confessed it. This person said that enlightenment was like diving into a pond without causing the water to ripple. She didn't know what this meant. It was probably just a line to get laid. But at this moment, those words struck her as somehow important again.

Turning back to the field, she closed her eyes and listened without effort or self-consciousness. She released from her mind the missed exit, home, the bed she had just been made on, and her wrinkled and subtly smelling clothing that looked as though it had been worn, abandoned for sleep, and taken on again too early in the morning. The sound of crickets disappeared. In its place came the wind's, a kind of low hush, as if it were hovering just above the ground. It whispered to the blades of grass, to the dirt, to the lake far off in the distance. It danced marvelously, spinning and sliding through the grass and fields like fingers through the earth's hair, scooping all of its troubles up into tiny pools of condensation as an offering to the morning sun. Weakened by an overabundance not of emotion but of complete surrender, like sleep or faintness, she stood like a needle stuck into the ground, the wind passing through her body and mind, which stood emptied, bordered only by her quiet breathing. The past fell from her like overripe fruit, and the future—or was it just anxiety— came to rest on her shoulder like a giant bird. She opened her eyes and looked around, confused, as if she had just been awakened from a trance. She didn't know how long she had been standing there.

But she knew that something was missing. Without realizing it, she raised her arms as if to embrace someone or something. She took one step forward, and the presence that was strong when her eyes were closed but that had pulled away when she opened them, pulled farther away again. She took another step and a coldness fell upon her like sickness. Her thoughts raced like bullets. She looked around to appeal to something. She found nothing. The wind had died completely.

"No! No!" she whispered. "Please. Please don't go," she said taking another step forward. Now she was deep into the long grass. She could almost see it fleeing from her. She reached out again but found nothing. "Please!" she said,

11

now yelling, holding her fists to the grass. It darted again. She rushed it, angry, then pleading. Stepping forward with weak steps, then angling slightly left toward a large pine tree, she took a hard left until she circled the tree, crossing her own path. She stumbled into a near run for several yards, trying to follow a sound—a presence—whose origin was impossible to determine and that kept moving. Finally, ending ankles deep in a cold, slimy swamp, she begged, "Why? Why? Please come back!"

She could sense that presence in the swamp, could feel it rolling over the grass and stalks and earth, over everything except her. Her anger and desperation was about to resume with renewed force, but then it stopped.

"No, no. God, no ..."

She looked in panic at the path she had made, her throat tightening. Behind her were crippled stalks and broken branches, witnesses to the destruction she had caused. It was as if she had traveled down a hallway into a room, leaving her to face walls of rushes with no apparent exit. She felt she was being told something horrible, something made all worse because of its beauty. But the message she longed for, the message she thought she had just received, was not accessible to her. The message was not for her. She was eavesdropping but couldn't fully hear.

"I'm sorry... I didn't mean to... please... please come back..."

Whatever she had sensed or felt or wanted had now slipped away, and was hiding in distances.

"I can't go. Please don't make me go. Please."

Steadying herself, she lay down on the stalks that she herself destroyed, the only ones she felt she could lay claim to. She whispered, "Let me near you." She lay there long after she knew that enlightenment, or something she identified as enlightenment, was to be forever denied her. She cried, knowing that whatever was out there had pulled away from her and that it should have. Finally, when that presence was no nearer to her than the moon, she got up, returned to her car, pulled back onto the highway and lit a cigarette, still heading away from her small, messy house.

After an hour of driving she finally exited.

There was only one main street and it was quite deserted. It looked as if everything had been closed up for hours. She glanced at the clock on her dashboard. 12:47. She wondered how it could have gotten so late so quickly. But this was academic. She didn't feel the effects of time and hadn't for a long while. It could have been seven in the morning, two in the afternoon, or this 12:47. It all felt the same. Sunup or sundown made no difference; it only changed the backdrop. She never felt fully awake or dreadfully tired. It was all limbo: strange, numbing, indifferent limbo.

Looking forward, she could see that the road was going to give up its businesses and revert to residences or fields or barns. These were things of no concern to her. At that moment, a small light on the right side of the road caught her eye. She slowed. Pulling nearer, she realized that it was a church, though not a very large one. In fact, it looked as if it might have been a government building at some point, maybe an old town hall. Yet it still exuded that melancholy presence that churches have. The entire building looked at her with drooping, sluggish eyes, eyes that would not be pleased with all they saw but that were sad enough not to reject anything. She pulled into its parking lot and killed the engine. The car seemed to lower itself to the ground in an act of surrender or rest. Her own body relaxed in the driver's seat and she sat for a while, wondering if she should go in. She knew that, like the building, the men inside would not reject her, no matter what the hour and no matter what her story.

She exited the car and headed not for the church but for Charlie's, a small bar across the street.

Entering the bar, she was taken back at how small it was. The bar itself ran the entire length of the place, which couldn't have been more than twelve feet. Between the stools and the back wall, in the space of only five or six feet, stood three unoccupied tables. She approached the bar and took a stool, leaving another in between her and the nearest person, a large man who didn't seem to notice her.

The bartender approached slowly.

"What'll it be?" he asked. His voice was deep, almost hard to hear.

"A beer." She paused. "Whatever you have on tap."

The bartender turned around, picking up a glass, and walked toward the tap. He returned shortly.

"Keep the change," she said.

He nodded.

She finished her beer quickly, knowing before she even started it that she wasn't going to have another. Whatever dim possibilities she had hoped this night might have shown were extinguished long before they had been given a chance. As she rose to leave, a man sat next to her and ordered a beer. With the abruptness and nearness, the timing with which he chose to sit next to her, she knew it was not coincidence. She had seen him enter a few moments before, occupying himself by standing in front of the television, feigning to make a call, surprised, as he patted himself down, that he didn't have change, then heading in her direction. She sat back down but was surprised when he ordered only one beer.

He was halfway through before he acknowledged her. Although surprising to her, he displayed a patience most men lacked.

"Hello."

"Hi."

"I'll have another beer," he said, turning away from her.

She frowned, defeated. There was patience and then there was rudeness and if he wouldn't flirt with her, he was rude. Perhaps she had been wrong. She looked at him. When he didn't acknowledge the weight of her glance, she peered hopelessly into her glass, which the bartender had not yet taken. After staring at the warm puddle of beer in its bottom, she looked to the stranger once more. Perhaps he hadn't felt her watching him. Or perhaps he had been too afraid to appear forward. Again he failed to respond.

"Not very polite," she finally muttered.

"What's that?" he asked uninterested, not looking at her but straight ahead at the back wall.

"Most men would offer a girl a drink."

"You seem quite finished." He turned toward her. "Or at least you seemed quite finished when I sat down," he added as an afterthought.

When he still refused to order her a beer, she did so herself. She was tired of every meeting with a man being part of some game she had no recollection of wanting to play, being told why she was playing, or how she was to win. But worse than that, she was tired of herself. She had the routine down cold: look lonely until a man approaches, act interested in everything he says, agree to go to bed with him. Oh, there were a few middle steps, like murmuring "I'm not interesting," when he finally asks about you, which usually takes an embarrassingly long time. Men love to talk about themselves. "I'd rather hear about you," you say with a smile. Men want to hear certain things, have their women a certain way, and listening is the only way to figure those things out. They mostly want the same things anyway: to be right, to have sex on demand, to do whatever they want, whenever they want. Reverse it and that was what they want from you. Not this time. Instead, she decided to just talk, to just push all the bullshit out of the way. She wouldn't wait for him to approach her. She would only act interested if he was interesting and she wouldn't agree to anything. But most important, she wanted to get as far away from herself as possible.

"I would have said this place was small or possibly charming or maybe even 'real' having no pretenses, a 'real,' bar, but it's not."

"No?" he asked, looking at her with sincere curiosity.

"No, it's a dump, a shithole." She did not lower her voice to keep it from the bartender who couldn't care less. "It's old, dirty. Look at my glass," she said lifting her spot-covered glass for inspection. "A real dump. And here I sit," she finished, self-satisfied, her loose speech a revelation. Her body fell back relaxed upon the stool.

"So what are you doing here then?"

For a brief moment she felt the compulsion to leave without a word or a backward glance. She even felt the pressure on the balls of her feet. She hung her head momentarily before looking up.

"I don't think it really matters, do you?"

"I suppose not," he said with a nod of the head. "But if this is a shithole..."

"I'm not disapproving. It is what it is. And I am simply recognizing that. I just want to be clear."

"You are," he said.

"Thank you."

"I'm Dan, by the way."

"Caroline," she said, downing the last of her beer and motioning the bartender for another. "And I suppose you're wondering what's on my mind, what's keeping me in this place at this hour?"

"I was a little curious. I'm just sitting here minding my business, enjoying a drink, when this woman starts speaking loudly about what a dump she's in. Especially when it was abundantly clear that from the moment I came in you wanted me to sit by you and wanted, no, expected, me to buy you are beer."

"I did want you to buy me a beer," she said as her fresh beer arrived. Smiling, Dan started for his wallet. "But not anymore." She waved Dan aside and paid herself. "I did want you to sit by me at first. Now I don't care what you do."

"So I offended you?"

"No. Not at all. I'm here for me now. I'm going to buy my own drinks and talk about whatever I want to talk about and you're going to listen, whether you want to or not." Dan did not move.

"So what *exactly* do you want to talk about?" he asked.

She knew she hadn't been wrong about him. This time, however, she was in charge.

"Who says there's anything and, second, who says that it's any of your business?"

"It's not. But really, what does it matter? You don't know me and I certainly don't know you. The odds of us ever seeing one another are... I don't know... slim. So just let it fly." As he finished he smiled at her, raising his hands in a gesture of acceptance almost as if he were waiting for a hug. She said nothing. She would not be bullied.

"You're like that sign there," he said nodding to a small, wooden frame with the words FREE BEER TOMORROW painted in black across it.

"I'm like the sign 'FREE BEER TOMORROW'? Gee, that's flattering. I'm really glad I nearly talked to you."

He pushed forward undaunted.

"You sit there with a pretty straightforward thing you want to say, or think you want to say, but you'll wait. You'll promise to tell me, or whoever," he said in anticipation of the interruption that was beginning to assert itself, "tomorrow or, in other words, never."

"Fine. So you want to know what I'm doing here at this hour. I have a friend that lives a little north of here in Litchfield. I was almost there when I just stopped here. Didn't call her to say I wasn't coming. Nothing."

"Why?"

"Because of the church across the street. I pass it every time I go to Cynthia's and it's so damn ugly I just had to see what it was like inside."

"Were you disappointed?" he asked.

"No. It was ugly. Then I saw this place and I thought a drink might be nice before I head home."

"And home is ..."

She gathered up her keys and purse, stood up, looked at Dan and said, "I'm leaving."

He waited until she was at the door before asking, "What's wrong?"

"I am not going to have this happen again!" she said, the door handle in her hand, her purse dangling furiously. "You're all the same. You act nice, considerate. You pretend to be interested in me and ask me all these subtle questions until you know where I work, where I hang out, and where I live. I know how this goes and I will not allow one more freak to follow me!"

"Hey, I really don't care where you work or live," he said, turning back to the bar and his drink. "You're not that interesting. I was just being nice. I'm sorry if you've had that happen but I'm not like that."

Caroline waited. She seemed to be weighing his words, trying to determine if he was sincere or manipulating her. But in fact she was so involved watching herself and the scene that she had just made that she was barely aware of him. She didn't realize how liberating lying could be. Slowly, she made her way back to the bar, a sustained look of suspicion on her face. She was aware of every move she made.

For the next hour Dan hardly spoke. Instead, he was treated to every sort of lie that Caroline could think of. She invented and killed off a sister she never had, nearly bringing herself to tears as she recalled how Annie carved her initials in a pew at church. *I don't think Mom was as mad as she acted; Annie was never punished. I can still see the light pink and blue dresses we wore. White on Easter. This was the real reason I stopped at the church across the street. I always feel her in churches.* She told him about her struggle with diet pills, her temporary conversion to Judaism. Dan did what she had always done—listened— though she knew he was calculating how to become intimate with her. Caroline smiled deviously. It couldn't work. All of his strategies would be based on a person who did not exist!

"Shouldn't you call your friend?" he finally asked, glancing at his watch.

Looking at him, she nearly confessed everything: the lies, how she happened onto this bar, how wrong everything was. How she had just had sex with another person who didn't matter to her, and who didn't want her after, and how it made her sad even though she'd never admit it. How she had missed her exit but couldn't find any reason to turn around and instead stopped at a field. But how could she tell him of that wonderful something she had experienced? How it left her and it was the worst leaving she had ever felt. How she wanted to say thank you even though it ran from her. But instead I destroy things, she would say. I fall on things. I wreck things. And why isn't happiness ever for me? "She's probably in bed," was all she could say, looking into her lap, ashamed.

Dan lowered his head in an attempt to catch her eyes. "What's wrong?" He touched her wrist but quickly withdrew.

"Do these pants make me look fat?" she said, still staring into her lap.

They both laughed.

"I've always thought that they did."

"You look all right to me," he said matter-of-factly.

"So do you," she said. "I can't believe I just told you that," she said speaking into her chest, blushing.

"Why?" he asked.

"You didn't really mean it in a come-on kind of way. You were just saying that I looked okay."

"And you did?" he asked with a grin.

"Well, yes. I guess I did."

"I would have said that to you as a come-on, but you looked kind of serious. Looking at you now, smiling, I will definitely tell you, you look nice. Why don't we move to a table?" he asked rising. He led her to the table. He was accustomed to dancing around things like attraction and, with her being so direct, he didn't know what to say once they had moved from the bar and the game to the table and honesty. He looked away, running his hand over his rough chin as he always did when nervous. He knew she was now looking at him and what her glance was waiting for.

"Just let me get us a few beers first. On me. If that's okay? Okay."

He looked to the bartender, as old and faded as the paint on the walls, who didn't notice him, and nodded. Looking back at her he laughed nervously. "Guess he didn't see me." Now she smiled nervously.

He rose from his chair and walked to the bar.

"You do look nice. No doubt about that," he stated as he returned with the beers, knowing that he was now coming on to her.

"Just give me a second," she said holding up an empty pack of cigarettes, stopping him before his come-on became too obvious and unbearable. "I need to get more."

"Okay, right over there, behind you."

She came back to the table.

"I have to confess something," he said with a wry half-smile.

"What's that?" she asked eagerly, leaning forward and crossing her legs.

"I really don't know how to do this. You're so honest. Don't get me wrong: it's refreshing. I'm just not used to being honest myself. I don't know if I can do it." As he spoke he looked up. Her face, full of pregnant joy, began to pull into its familiar frown, disappointed, like a paperweight lifted off a page that flexes back to its natural curl. "I guess I'm going to have to be honest," he said. She was again transported.

They sat in silence.

"So where do you work?" he finally asked cautiously.

She exhaled, strangely relieved. "I'm a customer service representative for GHT, a computer business. Dealing with ... fact is I don't really know what they do. All that computer crap. Who understands it anyway, right?" He laughed. "A bunch of nerds who couldn't have a good time if you let them loose in the Heineken Brewery in Amsterdam, for fuck's sake!"

"No doubt," he said, laughing. "You've been to Amsterdam?" he asked, impressed.

"Well, no."

"Oh, I didn't mean to … I haven't either. I know what you mean. I work for a small drafting firm—"

"Around here?"

"No, I have to commute into town. But it's the same thing. Dull as dirt. I really can't stand it but they pay me all right, so what the hell!"

"What the hell!" she repeated. "Do you know anything about Buddhism?" she blurted.

"No," he said smiling, shaking his head.

"Me neither. You wanna talk about it?" she asked her face beaming.

"Sure."

They sat in silence, each waiting for the other to begin. As he knew nothing about the subject (and neither did she), neither spoke. He pulled at the front of his shirt as if he were hot (he wasn't); she crossed her wrists in her lap and looked over his shoulder, slowly biting her lip. When their eyes met, their awkwardness converted into spontaneous laughter.

"Did you have anything particular in mind, because I know nothing here. This is virgin territory for me," he said, still laughing.

"Okay, I do."

"Hit me."

"I once read this book and this one line really stood out. You wanna hear it? Okay. It said that enlightenment," she smiled when she said this last word, her eyes widening like the remembrance of a first kiss or shared secret, "was like diving into a pond without causing any ripples. Isn't that great?"

He sat back in his chair. "Wow. That is great. Really."

"I know. It's the wildest thing I've ever heard!"

"I love it when I come across things like that. Things that are a little out of the ordinary. That push you into strange or new places. I need to really think about that one," he said, tilting his head to the ceiling.

"It's very hard," she said, nodding her head gravely, letting her eyes follow his.

⌒〟

"I guess the first thing I wonder is if it is even possible," Dan began as he approached the table, setting the beers he carried in each hand carefully on the slightly jiggly table. "I mean, is the writer being literal or figurative?"

"You're right. I never thought about that. I always assumed it was literal," she said, shirking her shoulders in an exaggerated shrug.

"Who wrote it? I guess that doesn't really matter."

She was sorry she didn't know who had written it. She was sorry she hadn't listened better to that nameless boy. She was sorry she had never read a book about Buddhism. At that moment, she could have been sorry for just about anything. She was having a wonderful time and the world was beautiful. And after a moment she said, "Do you think it is possible? I mean to actually jump into water and not cause any ripples?"

"I've never seen it done if that's what you mean, but that doesn't mean it's not possible. What do you think? Do you think it's possible?"

"I've never seen it done either," she said smiling. "But anything's possible, I guess."

"You think he knows?" said Dan, signaling the bartender over his shoulder, smiling.

"Fat chance," she said. "Probably can't even spell Bud-dhism."

Dan laughed. She was glad.

⌒〜

"Maybe it means … no, that's not right."

"I wonder if it has to do with …" began Caroline, trailing off nearly as soon as she began.

After several minutes they were again stumped, the conversation falling limply back to the awkwardness it had when Caroline originally offered up the subject.

"I have a great idea!" Dan said, turning around in his chair. "Can I get a Vodka Cloudy please?" he asked the bartender. He turned back to Caroline. "Go into the bathroom."

She rose and did as he asked. Her hand on the men's room door, she turned and asked, "Which one?" Looking over his shoulder, money in his hand, he said, "That's fine." She entered. She didn't even look in the mirror. After a minute or two he pushed open the thin wood door, holding not one but two thin clear glasses with the Vodka Cloudys.

"Follow me," he said, pushing past one of the stall doors that was nearly divorced from its hinges and into the stall. He placed one of the drinks on the back of the toilet. Standing over the water, he pulled an ice cube from the drink still in his hand, which quickly began to sweat nervously, and held it up to her. She nodded, impressed with his ingenuity, not at all curious why he didn't simply get two glasses full of ice. He held the glass out to her. She placed her thin, perfectly painted nails into the glass and pulled out a cube as well.

"Ready?" he asked, their bodies forming a triangle with the toilet. And with her approval, he dropped the first ice cube into the unmoving water. With the subsequent splash, Caroline eyed Dan who continued to stare into the toilet. Slowly he turned to Caroline's waiting eyes.

"Another?"

This time Caroline held an ice cube over the small pool of water. Before she dropped it, she let Dan lower her hand. It was much as they suspected: although the shorter distance caused a smaller splash, it did not eliminate it.

"This is not going to be easy," he said taking a sip from the glass. "You want to try it?"

"Sure; ew, what's in this?"

"Vodka, charged water, splash of coke."

"Tastes like pure alcohol."

"Yep. Cleans you out, that's for sure." His right hand seemed to be practicing fingerings for some instrument on his glass.

They tried several more ice cubes at higher and lower levels, at the center of the toilet and several off-center. The splashing continued.

"I have an idea!" said Caroline in a moment of inspiration. After another sip, she dipped her hand into the glass for another cube and held it near the side of the toilet without letting it quite touch it. Dan watched transfixed. As she let go, it caught the inside of the toilet and slid around, following the circular wall until it slipped into the water. "Did you see that?" she asked, excited. "There was almost no splash!"

"You're right. There are still ripples," (at this she began to frown), "but I think you're onto something." She hugged him ferociously, spilling much of the Vodka Cloudy on his sleeve. She pulled back, suddenly near tears.

"Oh, I'm sorry. Let me get that. I'm so sorry." She reached around him to the toilet paper dispenser, balling up mounds of toilet paper like gauze, tapping the cloudy wound tenderly if a bit desperately.

"Not a worry, believe me."

"Are you sure?" she asked, dabbing at his sleeve.

"All for enlightenment, right?"

"Right."

She hugged him again, this time more cautiously.

"I think you're onto something. Here, let me have another ice cube. I think all we need to do is just add a little finesse to your technique and we'll really nail what we're after."

Taking the same position as Caroline had moments before, he held the ice cube near but not quite touching the side of the toilet. Only when he let go of the ice cube did he pull his fingers back (to make its release lighter, he explained). They watched as it dropped down the side of the toilet like a child down a slide, entering gracefully, with a slight splash, still causing ripples across their little lake.

"So much for finesse," quipped Dan.

After twenty more minutes, two beers, and four more Vodka Cloudys worth of impromptu experiments, they reappeared from the bathroom and took their previous seats. Dan sat back deep into his chair, happily exhausted. Caroline attentively lit a cigarette, watching him.

"I can't believe we never got it," she said. Never had disappointment beamed so brightly.

"I'd love to know who solved that one."

Slowly she pulled the folded piece of paper from her purse and asked, " Do you want to hear something else kind of interesting?"

"Absolutely."

She handed him the paper. He unfolded it, the creases down its front and middle deep and worn.

"Let's see," he said holding it up before his eyes, "'*Hate or how a typewriter is better than a wife.*' Interesting title," he said with a sardonic laugh. Looking up, he saw that she obviously didn't want him to joke about this. He buried his eyes in the paper.

"He really likes Frank Sinatra," she said, having never taken her eyes of him while he was reading. "One of his newest obsessions."

"Your boyfriend wrote this?" he asked coolly.

"Yes. Well, my ex."

Clearing this obstacle safely out of the way, he began to really read. By turns it was angry, sad, eloquent, defeated. He talked about love of objects and people. Dan read aloud, "'*The love of objects is a selfish love: they do whatever we ask of them.*' That's because people can't," he said looking up briefly at Caroline. He continued to read aloud, "'*Things do not resist temptation; people do.*' Some of this is really good. '*Two people cannot penetrate each other.*' Or this one, '*It is not oneness the lover seeks but its opposite. And this must be sought, as it is all that is possible.*'" Looking up he read the author's final summation of love: "'*Love becomes a condition of proximity: I will marry you; I will live with you; I will have intercourse with you; I will procreate with you; I will grow old with you; I will die and be buried next to you. No matter how hard they try, no matter the sincerity or strength of the attempt, two lovers are merely bookends to the alienation between them.*' It's good. Dark, but good." He longed to know what was between this ghost author and this woman.

"This is about you, I presume?" he asked.

"Yes. After he moved out. There was someone else involved. It was pretty ugly. And no, it wasn't him, it was me. Stupid me. Don't be sorry. I can see it in your face, that you're sorry," she said, lighting a cigarette, very forcibly changing her mood. "I just wondered what you'd think of it is all," she said cheerfully.

Setting the paper on the small round table, he said, "It's pretty. But pretty words don't compare with pretty people," he said awkwardly.

"That was bad," she said shaking her head.

"I'm terrible at delivering lines."

"That wasn't much of a line," she said, exhaling smoke.

"You don't have to tell me." He stretched deep into the chair. "I get so tired of sitting all day, don't you? Desk jobs are terrible. I used to be in the best shape, and now..." he said, pointing to his gut. "Not to mention hanging out in bars all the time. Alcohol and smoke and fatty foods—great combination."

"Oh, is my cigarette bothering you?" she asked, quickly extinguishing, it her entire body jumping.

"Not at all," he said.

"What do you want to talk about now?" she asked, excited. She would have talked about anything.

"I didn't realize how late it had gotten," he said.

"You're right," she said, looking at her watch and thinking he was apologizing. "It doesn't feel that late. I'm not tired at all. I could sit like this all night."

"We'll be hurting tomorrow when the morning comes. I hate working hung over."

"I don't care. I hate my job anyway," she said. "Don't worry about me. I can hold out as long as you can."

"Really?"

"I'll be fine. I'm made from strong stuff," she said.

"Okay, I believe you. Still I don't think you should be driving. We've both had a lot and if something happened to you I couldn't forgive myself. I'll be okay. I just live around the corner. I've walked home plenty of times."

She thought it over. He had a point. She had drunk a lot and did not want to get pulled over. But something wasn't right. Then she remembered how this had started: speaking boldly.

"What are you doing?"

"What do you mean?" he asked, too innocently.

"You're being weird. Are you drunk? I knew you were drunk, but now you seem even drunker."

"*I'm* not," he started loudly, catching himself immediately, "drunk. I just don't want you to drive. You've drank too much."

"If you're feeling responsible because I'm drunk, don't. This isn't the first time I've been drunk and had to drive a long way. I'll be fine, so you don't have to beat yourself up. I've been having fun. Let's keep having fun."

"I don't feel responsible. Well, I do, but that's not what I was trying to say. What I was trying to say was that I think it would be fun, not fun, well, it would be fun, but more than that, I mean it would be nice, as we are getting along so well, if we …"

"If we what?"

"I mean, we've been getting along great. I never met anyone like you. I was wondering, what you would think of … Do you want to come back to my place? I mean, only if you want to. It's no big deal, I just thought, you know, to hang out or talk."

"What?" she asked, pretending to be surprised. She let the rest happen as if on automatic pilot.

"I'm sorry, I just thought …" he stuttered, panicked, back-pedaling furiously.

"Oh, oh, I didn't know what you were asking. I thought you were drunk. Sure. Yes. Yes. Yes. Do you want to leave now or …?" she asked, beginning to reach for her purse if he indeed wanted to leave at that very moment.

Not expecting this response, he was momentarily dumbfounded.

"Why don't we have one more beer and then we can take off? Does that sound alright?" Her response had left him stunned, like a bird that had struck glass. He needed time to recover before knowing which way to proceed.

"Yeah. Yeah," she said setting her purse down. It was always the same. It didn't matter how great a guy was or how different he was from all the others, when it came to sex, they were all the same bunch of babbling, nervous idiots, playing by the same rules, rules that transformed her against her will back to her old self. "Let me get these," she said, pulling her worn wallet from her purse, walking to the bar. Setting his beer in front of him, she was, Dan noticed, standing directly next to him, her face only inches from his. He thought that perhaps she was going to kiss him. His body prepared itself. "I won't stay after," was all she said before sitting down with a gravity that told him to neither object nor question.

A WRITER'S LIFE

3

As the door to the office closed behind him, Lipman slowed his step and leaned against the wall. Sighing, he threw his tie over his shoulder, reached into the front of his pants, untucked his shirt and pulled out the book he'd serruptiously slipped under his shirt. He couldn't read at his desk and had to smuggle any book he brought out. It rested on his palm, looking up at him like the reminder of an unfulfilled promise. Looking around impatiently, and pleased to find that he was alone, he straightened himself out and entered the bathroom. Finding the stall farthest from the entrance, he unbuckled his belt, loosened his pants, dropped them, sat down, and began to read. Or to be more specific, he opened the used copy of *Death in Venice* to the spot he had last stopped at, leaned back, and let the words transport him, *"It was the urge to escape—he admitted to himself—this yearning for the new and the remote, this appetite for freedom, for unburdening, for forgetfulness."* And there it all went. Every command, every pressure, every obligation foisted upon him from the outside that he hadn't the courage to shake, every sign that he had gone mainstream, disappeared in the space of one sentence. If anyone else had been in that bathroom he would have heard Lipman's deep expiration of air, a sigh that the stranger couldn't know was an expression of bliss.

Lipman read on, but with every movement of his feet on the gritty tile, with every turn of the page, even with every breath, time, like the shadow of a bully, fell upon him in the silence and the echoes with a harsher, sterner force that usual. A paragraph into the third page, he felt the words looking back at him like smoldering eyes. Decorum allowed him only two pages; after that people began to wonder. The stuffy silence of the bathroom was inversely proportionate to the tornado of voices, meetings, numbers, and the unexpected emergencies that occurred every day and were poised outside the stall waiting for him. Slowly, with a painful swallow, he closed the book.

Rising off the toilet seat, he felt a fierce stubbornness ignite inside of him. Sitting back down too hard, he reopened the book, his posture straight, defiant. He coursed through three more pages, the exhilaration accompanying this insurrection brief. He hung his head in what was all too clearly a hollow victory. He had scanned the pages, his eyes, the tools of his rebellion, merely passing over the black letters, peering through the stall door, beyond the bathroom and deep into the offices where his duties chastised him. The voices, the deadlines, the pressures would always be there, waiting. And not just here but at every job like it, which at this moment was every job he could imagine. There would never be a time when his responsibilities to reading (that is, to his life) would outweigh the responsibilities to everything else. Not to mention the writing. Looking down at the book, he shook his head. He had comprehended nothing, his bold act only signifying how far gone he really was.

Having become the top Minnesota Admissions Representative at National College after a terrifically difficult start did not ease his suffering, but intensified it. He had never done sales and, while having the presentiment that he would excel at it, he had no suspicion of the pressures, internal and external, that came with its success, or for that matter, its real or threatened failures. Pride, competitiveness, and the desire to dominate on the one hand; the pressures exerted from the university to continually enroll more students than the quarter before while retaining 90 percent of those enrolled the previous quarter, on the other. The fate of the college rested upon his shoulders, something which all of his superiors never failed to remind him.

But this was nothing compared to the money.

There was no substance more poisonous and he knew it. Once, after he had been out of college for several years, he ran into a girl he had known since high school. She had a job that was prestigious, challenging, and paid her well, very well. She hated it, loathed it with all of her being. She couldn't stand waking up in the morning and was certain she had aged six years in only three. Then find another job, he stated obviously. I can't. Why? The money was too good. She had grown accustomed to everything it afforded. To quit and follow her dream was now impossible; it didn't pay enough. This pretty much said it all. At the time he didn't judge her. He didn't pity her either. All he felt was an overwhelming satisfaction that money never got its hands on him. He had gotten sick from it when he first tasted it but after that he grew quickly immune to its poison. Besides, he liked mornings.

He had come to his conclusions about money from his earliest days and acted them out once he was old enough to work. He had only taken jobs that he enjoyed, jobs where he was alone. Jobs where he could read. And think. (All of which led up to his need to write.) As long as there was enough for rent, food, and books he was happy. Such ideals are easily attained when one is young. He did not pay rent or buy food living at home until his second year of college. And used books were never a burden to anyone's pocketbook no matter how many you bought or how little you made.

Lipman, however, would object to calling what he valued "ideal." He knew that what most people called ideals were abstractions of perfection that were impossible to imitate, their unreachability a justification for people's abandonment to the below-par life they lived. People did not *outgrow their ideals* to see life *as it really was:* they never had ideals in the first place. Lipman would live his way. It was not money, but one's attitude toward it, that could prove crippling.

The darker, less self-satisfied truth was that Lipman feared money. It was money, not sex or fame or even power, that was his great tempter. Not a tempter to "sell out." Lipman did not believe in such nonsense. Being a good American, he supported free enterprise. Understanding the Marxist critique of capitalism, he knew that the artist couldn't escape this. If he were to have the opportunity to sell his novel, he would do it; the reason you published a book was to have it read. But wanting a book published—even publishing it—doesn't make it art. It doesn't matter if one published to become famous or to move people or both. This could not affect the value of the work. It was either art or it wasn't.

But publishing is the least important part of the process. The reason to write was because you had to and if it never got published it wouldn't ever matter. Writing a manuscript and publishing a novel were completely different. No, what Lipman feared about money was the way it could ease one's worry, something that atrophied the muscles of discipline. Money offered too many distractions, made the unnecessary interesting, and ended by causing you to betray yourself. Fitzgerald. Faulkner. It destroyed artists and art. He knew how strong these temptations were and he did not know if he could resist them.

Almost as if to prove this he became an English professor. He made enough to pay for his spartan essentials (he could pay rent, had money for socializing and, as always, for used books), he was near his most passionate subject. Most important, the combination of morning and night classes allowed him ample time to write.

Now, at age twenty-seven, he was an admissions representative, a position that offered more money—a lot more—than teaching. (Of course, what didn't?) Yet this was not just a different job but a momentous step toward conformity, toward a denial of the value of thought, of his art, of the entire life he had lived up until that point. There was just so much stuff that required his attention. He had a fiancée. There were the wedding plans, there was the house to close on, and he had a car that he could barely afford (he had never had a nice car in his life, much less one that required monthly payments), and then the honeymoon: Cancun or Paris? Then there were the *smaller* expenses. He had moved into an expensive apartment, with a garage, cable television, and its own washer and dryer. He took French lessons. He belonged to a health club. The *Calhoun Beach Club* no less! Did he really need a view of the lake while he did cardio? The events that had ushered in this new era had been so slick, so seemingly out of his control that he balked when he thought of it. Time had become his willing accomplice. Time offered itself whenever he did something beyond his nature: it was time; the time was right; it seemed time. Whatever made him come to these conclusions made him despise himself and everything he had.

No longer was he a writer who worked. He was a salesman who wrote *on the side.* His passion had become his hobby. So integral had writing been to his existence that he had never experienced the desire to do it, like one desires water when one is thirsty. He didn't put on writing like a beautiful hat. It was a part of his central nervous system: it did as it pleased, and it made him who he was supposed to be. *"I do not want myself to become other than I am,"* Nietzsche had once written. At one time Lipman had found the force of these words liberating. Now they mocked him, nearly stopping his heart cold. It was as if he was weak from months of hibernating.

Reopening the book in a fury, he searched among the heavily underlined passages until he had found the one he was looking for. *"If they were so excellent in both composition and texture, it was solely because their creator had held out for years under the strain of one single work, with a steadiness of will and tenacity comparable to that which conquered his native province; and because, finally, he had turned over his most vital and valuable hours to strains of production."* What had *he* held out for? Where had his *most vital and valuable hours* gone? The only answer was a negative one—not to his art. The worst of it was that there was something inside of himself that stopped him. The daily obstacles and his worthless job impeded progress on his book. But in those precious moments when he was alone, he found himself lethargic, uninspired, indifferent, tired, lured by procrastination, his creativity blunted. Instead of inspiration he was visited by ghosts. All the ideas he had believed and *still should have* believed in were suddenly resurrected the moment he read this passage. Every day was the Easter of his past. "And I'm reading in a fucking bathroom!"

Then, as if time were leading the counterattack that Lipman had just made on behalf of his forgotten self, the lights went out. He sighed as the light seemed to escape through the crack under the door. Having failed to register movement, the motion activated lights timed out. That had to be metaphysical, he thought aloud before shaking his arm in the darkened air until the lights came on again.

Standing up and stuffing the book into his pants, Lipman made his way through the bathroom and into the corridor, back to the office, to his desk, finally pulling out the concealed book and once again hiding it, along with his hidden life, in the bottom drawer. It was nearly three. There was always a meeting at three.

⌐〜〉

Lipman hadn't heard her get out of bed. It was only the subtle rising of her side of the bed that made him aware of her rising. He was surprised and immediately anxious.

"Where are you going?" he asked, his voice still holding onto sleep. She was heading for her purse, determined.

She said nothing.

"Sweetie, is something wrong?" he asked as casually as possible. He looked at the clock. She didn't have to start getting ready for another half an hour. "It's still early." He could see that she was digging through the various pockets in her purse but he couldn't begin to guess for what. All that was clear was that she was focused and determined to ignore him. After a moment she started to cough exaggeratedly. She must be calling up an alibi for a fast departure. He laid back and frowned.

What is it he could have done, he wondered? Everything had gone perfectly last night. They both had to work late so they began the evening with a late supper, followed by a backrub. After that, they crawled into bed and talked for what later seemed quite a long time, about work, possible vacations, the dread of having to get up in the morning and do it all again, after that—he caught himself. It occurred to him that at that point in the conversation she had placed her fingers over his mouth to quiet him. He thought it was because she wanted to make love. Maybe she was really upset? She often told him that his anticipation of unpleasant things in the future greatly put her off. Or to be more accurate, the way in which he concluded speaking of these things, acting as if they weren't negative at all, soured her. This had to be it. He must have said something.

But she had stayed the night. They had made love. And not one of those we're-nearly-asleep-quickies. The length of the session and depth of the feelings it stemmed from and in turn produced were immense. He had fallen asleep with no doubts about this woman; he was in "Capital L" love with her (compared with all the "little L" loves he had almost exclusively known). He had slept well. Did she stay because she was too tired to drive? Had she placated him? Had she just wanted to shut him up? She had fallen asleep at the wheel a number of times and they both knew that if she left this was bound to happen. But she had already stayed over once this week. He knew how badly she wanted to move in with him, but he always gave excuses why she couldn't yet. He knew this wouldn't do for long. She had already told him that either he get serious in the relationship or she was gone. She needed to know if they had a future. That had to be it: she'd stayed to pressure him into finally making a decision about their life and if there was anything Lipman hated, it was being pressured. As he was about to confront her, something odd happened: the phone rang.

He looked at it in disbelief, shocked out of his anger. There was no one who would call him this early, not even someone from the school. He picked it up warily.

"Hello?"

Before he knew what was happening, Leslie was turning to face him, and speaking into her cell phone, asked how he was.

"What are you..." he began to ask, partially dropping the phone. She pointed to his phone with a smile as big as the sun. He put it back to his ear, "What's going on?" He was relieved.

"Nothing. What about you?"

"Not much. Did you get enough sleep last night?"

"Well..." she said drawing out the syllables. "I tried, but something just kept me awake."

"I see. I see. I have that problem sometimes too."

"Are you going to have time for breakfast this morning?" she asked.

"Maybe a quick one," he said with a confident nod of the head.

"What would you like?'

"Oh, a bagel and maybe some eggs."

"How do you want those?"

"Sunnyside up, please."

"No problem. I bet you look cute today."

"I'd prefer to look at you, love."

"That can be arranged."

They both smiled, never once having taken their eyes off one another.

"I don't care where we are, a day can't go by without our morning call."

She was quite right. Every morning for the past two years precisely at 8:30, after she had finished showering, dressed and put on her make-up, Leslie would call Lipman. Even though they only were able to talk for ten minutes, it had become so much a part of both their lives that it was unbearable to think of having to go without it. Even when her job had sent her abroad, one of them would set the alarm, waking at an ungodly hour, just to talk about next to nothing for ten minutes before drifting happily back to sleep. Lipman was just happy that she wasn't pressuring him to move in together; maybe it was time to ask her, then.

As they continued their phone conversation *(How did you sleep? Fine. You? Good. Big day at work? Nah. The usual.)*, he sat in awe. While it was true that he had known Leslie six months before Roberts' costume party, it was this event that Lipman considered their official meeting. He first took note of her because she was allergic to bread and passed on beer in favor of a very specific type of wine that she had brought with her. His interest in her was confirmed when, going out for coffee, she pulled from an inside pocket a small glass jar of soy milk (she was lactose intolerant too), and he fell in love with her at a Lipman family function where she handed out gourmet chocolate bread as a gift. He was convinced that her allergies were a psychosomatic response to middle-class values, but in the grandest, most artistic sense. He convinced himself that if he were going to enter the mainstream and give up his independence, which to him meant sacrificing his time to write, especially in the mornings (there would be evenings and weekends, although not lately), it needed to be with one whose life was tempered by an artistic temperament. She was his compromise.

"Well, I guess I better go, don't want to be late."

"Yeah, I should get up too," he said.

"Bye."

"Bye."

"Don't forget your eggs," she added quickly before hanging up.

With that, they both hung up their respective phones, smiling, and once Leslie crawled back into bed, they made love.

He removed the paper from typewriter, his eyes pulled by the straight and curved black lines, by the whiteness of the page, that popped out of the black depressed letters that had been stamped on paper with such force. They could not know that, when uttered, they evoked sound, that when read, they produced thought. Placing the page facedown on the desk, Lipman quickly forgot it and rolled in a fresh sheet of paper upon which his thoughts would roll out in black-inked symbols and white spaces.

He had decided to articulate for posterity an idea that had originated earlier that week and he wanted to get it on paper while the idea was still sizzling. At times, his fingers glided over the keys with the grace and ease and fury of Mahler's baton over an orchestra; at others, they resembled a child's hand pointing at fish in a tank—this one and this one and this one! At others they marched, at others, reprimanded. At any rate, thought formed long ago translated itself into the motions of his fingers, which was released onto the page. Only later, when he looked at, read, and brought them back into his mind, did Lipman revisit and then severely edit them. At the moment, they glided.

"Dammit."

His hands came to a halt. He opened the top drawer of his desk, pulled out the little white bottle of Liquid Paper, and lightly brushed away his mistake. He sat back in his chair, giving it sufficient time to dry. His hands danced nervously on the desktop, spelling the words they longed to be giving to the page like a martial arts expert practicing the forms of hand-to-hand battle. He sighed. There was nothing more irritating (aside from the glitch of motion, the possible wilting of inspiration, and the mistake itself) than typing before it was completely dry: he would have to start the whole process anew. Lipman had no tolerance for blemishes.

While it dried and his hands danced impatiently, his thoughts fell back upon the fictional scenes that were already well established in his mind. Having the nostalgia of real memories, they only needed to be extricated from within. "I saw the angel in the marble and carved until I set him free." This claim of Michelangelo's expressed perfectly how Lipman felt about writing. Everything that needed to be said was already there in his mind. It was simply a matter of chipping away at the excess thoughts, words, music, ideas—of editing out the superfluous to find the buried words, the real truth. In that sense, nothing was fiction. He thought it beautiful.

Lipman, however, had come to writing quite accidentally. And although it was his passion, his most serious and important endeavor (to use his own words), that which made him feel he wasted time on everything else, it had started out as just another class activity in school, in seventh grade to be precise. Lipman was always an above-average student in all of his classes and, succeeding in all, he never preferred one class to another. He had no reason to; school was simply another thing he did. Thus, when the entire class had been given the assignment to write a five-hundred-word descriptive essay recalling a place that had struck them as interesting, Lipman did so. The teacher, Miss Hass, the toughest at Eisenhower Middle School, had made it clear that each of the senses were to be engaged throughout the essay.

To help the students get a sense of what she wanted, she told the children to take a notebook and a pen and to proceed to the gym. All of the children were excited beyond belief at this proposition. Not only did they get to leave the classroom, which was old and depressing and resembled social studies films depicting life during the fifties when children had to fall to the floor, heads in hands, to practice for the drop of the bomb, but they got to go the gym. This was second only to going outside and just above going to the lunchroom. The best thing, of course, was leaving for the day.

They were all visibly disappointed when they were told that they were not to interact with the class currently taking gym (who really seemed to be having fun, more fun than their own class ever did during gym), but that they were to observe them and describe them in their notebooks (they should have known!) They were to describe, Miss Haas said, everything they saw, heard, smelled (many giggles), tasted (perplexed looks and giggles), and felt.

Naturally, they were resistant. But when they reluctantly accepted the reality of their situation (Miss Hass was never a softie), they began to move their pens, slowly at first, but later with much speed. Miss Hass would have liked to believe that their enthusiasm was the result of a whole new world opening up to them, the rediscovering of the senses they lived with every day and had allowed to become dull, but the speed of their writing belied a desire to be finished and just watch the other class playing dodgeball without having to work.

A few weeks later, Miss Hass returned the descriptive essays to the children who had forgotten all about them, even though they had just written them. She said many teacherly things, letting them know that, overall, she was pleased with the essays, that she learned new things about everyone (something that she particularly liked doing), that a few concentrated only on one sense and that sight wasn't the most important (adding that this was a common mistake), that comma usage still needed major work (an observation that lowered even the sturdiest of shoulders), and that anyone who did not find a grade on his or her paper was being asked to re-do the assignment. It was nothing they hadn't heard before.

As always, she singled out an essay or two for special consideration and recognition because of the fine quality of the writing. Miss Haas (herself a failed writer) took this very seriously; she believed that teachers, good teachers, could change lives. The students listened to her proclamations with the same indifference that they did everything else. This time, however, she seemed particularly insistent about one of the essays. She told the class, as she walked up and down the perfectly straight aisles, that not only was a certain essay of a quality superior to others but that she wanted the permission of the author to copy it and use it in future classes as an example of fine student descriptive writing. The class was surprised by her use of the term "author," a most important designation, they had been told, an authority, not one who merely put words on the page. Heads began to turn in anticipation.

When Miss Haas spoke the name Mr. Lipman (she always used a Mr. or a Miss in important times), all the class predictably turned toward him with a mixture of excitement, surprise, and envy. Lipman, whose head was turned toward the back of the classroom and who was talking to his best friend, Derek (who never, ever brushed his hair, but rose from his bed and darted barely dressed to the bus stop), had not heard his name called out. When finally aware of the overwhelming and focused silence, he revolved back around to the glowing faces of Miss Haas and the half-envious, half-awed faces of his classmates. He stopped talking.

While he nodded in acceptance, his mind searched, but it was of no use; he couldn't remember what he had written. He stared at the paper Miss Haas was holding up. His eyes brightened, recalling the adventure story he had written! Now he remembered. Oh, how he liked that one, as far as stories went. It was filled with canyons to leap, mountains to climb, swamps to wade, explosions, spies, rain, dangerous animals, natives from strange countries, Nazis, and a pretty maiden. He included her because these stories always seemed to have a maiden, not because he wanted a girl in his story. The main character was a protégé of Indiana Jones, complete with an "Indiana Jones hat" (he did not know the word "fedora"), leather jacket, and bullwhip.

He was confounded when what she read aloud a page and a half that described trees, leaves, rain, snakes, chipmunks, raccoons, lakes, boats, the wind, the smell of barbeque, the sky and the sun, and his dad standing on the hill overlooking the lake, saying, "Doesn't it seem sad sometimes?" He barely remembered this scene. Then he remembered forgetting about the assignment until Sunday night and writing, in a panic, about a vacation his family had taken on a small lake in Wisconsin. It was nice enough all right, but it was no Indiana Jones adventure and it was certainly not worthy of Miss Haas's high praise. The other one was maybe; but this one full of trees and grass and sad fathers?

Walking to the front of the class, the eyes of the world on him, he realized that some people are special, different— better. They can do things others can't. He didn't know at the time, but after this, he would be asked to give speeches at school functions and would be allowed to leave classes early to work on them. He would be treated like a peer by the teachers: he would be called on first and expected to be right (and he always was or at least was close enough); they would think his clowning witty, the sign of a superior mind. The girls would want to be near him, the boys would envy him. He would get away with anything. He would be considered an authority. Turning around and facing the class, Lipman now stood taller, happier, and in awe of that "something" he possessed.

At his desk, looking at the back page of his essay, with its bright red "A," and the message asking permission for its use, it was decided: he would be a writer. He didn't make a conscious decision; he didn't say anything or have a vision. Fate was not like flying, the sky opening into endlessness space in which one could maneuver freely at will. Fate chooses its subject, soaks itself into it until it does its bidding. This isn't to say that things chosen deliberately are more meaningful, more of an expression of free will. On the contrary, most choices have little or no reason behind them. And all the feelings, desires, logic, and preparation are merely events of the mind; people only think that they have free will and only think that they can be held responsible. Later, much later, Lipman would come to know this. He would know that the subjects he wrote about, his writing style, writing itself, and the existence he lived that produced those things, in short, the series of paved roads he thought he chose, were pathways that he couldn't have avoided. He would know that his mistake, that the mistake of all travelers, is to think the journey, the roads along the way, and the construction of those roads were commissioned by the traveler, not chosen for him, that the world conforms to the individual and not the other way around. And from that moment, he worked.

Pulling the last sheet of paper from the typewriter, he placed it facedown upon the others and picked them all up. Flipping through the unfinished story, he sighed. They were all there: Leslie; his best friend, Roberts; himself; people and experiences from his past. He omitted no detail, left no truth hidden, no matter how ugly, unflattering, or black. Opening the black file cabinet to the right of his desk, he placed the story behind all of the others that he could not use or finish, and locked the drawer.

"Okay, we don't have much time," started Leslie, frantically, before the door was even open. "It's..." she squinted at the clock across the room, "5:30 now. The dry cleaners close at 6:00, and we have to meet my parents for dinner in an hour. After that we should be just in time to meet Jim and Liz at *Sunsets*. Just in time for their late-night happy hour, which you always like."

Before she was finished speaking she had already pulled off her heavy coat and scarf and most of her work clothes, and was rummaging through the closet for the perfect outfit; one that would accommodate both dinner and drinks, as both places were quite different, her parents preferring a conservative atmosphere, her friends a hip, edgy one. She would try on four or five outfits before she'd find perfection. Several minutes later he heard her calling him from the walk-in closet.

"Here, this coat looks good on you," she said as she came into the dining room. Now that she'd found perfection, it was his turn.

He looked up from the dining room table, pushed back in his chair, yellow notepad in hand, and said plainly, "I can't."

"Alright, alright, I don't know why you hate this one so much but I just thought I'd try. It does bring out your eyes wonderfully. Can't blame an egg for trying."

She went down the hall to the closet and brought back a new jacket, a pair of soft tan slacks, and a crisp white shirt with an odd, yet strangely beautiful American Indian insignia on a flap that, acting as a kind of tie, folded over the three buttons at the shirt's top. He lightheartedly ignored them as Leslie placed them somewhat carefully over the couch arm. She continued talking as she headed back to the bedroom.

"Do you think we'll make it to the dry cleaners? There are a few things I really have to pick up. I have that big meeting next week and I really want to wear my pantsuit to that cocktail party." She looked at herself in the mirror, feigning a criticism that was self-mocking at best. "It's the one I wore when you fell for me," she said drawing out her last words playfully, pleased at the resurrected memory.

After smoothing her clothes and heading out of the bedroom, she stopped in her tracks when she saw, at the end of the hall, the pile of Lipman's clothes. Although they hadn't been touched, they seemed looked over and disregarded by Lipman, who sat tilted back in his chair, smiling quizzically.

"You're not ready," was all she could come up with. It was almost a question.

"You know I'm not going," he said with a befuddled smile on his face.

"What are you talking about?" she asked, almost allowing herself a hint of anger. But before it could really materialize, she walked far enough to come into partial view of the kitchen and the calendar tacked haphazardly over the sink. "Oh, it's the 23rd."

"Fraid it is." He sighed a laugh.

"There's no way you can go, not even just for dinner?"

He shook his head.

"You know how much I've been looking forward to this, not to mention my parents. They've only met you a couple of times. They're starting to doubt how great you are. I tell them all the time you know. I just want them to understand what I understand. Am I way off base or—?"

"Sweetie, you know the rule."

He hated to invoke the rule at such a moment, especially since Leslie was so giving, so understanding of him. It could only feel like an attack, an I-told-you-so of sorts. Not that it nullified any of her points; it didn't, it simply superceded them. He was scheduled to write tonight. Since she had moved in it was the only way he could write at all. It was ridiculous and it didn't work well, but it was all he had.

"Yes. I know. Still wasn't there any way to finish before I got home? You've been here for hours."

"It doesn't really work that way. I have to think, reflect, wait," he said with what he hoped sounded like levity, looking up toward the ceiling. The flippancy of his words disguised what was to him very serious, something nearly impossible to communicate and which, when he tried to explain it to others, often sounded abstract or absurd. He felt smoldering resentment rising.

"There's no way?" she asked pleadingly.

"As much as I want to …" he trailed off, the silence finishing his thought for him. Now he just wanted her gone.

There was a momentary and terse silence. Soon she brightened.

"Alright, alright, you're right. I knew or I forgot while I was at work. I don't want to disturb you. Really," she added, with the proper amount of heaviness. She lifted her head and smiled. "I love you." It was clear she meant it as she crossed the room to kiss him on the forehead. He pulling slightly away, already concentrating. "I'll see you when I get back, then maybe you can show me what you have."

"Come on now," he said scolding her softly without looking up.

"Can't blame an egg for trying."

"You're not scheduled tomorrow night are you?" she said heading into the kitchen. "Because—"

"No."

Although smiling, he was so angry that if he did not quell it he would be unable to work. It was nearly impossible already. He took several large, canyon-deep breaths. As she opened the door to leave, she heard the sound of the pencil across the yellow legal pad like the scratching of an insect's leg. The moment she locked the door behind her, Lipman stopped writing. Tilting his head back, he transformed his breathing into a low, crawling moan. When he finally looked back at the notepad, he saw that they were still there: Leslie, his mother, past lovers, and himself, always himself. Trapped.

Dropping the notepad to the floor, he wandered listless through the apartment. With the exception of those in the living room, no lights were on. Everything was covered in a gray indifference. Ending up in his study, he looked at the bookshelves lining the room and the pile of books on his desk: Kant and Kant commentary. So obsessed had he become with Kant's ideas that for a year it had been his only reading. Finally feeling overwhelmed, he had abandoned Kant completely. Picking up the top volume, he flipped through pages darkened by underlining, marginalia, stars, exclamation points, and boxes around entire paragraphs. Stopping at a particularly marked-up page, he read in the gray darkness what he had underlined. *"Beauty, Kant reminds us, is a definitive 'symbol of morality.' The stance that we take toward art is similar to that which we take towards other human beings when we are properly respectful of their dignity."* He set the book down. He needn't read the rest. He had come back to these words so often they were an indelible part of him.

Pulling the chair out from the desk, he slumped down. From the corner of the desk a picture of Leslie and himself, all smiles, sitting on large rocks, stared. He remembered their trip to Duluth well. That was where he asked her to move in with him. He asked with the seriousness of a marriage proposal, something which would come some months later. How could she know that he hadn't finished anything since they had known one another? Not a story, a poem, much less his book. He couldn't tell her. He didn't even really want to. It wasn't all her. It was their life. The job. The people. He had become infected with their values, their morality. He needed only a few words to describe his condition: hypocritical, in denial, assimilating, and the idea that somehow he was or always had been a sinner. It didn't matter that he had completed nothing, that the unfinished manuscripts stuffed his file cabinet. Inside of his head they were complete; everybody he knew and everything they had all done were waiting to be transformed, waiting to be sinned against.

Putting his coat on, he left his apartment.

⌇

Stated the educated man (as his brains were failing him), "Need I remind you that according to the Buddha enlightenment is open to all?"

He was about to enter the bar when he shuddered so intensely he nearly dropped to his knees. He steadied himself with the iron armrest of a bench bolted to the bar's front porch, and lowered himself slowly, fearfully. He gazed at the sky for a long time but saw nothing of it.

"You can change what you do—not what you are," he said, his entire body resisting the idea the minute he uttered it.

Coming out of the bar, a man tossed his cigarette to the ground. The snow seemed to swarm around its glowing end like piranha to flesh, suffocating it in a few short moments; a flat line of smoke rose and died quickly.

"That's more accurate," he said quietly, his voice trembling.

Lipman stared at the lifeless butt as his thoughts continued to fill his head like smoke.

"It wasn't supposed to be complicated. I changed the course of my life yet remained a writer. Forge a private life of creativity with a public life *no different* from anyone else's, I told myself. I had no idea what kind of mistake this was, or the kind of energy it would require.

"That the appearance of things is a betrayal of my life is embarrassingly apparent with every line I write; the inevitability that I am supposed to be in *every* aspect of my life surfaces in the work, exposing the hypocrisy that is my life. I am not living what I believe. A man, his imagination, and his life are one. It is this unity that rips me apart every time I write, or every time I don't. I don't even know what I'm doing."

Standing up to open the door to the bar, he thought, "I'm weak."

Walking through the door, Lipman felt the rush of heat blow over his face. Its contrast to the coldness of the newly arrived winter, which always seemed to enter the world like a houseguest who refused to call beforehand, was an unwelcome respite; it made him momentarily nauseous. He began unbuttoning his long overcoat, scanning the room for Roberts and Kilzer who he knew were there. The bar was dense with people. The sound of conversation was similarly dense, drowning out most of the music, leaving only the deep rumble of the bass in the floorboards and walls. As he adjusted to the temperature, he heard the door open behind him, followed by the dry howl of the winter wind and voices talking. He stepped away from the door.

At the same time, he noticed a head toward the back of the bar pop up above the crowd. He recognized Roberts. He was looking toward the entrance, his face distorted in his attempt to make out the faces of the people just arriving trying to get tables. Lipman made his way through the crowd and back toward Roberts who still hadn't spotted him. It wasn't until he was within three feet that Roberts' face lit up with the spark of recognition.

"Hey, I didn't see you come in," he said, again looking toward the entrance as if he still didn't believe Lipman had gotten past him. "I wasn't sure if you were going to make it."

"You're not the only one." Lipman took his coat off and threw it over the back of an empty chair. "I've never seen this place so crowded," he said, glancing around. He had expected Kilzer to be with Roberts.

"I guess there was some kind of private party upstairs." He paused to sip from his drink before continuing. "Apparently, they were only expecting forty or fifty people and nearly two hundred showed up. They ran out of food half an hour ago."

"Really?"

"Well, the complimentary food."

"Oh," Lipman added, vaguely interested. He was late and he felt bad that Roberts had been waiting alone for over half an hour. He decided that he would buy the next couple of rounds.

"People can't live without free food. They act so mad. But it's free. Just have a good time. There's Kilzer," Roberts said. "Over here."

Kilzer approached the table. "Man, it's busy," he said taking a seat.

"You're telling me," said Roberts.

"How's the job going?" asked Lipman.

"Oh God, why are you asking him that?" asked Roberts, utterly exasperated.

"What?" asked Lipman, innocently raising his hands.

"You know Kilzer can't say a bad word about anyone no matter how much they obviously deserve it."

"Bad job or something?"

"The job's fine," began Roberts, answering for Kilzer, "it's the asshole running the place that's in need of a good belt, that's all. Not that Kilzer would ever let on."

"He's all right," offered Kilzer plainly.

"See! See! What did I say?"

"Well he is," Kilzer said dismissively.

"Oh, he is not. The hours he makes you guys work. And the money, it's ridiculous. Just admit it, right now, in front of Lipman, me, and the world. Admit that you can't say a bad thing about anyone."

"I will not because it is not true," he said, stopping Roberts's objection before it began. "I just believe that you can't fault people for who they are."

"Free will has left the building," shouted Roberts, cupping his hands at his mouth, his voice mimicking a loud speaker. Lipman turned away tired. "You don't see a contradiction here? That something unchangeable is still capable of free will?"

"That is free will. You can always struggle against what you are," said Lipman.

"See that girl over there leaning against the bar? The one with the dark brown hair? Do you think she's attractive?"

"Without talking to her, without knowing her story, I couldn't say. Even after that, I don't think I really could."

Lipman furrowed his brow, pulled into the conversation not out of habit or even curiosity, but only in order to bring the conversation to its usual, stalemated end quickly. "So how do you make the determination?"

Kilzer had to think about this for a moment. Roberts smiled. "I just like getting to know people. It's not about how they look or how smart they are or anything like that. It's who they are. So I guess I'd talk to almost anyone."

"Is there anyone that you could find unattractive?" asked Lipman.

"I don't know," he answered sincerely.

"I see our friend here has a running start on us. What do you say we play a little catch-up? Beer?" asked Kilzer before pushing his way through the crowd toward the bar.

"God, I haven't seen him for a while," offered Lipman, still turned toward the wall of people that had swallowed Kilzer.

"He took his two-week vacation in England. Holed up researching that Blake biography."

"He's always been big into Blake," he said stoically.

"You always just turn away at the mention of Blake."

"It's not that I don't like him. His talent can't be denied. I just get tired of all that cosmogony stuff."

"I should have supposed," said Roberts. He took small, methodical sips from his glass, which Lipman knew contained Morgan and Coke. Although Roberts drank quite rapidly, he never gulped (he thought this ungentlemanly), and Lipman found this odd. Roberts was in no way gentlemanly. Watching him take his quick, small sips, Lipman couldn't remember him ever drinking anything else. He searched his memory to contradict this but he could not. Lipman found this little trait somehow pleasing and he smiled to himself as Roberts took another series of baby sips. "He should be done with it in a few months, depending on how much he can work on in during his off-time," he said, setting his glass down.

Their conversation was interrupted by a loud commotion in the middle of the bar, a rumbling they had both heard earlier but had disregarded. Turning to look, they saw two men of unequal size. As the bigger of the two men approached, the other, smaller man scurried to get off his stool and brace himself for the imminent fight.

Of course, this was only half true.

Looking at the two men, Lipman identified with the smaller one, the prey that longs to be predator. Throughout history people have set small men in their image to destroy the larger men in their path. David destroyed Goliath. Charlie Chaplin stooped to conquer. He thought of all the underdogs that he had worshipped—yes, worshipped—in his lifetime. Lipman longed to fight.

The entire crowd, swaying involuntarily, formed a circle around the fighters and followed the smaller man as he was pushed toward the back of the bar. He staggered to find footing in the throng of arms and chests and faces. It seemed to be taking him longer than it should have. This confirmed what Lipman already concluded: the smaller man had already been defeated. When Lipman saw the smaller man scurry off of his chair, he knew who would be the victor. Any ground gained now was only to lessen the defeat, or rather was to elongate the distance between him and defeat; defeat would never be diminished.

He rushed the giant, a man with curly black hair and a salt-and-pepper beard, whose tightly tucked-in shirt hugged a soft bulging gut. For a moment they locked like praying hands. The larger man attempted to peel the other man off of him by grabbing at his back. But he merely untucked the smaller man's shirt. He staggered back, his flailing arms searching until he got a firm grasp on the smaller man's pants.

The smaller man attempted to take advantage of his opponent's imbalance, throwing and connecting two quick punches: one to the man's gut (which just absorbed it) and one intended for his face, which wound up sliding off of the man's cheek, landing, quite ineffectively, on the man's right ear. The larger man quickly grabbed him and tossed him backward into the crowd, which surged like an ebbing tide that did not break. It would only open when the fight was over and one of these men was lying unmoving on the ground.

As the smaller man tried to extricate himself from the web of torsos and arms and faces, the larger man stood alone, waiting, in the center of the circle. He was about to break. You could see the change in his eyes; they had the stillness of a cat the instant before it pounces. The smaller man was attempting another run at the man when he got caught by the neck and belt and flung catapult-style into the jukebox.

Amazement was as tangible as the discarded peanut shells on the floor. There were a few seconds of astonished silence. The victor straightened his clothes and took his seat at the bar, and the room quickly regained its hum of conversation. Kilzer found his way back to the table. The fight had lasted under two minutes.

"Thought I was going to lose these babies, but we made it here unharmed." Setting the bottles on the table he pointed toward the bathroom and made hastily for that direction.

Roberts looked up thoughtfully from his drink. He pointed in the direction of the fight, "Now that's morality." Lipman hadn't heard him. "That," and again he pointed, "is morality."

"Yeah, it certainly makes you think. That guy could have been killed. I mean he didn't get that much height but—"

"Not *mortality*, Lipman—morality!"

"Morality?" he asked astonished. "What does that have to do with morality?"

"Two men," began Roberts, "those two men had a conflict of interest, which is always the starting point of ethics, and it was settled the way every conflict of interests is settled, by force."

"But we don't even know what it was that they were arguing about, most likely nothing. The little guy probably thought the big guy was looking at him funny or something and decided to have it out with him. He was probably trying to impress a girl."

"Didn't you notice that long vacuum of silence after the fight? What do you think the reason for it was? Nobody in this joint made a move, a sound, until he the victor sat down. They were acknowledging him as king... master... God. That silence was a silence of respect and understanding, that he," Roberts said, nodding at the victor, "is the law."

"Because he kicked somebody's ass?" Lipman asked sarcastically. "Come on. They weren't giving him respect—it was fear. Plain and simple."

"Now what you are correct about," Kilzer began, as he sat down, lifting his index finger from his glass and pointing it toward Roberts, "is that that man will be obeyed as a law. Where you are incorrect, where you are always incorrect is that *he is* The Law. His actions make no claims on how others *have* to act. He is only obeyed because people *think* they should."

"Power. Power. Power. Any way you look at it, it has to do with who has the power, either physical brute power or control over agents of force," said Roberts.

"All that man demonstrated is how social order is created. He is not the indifferent force of nature you think he is. Neither is he The Law. There is nothing transcendent about what he did. There is nothing transcendental. There are only private prudential choices. All he did was obey himself, which simply recognizes conventional morality as just that, a matter of mere convention. Socrates is the best example of this," said Kilzer.

"You're not really saying anything different from me," said Roberts. "You're just being a pain in the ass."

"Socrates?" Lipman asked, astonished. "Socrates would be appalled. What you are both talking about leads to immorality. If you live in this way, like that brute, you will be caught, prosecuted, and punished."

With a wave of his hand and a smile Kilzer denied this. "You know as well as I do that that makes no difference."

Lipman groaned.

"Only a Christian would assume a private choice leads to punishment. All I know—all you know—is that I have to create my own values or—"

"Be enslaved by another man's," interrupted Roberts, finishing the line in unison with Kilzer. "Is that your favorite line by Blake or don't you know any others?"

"That's what I love about you Roberts," said Kilzer with sincere affection. "You readily confirm Blake's truest statement that opposition is true friendship."

"You guys are still missing the point," began Lipman. "You are not talking about morality but something that destroys morality. By definition, morality is what benefits everyone. It is universal. It is not for a single individual to do as he pleases! And if the principles of morality are universal, they have to be something that can be applied at all times to all people. Your victor over there is not an example of that. We cannot *consistently* apply the principle behind what he did; it doesn't work. It is in conflict with itself. It logically fails. It's like when you break a rule in a game; the game falls apart."

"You can prove *anything* with logic," mocked Kilzer. "And that man *can* consistently apply this principle, though he'd likely get defeated eventually. However, if everyone were to adopt this principle, to beat up others when you want to, things would be chaotic. If the reason to abandon this principle is this, then your reasons are *practical* or prudential, not logical."

"Here," Lipman said, frustrated. He lifted his glass, yanked the napkin aside, and pulled a pen from his inside coat pocket. "Let's say that we're all at a baseball game and the man on first tries stealing second. The catcher's throw comes up a little short and we wonder how far he actually has to throw from home plate to second base," he said, drawing a baseball diamond. "We know that the distance from home plate to first base is ninety feet. What we need to do is draw a line from home plate to second, creating a right triangle on either side," he said making two triangles. "This line," he said, pointing to the line from home plate to second base, "and the square of this line equal the sum of the squares of the other two sides. 90 squared plus 90 squared, is 8,100 plus 8,100, is 16,200. The square root of this is 127. The same relationships would hold true if I needed to figure out how long a guide wire needs to be that I'm going to put on my flagpole at the house to secure it," he said, flipping over the napkin.

"You don't have to go any further. You're going to create another right triangle and use the Pythagorean theorem to do the same thing in two different yet similar situations. You're going to tell us that whether the example uses flagpoles or baseball fields is irrelevant. That when a mathematician follows the rules of a proof, the conclusions reached will apply not only to the particular situation but to all relevantly similar situations. The universals patterns transcend specifics and you'll say that living morally and *artistically* is no different from seeing the world as a mathematician sees it. Is that about right?" Kilzer asked a deflated Lipman.

"We've heard this a hundred times," said Roberts.

"Just because you've heard it and are bored by it doesn't mean it isn't true. I'm talking about the application of a universal. It tells you *exactly* what to do in every similar situation: is there a right triangle? Then here's what to do. Morality is not dependent upon particulars; it isn't determined by your desires, or the consequences you want to bring about. I don't know why you guys resist this so much. If it isn't universal it isn't morality."

"I can't disregard my individuality and my emotions," said Roberts.

"Our context," said Kilzer, finishing Roberts's list. "Fuck triangles and to hell with universals."

"Thinking universally eliminates doubt," stated Lipman emphatically. "There is something to always reference. It's not all on your shoulders. You don't have to *wonder* if something is right or wrong. You don't have to second-guess yourself. If it is wrong to lie in one situation it is always wrong to lie in similar situations."

"Seems to me you don't have to think," said Roberts. "Like a slave obeys his master."

"Let's be honest here. What you're really talking about or talking around with all this Kant 101 stuff is hurting people. You don't want to hurt people," said Kilzer to Lipman. "And this from the guy who used to tell me that the easy way out is to be commanded rather than to command and only cowards take the easy way. Back in your Nietzsche days. What happened to that?"

"No, no, no," said Lipman. "You're wrong. I know where you're going with all of this and you're wrong. You're wrong about Kant too. We're not slaves. We can reason. We do reason. Just as we can figure out the hypotenuse of triangles no matter where we find them, we can figure out how to live. You think it's like following some tax law. Having emotions and a personal perspective doesn't mean we can ignore following what's unchangeable and ingrained in the universe, in the very requirements of reason! You talk about me acting like a Christian? You guys are Jesus in the garden. You didn't see Socrates weeping before his death. He followed the law," stated Lipman with a dignified air.

"The thing that's most paradoxical about your stance is that you think that, by referring or defaulting to this universal moral principle, you keep from hurting others when, in reality, it's this stance that leads to injury. It's World War II and I'm hiding a Jew in the house and a member of the SS comes to my door and asks me if I am hiding a Jew. Based on your theory, I have to tell him the truth. The circumstances don't matter. Or," he said before Lipman could interrupt, "if murder is wrong then so is self-defense. If abortion is wrong I can under no circumstance abort a baby, even if I'm twelve years old, or have no money, or was molested, or raped. You know it and I know it. So quit trying to force something that does not work; you're trying to convince yourself that you're something that you're not, because you're trying to forget something, because you feel terrible."

Lipman turned away exasperated.

Roberts stopped abruptly and began taking a series of small sips from his glass. Quickly finishing what was left of his drink, he caught the eye of a passing waitress and ordered another. Then, out of what can only be called an immense swell of affection for his friend, Roberts got an idea, stood up, and walked through the crowd to the bar.

Lipman looked to Kilzer and back to Roberts fighting his way through the still substantial crowd.

"Hi, I'm Dean Shwindel," said Roberts to the bartender. "I'm with the manufacturing company that supplies your glassware, and I need to look at a couple of your glasses. Whatever you have is fine. A couple mugs or wine glasses, even a few snifters would be fine."

The bartender, a heavyset gentleman in his late forties, eyed him with a combination of distain and mistrust.

"Why?" he asked coldly.

"Well, we've had a few complaints that your distributor is messing with our glasses, lowering their quality. We had one customer in Duluth who actually lost a tooth as a result of the sabotage. Which is exactly what it is: sabotage. I hate to use strong words like that but that's just what it is. A poor man in Des Moines cut his lip up pretty bad; the glass shattered and shredded the guy's lip. Never could get all the bits out. Hurts every time he lifts a glass to take a sip. See, we happen to know that another glass company is trying to get rid of us. So they are trying to discredit us by placing insiders in this distributing company. Unfortunately, money still talks, you know. Honest work like the kind you do here just means nothing these days. So I just need to make sure none of our product has been messed with. It's really beneficial to both of us."

Slowly the bartender placed a glass on the bar in front of Roberts.

"I'll need two."

With even slower movements and without taking his eyes off of Roberts he placed another glass on the bar.

Roberts picked one of the glasses up, held it up to the light, turned it to and fro, rubbed it, and squinted deeply.

"Yep, these are certainly ours. High quality, if I do say so myself," he said shifting his eyes from the glass to the bartender. "You can tell by the lip of the glass specifically. See the little ridge," he said holding the glass up the light and toward the bartender. The bartender leaned forward barely looking at the glass. Roberts gave it several light taps on the railing that surrounded the bar, turning it as he did so. "Well, this one certainly seems okay." He handed it back to the bartender, who looked at it curiously before putting it back.

Without a moment's hesitation he raised and smashed the remaining glass on the imitation bronze railing; glass flew up and out in every direction. Lipman stared on in awe. "He should take a pen from his pocket and write something on a nearby napkin about the quality of the glasses. That would be a nice touch," reflected Kilzer.

The bartender stared, waiting.

Before all the pieces of glass had struck the floor, Roberts had already turned around to Lipman and Kilzer, "You see, all he had to do—" And before he had finished his sentence, his head quickly turned left and right, showing surprise at the man that grasped him from behind. The bartender had alerted the bouncer long before he had given Roberts the glasses.

"Take him out of here," said the bartender steadily in a deep, gravelly voice. The bouncer already had Roberts halfway out the door. "Get his friends out of here too. Those two over there," he said. The bouncer turned his head around as he exited the bar to see the bartender pointing at Lipman and Kilzer, who were already beginning to stand.

Lipman, who dropped his head severely even before Roberts broke the glass, put on his coat with an exaggerated laboriousness that stunned and disappointed Kilzer, who had been smiling with delight from the moment Roberts left the table. He finished his drink as he walked toward the door, leaving the glass on the hostess' podium, giving a casual salute to the hostess. Lipman mumbled a quick, unheard apology.

Outside the bar, Lipman, Roberts, and Kilzer sat on the curb across from the bar.

"So, here we are," said Roberts gleefully, scanning the area.

"We sure are," said Lipman. "I can't believe you." He quickly added, "In all the years I've known you you've never done anything like this."

"And I've never seen you so timid," threw in Kilzer to Lipman.

"I was overdue really. Something just came over me. But think about it later."

Kilzer pulled out a cigarette, lighting it promptly.

"You kill me," laughed Roberts.

"Why's that?" asked Kilzer curiously watching the smoke exit his mouth.

"You won't smoke inside in a bar, the one place left in this country where you're still allowed, but once you're out here…"

Kilzer simply shrugged.

"It's cold out here," commented Roberts. They all agreed. No one moved. "What can I say? Force is morality. I proved it. That bartender didn't say or even have to say that breaking glasses was right or wrong or against policy. He didn't like it, so he threw me out. The only explanation he *had* to give was in calling the bouncer. I mean, he can have me thrown out just because he doesn't like me. Morality is power," he said, smugly pointing at them sitting on the cold, hard curb outside of the warm bar with its softer seats.

Lipman leaned back. "I don't think so."

"You know what concerns me about the whole thing?" asked Kilzer, "is that we're all greasy salesmen, the whole lot of us. You say morality is this, Lipman disagrees and says it's this, and I disagree with both of you and say this. That's why I liked what Roberts did."

"Oh, come on," groaned Lipman.

"I agree it proved nothing, but it did get at something very important. It made me think about the point of all this goddamned talking. We've been doing it as long as we've known each other. Do we get so wrapped up in abstractions that we forget reality? I don't ever remember reading anything about a guy asking Socrates if he should be faithful to his wife or how to get ahead at his job. I mean, someone must have asked. Get any notoriety and people, dumb, well-meaning people, will ask you anything. I can just picture it, Paul or Luke or John sitting at their desks, thinking the same thing, 'Should I put it in there?' And they're all picturing that same, bald, fat ordinary guy making his way through the crowd, asking Jesus if he could touch him to get rid of his hangover.

I know it happened! And they're all sitting there saying, 'It happened, should I put it in there? Or let it go?' Why don't we apply any of it to real life? Because really most of us don't. We learn and learn and then when it comes down to it, we either fall back on all the crap we learned when we were five years old, which in my mind isn't really acting at all, or we find some way to avoid acting, which is bullshit. I know I'm not being as clear as I could be, but I am a drunk."

"Yes! Yes!" said Lipman for the first time genuinely excited. "I completely agree!"

"I don't know how you can say that," said Kilzer, sincerely concerned.

"Why? That's my whole thing."

"I've read Kant. Don't the things he discounts—individuality, emotions—enrich our life and make us happy? Aren't they the essence of life, of art? How can't they be a part of a person's life? And then you sit there and agree with me that ethical theories don't apply to everyday life. How can you? I mean, really, I'm asking. Do you really think that's ethics? That's happiness? I mean, you're an artist."

"I guess it matters if you agree with *that* definition of happiness," Lipman said soberly.

"I'm sorry, man. I'm not trying to rag on you. It's noble what you're trying to do. And I'm probably the one contradicting himself. Or at least being a hypocrite. But don't ethical ideals take good ideas to extremes in ways that can't be carried out? It seems to me that every time someone fucks around on his wife, or betrays a friend, or lies to himself, he's inflicting a very real pain. We overlook this. All I know is that you'll never kill and you'll never kill and I'll never kill, most of us never will, so what good is all this value stuff if it doesn't deal with things that happen to most people most of the time?" Lipman looked away. "I tell you, it's the small paper cuts we inflict every day; they're much worse."

With that Kilzer finished his cigarette and found his way to his car. As he passed them Roberts looked at Lipman, "I don't know if he's right or not but it's no coincidence he mentioned hangovers."

"No doubt," agreed Lipman.

After a pause he asked, "Don't you have to get going?"

Lipman considered. "Not yet."

"Won't Leslie be home soon?" asked Roberts.

"What time is it?"

"Nine-thirty."

"That's odd. Feels like a million o'clock. She's meeting some friends. She told me she wouldn't be home until ten-thirty or eleven o'clock. So we've got a little time."

Roberts nodded his head, pleased.

"Hey, you guys, get outta here!" came a voice from the bar's entrance.

"I was thinking about going to Europe. Paris."

"Oh yeah? That'd be nice," commented Roberts.

"Hey, world travelers, get the hell off my property. Go home! There's gotta be somebody waiting for even you two."

Looking up, Roberts said, "That's a strangely comforting thought."

"I guess we gotta go."

The man stood at the entryway to the bar until they were deep into the parking lot, well out of sight.

"The lawmaker strikes again."

As Lipman opened the door to his car, he looked at Roberts, "You know, I'm not convinced."

"Yeah, but we did have some fun."

"You sound like a character in some damn bad movie," said Lipman over the roof of his car.

Both men lowered themselves into their respective cars and, having discussed morality's categorical imperative, drove home drunk.

⌒〜

Brushing his hair from his face, Leslie smiled at Lipman, "I wouldn't worry about it." She paused for a moment, attempting to catch his now-revealed eyes that he had carefully turned away. "You were working hard last night. You were up long past when I went to bed. I didn't even feel you crawl in. Must have had a productive night. I'm glad. And don't worry about my parents—"

"I wasn't."

"I explained it to them and they'll understand eventually. They just don't get art. Once they know you, they'll love you."

"They know me," he said defensively, pulling the sheet over his exposed stomach.

"They've met you," she said, "several times, and you've made a good impression, but they haven't seen you enough to know you—really know you. They will. Dinner was good, though. You would have enjoyed it. And you would have really loved the place. It was a little posh for me, but the bar was all backlit with this deep orange light and there were candles everywhere. I thought of you the entire time. The food was okay but we were really paying for the atmosphere. I thought it would make a great place for one of your stories," she said waiting for his response.

"Sounds nice," he said without commitment, resenting her intrusion into that world.

She looked at him again, her head titling softly to the side, "I'm going go take a shower."

"All right."

Lipman watched as she pulled herself out of bed and made her way to the bathroom, making a shield out of her pajamas to prevent herself from being completely nude. He thought it was very strange that this woman, and in reality all women he'd known, when sheltered by the anonymity of the dark (which, as anyone knows, disappears once the eyes adjust) will let you do any of a million things to their bodies without question or a hint of self-consciousness. But the thought of that same man witnessing them naked in the confessional eye of light provokes inestimable horror and shame in them. Lipman thought, this is true whether I've just met the woman, or as with Leslie, whom I've known for many years. Did people make love to become anonymous? Perhaps the only purpose of the darkness was to make the other person disappear. Or to make surrender appear. He was too tired to deal with all the melancholy answers to this question. He decided to forget it, although he did make a mental note to explore this theme further in a short story or novella. Of course, when transposed (Lipman's terminology) into fiction, his scene would contain a woman struggling to shelter herself with discarded street clothes, a jumble of jeans, t-shirt, socks, rather than pajamas. It was safer that way. And a stronger image.

Once he heard the bathroom door close and the flash of the water explode from the shower head, he lay his head back on the pillow, which was unnaturally warm, and tried to forget the past few hours. He found this took immeasurable strength, so he just let his mind lie as warm and uncomfortable as the pillow. He couldn't figure out what had gone wrong. He was usually his best in the morning. No prep work, he thought. He laughed indulgently. Listening further to the sound of the running water, he almost dozed.

A few minutes later, he was pulled from his lethargic state by the harsh sound of the door being yanked open. He opened his eyes instantly, searching the room for Leslie. It took him several seconds to figure out that she had only opened the door a crack to let some of the hot air out of the bathroom. He lay back again.

"How was Roberts?" came Leslie's voice from the bathroom.

He didn't know how to respond. But before he could, Leslie peeked her head out, smiling, "Didn't know I knew, did you?"

"No. Sorry."

"Don't be. You don't see those guys enough anymore," she said, disappearing back into the bathroom. "Having a block?"

"A little. Had a lot of ideas when I came back. That's why I got to bed so late," he said by way of justification. After a moment he asked, "How'd you know?"

"Your clothes," came her echoey voice, "they smelled like smoke."

"Ah," he said. "Sorry."

"Honey, stop it," she said, her voice firm but warm. "I know how important those guys are to you. All that talk you guys do. Way over my head."

"Don't say that," he said, sitting up against the headboard.

"There's a lot of things I can do and one I most cannot do is talk about philosophy."

"You could if you wanted," he said under his breath resentfully.

"So what did you guys talk about? Wait, hold on, I have to blow dry my hair. Hold on."

Lipman, hearing the buzz of the hair dryer, waited. It stopped and then started again. Finally, it stopped.

"So what did you guys talk about?" she asked from the bathroom.

"Oh the usual. But I don't know. It was okay."

"What happened?"

"Nothing. We just talked."

"Something happened. Did you guys disagree about something?"

"Kind of."

"What?"

He could hear various tubes of make-up snapping open and closed. He could picture her, leaning close to the mirror, applying the various items, and then leaning back to examine what she had done. Then leaning in for minor fix-ups.

"Nothing really."

She waited in silence for the answer.

"We did get thrown out of the bar, though."

Leslie pulled the door open to see his eyes, unsure if he were lying or not. She saw him, sheet pulled up to his mid-chest, fiddling with a corner, not even looking in her direction. She knew immediately that he was telling the truth. After a return to the bathroom and ten more minutes of silence, Leslie emerged completely dressed for work from the waist down, but from the waist up, only in her bra; she claimed it gets too hot in his bathroom. She ran her hands through her hair one last time, trying to make it fuller than it really was. Lipman was still lying motionless, his eyes looking past everything. Despite their conversation, she knew he was still embarrassed and was trying to hide himself behind that blank, motionless stare. She stood in front of him putting her earrings on.

"Why were you kicked out? Was there a fight? Was anyone hurt?"

"No, no, nothing like that. Well, there was a fight, but it didn't involve us. Not directly. We were just talking about it. I mean… Roberts was just… he just smashed a glass in the bartender's face."

"Why? That doesn't sound like him."

"I don't know. He was being an idiot."

"How did this happen? I don't understand." She was finally putting on her shirt.

"We were talking about the guys who got in a fight and whether or not aggression was a basis for morality. It sounds kind of stupid now but… That's what we were talking about."

"Sounds interesting," she said, buttoning the last button on her shirt.

"I guess."

"What did you say?"

He thought a long time before he spoke. "I said it wasn't. Roberts said it was. And Kilzer went a totally different direction."

"Sounds like him."

"Tell me about it. A couple things he said really got to me."

She approached the bed and sat on its edge.

"I have to leave, Don. But I want to hear all about it tonight. What Roberts said, Kilzer, you, okay?"

He nodded.

She stopped and looked at the shape of his body revealed by the single white sheet. She noticed how much smaller he looked without his clothes on, especially his work clothes. She felt her attraction for him grow. You have awful timing, she thought. He'll think you're pitying him. You don't have time anyway. There's always time, she countered. She kissed him on the forehead (which she knew wasn't any better) and said softly, "I have to take my grandmother to the doctor and then make a late meeting. I'll see you later tonight for dinner. Just you and me. Not like what we will have to endure a few weeks from now," she said with an anguished, wise laugh. "And our anniversary, Steve's birthday, Thanksgiving, Christmas, and the rest of those horror shows."

She rose. As she reached the bedroom door she turned and as she put on her black pea coat and gloves, she whispered, "You are probably just preoccupied with your work." She smiled and added sweetly, "What am I compared with immortality?" Then she was gone.

Deep in thought, he whispered flatly, "Yeah," unsure if he meant this ironically or not. He was momentarily distracted. Lipman didn't care for irony. He always felt like he was being laughed at when he tried to discern if others were being ironic. Having to guess if he understood something or having to choose which meaning was the "more correct" always angered him. Was it ironic that, at the very moment he was angry at the thought that Leslie had been pressuring him to live together, he decided to ask her to move in? He was greatly pleased when he discovered Rilke's pronouncement that irony "didn't dive into the depths." He wrote an entire story based on this, a good story, but his enthusiasm for this line had caused him an even greater sense of humiliation when he realized that Rilke too might have been indulging in irony. He burned the story. He also burned his copy of Rilke.

Finally, he got out of bed and headed for his study. Disregarding irony (there might be a sequel to the burned story, one to counter it) he played with his earlier thought once more. Was there something about being seen in the nude that was more exposing than being touched, even in the most intimate of spots? He looked down between his legs. "Maybe." Unwilling to push his questioning any further, he entered his study.

It had been his habit to go to his typewriter before breakfast and write a few lines to loosen himself up. Just like a runner stretching before a race, he would say to himself. Once the mind got going, there was no telling where it would go. Rolling a sheet of paper into the machine, he began with some automatic writing. He typed only two lines. Looking at what he had wrote, he exclaimed in anguish, "No! Not again! Why? Why?"

He pulled the paper, which came out with a harsh zipping sound. On the page were the two sentences, which he instantly recognized as written by Oscar Wilde:

> *I have put only my talent into my works.*
> *I have put all my genius into my life.*

He lowered himself slowly into his chair, his legs tucked automatically beneath it, his head dipped in utter defeat, his shoulders shrugged. Being a writer was his sole identity. He understood his life in terms of placing his genius into his works. Those terrible eighteen words mocked his life's pursuit, emptying everything he believed in of meaning. In his youth those lines had filled him with rage and he challenged them by obsessing about his art. He succeeded in keeping them at bay. But now those words appeared more and more. They seemed to declare his defeat, asking for his surrender. Looking at those words, he knew he had betrayed himself in the worst possible way. He had laid down his art for his life. The paper slipped from his hands, hitting the edge of his lap and spinning before it settled face up on the floor. He sat long into the day, paralyzed, unable to move or think.

JOE AND HIS WOMEN

4

CONSTELLATIONS

There would be a time not that far in the future when the room on the second story of the yellow house on Snelling Avenue would forever be bittersweetly remembered as the place where Joe fell in love for the first time. Was it funny that a rundown building should be the birthplace of love? Not really. Joe would come to know that love is less a discovery than a circumstance, an accident. Its symbolism has the same genesis as a chalk outline marking the arbitrary spot where you, not looking, were hit by a speeding vehicle. What is called being in love is really the second of two steps. One must first be struck down.

It was the dim yellow glow, deepened by the thick, cheap, always-drawn curtains, that first caught his eyes and drew his head upwards as he turned at the corner of Dale and Louisiana, a young, blond-haired girl named Caroline fastened proudly but submissively to his side. It was that light that told him that he was about to leave the silent rows of residential houses, made black by sleep, and reenter the city, an insomniac running nervously along Snelling Avenue. And it was the sound of the creeping cars that grew steadily louder that

caused his body to stiffen, his shoulder to pull back uncomfortably as if from a persistent itch, until he finally freed himself from her. Within a few paces her body caught up to his,
no longer expressing the tenderness of a lover but slipping on
indifference like a robe: they were like two anonymous people
walking together sometime after two in the morning.

Joe had been pursuing Caroline since the beginning of the
school year, even inviting her to a Halloween party where his
girlfriend would be. It wasn't until after spring break that she
first agreed to meet him at Whitman Park. It was four in the
morning and he had desperate, sweet words for everything:
how attracted to her he had been for so long, how he longed
to be with her, how special she was. He had a girlfriend. He
explained why he couldn't yet break up with her. By the time
the sun had come up, they were sitting on the swings, kissing
and talking.

It made little difference to him that her face would curl in
anguish when she saw him walking arm in arm with Laura,
that other woman who looked so much like her and was a
senior. Or when he would whisper to Monica, another senior
girl he was seeing, in front of Old Main, making her giggle,
or kiss the top of her head in the cafeteria making her smile
gently. Even eye contact couldn't make him flinch. At first,
she believed these were only the garments of painful neces-
sity, but in her heart she knew that it was much more. She
knew that, as long as the sun kept its teacherly eye on the
earth, and as long as his smiling, arrogant face soaked up the
warming rays of devotion from Laura and Monica, that *she
did not really exist.*

Walking around, she would look at her hands, touch her
face, and pull long strands of hair in front of her eyes to prove
that she existed. She would look at her reflection in store windows, in hoods of cars, and in spoons just to see her image.
And as pleased as she was when it always appeared, there was

something false about it, like an empty promise. Only when she looked into his face, the only real mirror, the only absolute proof, did she know that she was alive. Even if it was only true in the nighttime hours when they were able to see one another. In the day, her glance would come up blank. Empty. He was there, but she was not.

One day she sat in her lonely, sparsely decorated dorm room smoking. Opening the window, she accidentally set her cigarette on a piece of paper. Swearing, she quickly picked up the burning paper and set it in an ashtray. She noticed the paper's small burnt hole and how the remaining paper seemed to pull back in horror, trying to escape the nothingness that rushed toward it on all sides. She pulled back reflexively, almost nauseous.

Again she picked up the cigarette, this time placing it deliberately on the paper, letting it burn. She marveled at the fear the paper showed as it tried to escape oblivion, at how much character the hole, the emptiness, seemed to have. Fire consumed the paper with vigor, aggressively and monstrously. How difficult to be that in which birth and death coincide. No matter how much character the fire possessed, eventually it would snuff itself out.

"That's me," she thought. "That nothingness is just like me."

Putting her cigarette out before she vomited, she was determined that tonight would be the last time she ever saw him. Yet, when he appeared from between the trees as if from some deep part of her own hidden nature, his face hidden by shadow, she knew her words had been untrue even as she had thought them. Only he had the power to snuff her out.

For as much pain as his nightly leaving caused her, it caused an equal flowing of joy; she was his secret lover. And secrets imply great value. She was so special that he could share her only with the unspeaking night, that keeper of all the world's secrets. And she possessed something rare: a man who *asked* to hold her hand, a man who grew melancholy pondering the stars and who shared, in unabashed tones, his sadness. Looking at the horizon, she no longer saw a thin line that seemed to connect earth and sky, but two hands clasped in silent prayer, a prayer she alone understood. Exposing what they had would lessen its worth. And as sure as the approaching street confessed that their secret would evaporate under the public's prudish eye, so, too, would she return home alone.

Entering the small room across the street from him, she disrobed immediately and slipped quickly into her bed, making sure her discarded clothes were safely hidden in the small wicker hamper. So sharp had her sense for him grown that the scent of him on her clothes would keep her from sleep.

No sooner had she lain down to gather whatever sleep was left in night, and turned off the overhead light (she left the small bedside table lamp on), then she began her nightly ritual of examining the painting that hung on her wall opposite the bed. It was a simple work depicting a man largely in silhouette, his back turned to the viewer, peering suspiciously over his shoulder. None of his features could be made out except the outline of his face. It was the strength of his forehead, the vulnerability in the lowering of his chin, that made her see the resemblance. Each night as his goodbye resonated in her ears and the eager day chased him, the night, and her existence away, she would focus on this painting and fill its blank form with a new feature she had somehow overlooked. There wasn't a night when she didn't discover a new attribute, just as there wasn't a day when her roommate, Julie, a plain and simple girl, failed to shake her head, saying, "I don't see it." But this didn't matter. To her, it was the difference between connecting the dots and mapping out the constellations. It didn't take long until she believed it the most wonderful painting in the world.

And while it was true that he idealized her, it was an idealization of a wholly different kind. In his mind, he took her form and emptied it of all familiarity until it ceased to resemble her at all. In her stead was placed everything he wished to be. When he recalled those nights, he saw an autonomous man and a world that leaned on his shoulder as if he was *its* axis. His soul thrilled at the way she looked at him with bated breath, malnourished without the words that he alone could feed her.

When he lay alone in bed, thoughts of her disappeared as quickly as sleep descended. She was first replaced by dreams and then, in a matter of hours, by a daytime love named Laura. And if the next day someone pointed out to him the one he called *love* with such force at night and he asked him her name, he would be unable to answer.

THE NOTHING GIRLS

They sat tucked into a back pocket of a dead-end hallway, several feet from the last dorm room door and overhead light, the last several yards of hallway quickly snatched up by shadow. Joe sat with his back to the wall, legs pulled up to his chest, looking left past the girls, his chin aligned with his shoulder. Laura sat on his right, also against the wall. Long hair, blond. Longer legs. One tucked beneath her, the other stretched out in front of both her and him, her left hand gently resting on his right knee. Monica sat cross-legged in front of him, a little to his left (north-by-northwest, he would later think) with a look so determined she seemed directly in front of him, her hands placed gently on his feet.

Laura's not as pretty as Monica, he thought. And she's not a good kisser. Her underbite makes her mouth too small. No room for your tongue to move. But she's smarter and easier to fool because of it.

There had fallen on them that tremendous silence that is the natural coda to the exhaustion of words. Joe knew that endeavors of the heart cannot be explained, resolved, or understood with words. And so, like anyone holding the failure of words in their hands, they sat in silence, waiting for the antidote of more words.

"It's just so hard," offered Joe, saying nothing else, his last words fading out, still careful not to look at either woman.

Monica's and Laura's eyes blazed toward him, like fires flaring for a brief moment before dying again. Their heads fell.

Of course, that flame rose for only one thing: consummation, not merely in the crude physical sense, but in the parallel (although not necessarily deeper) longing for intellectual, spiritual, emotional ownership. There was a uniformity to that silence: the anguish of longed-for and denied communion. Monica's and Laura's desires were simple: they longed for him. (It was true that what drove those desires was very different. Laura was spurred on solely by his intellect, whereas Monica was pulled forward by the insecurity she sensed behind his attractive, confident exterior. Nevertheless the end result of their desire was the same. The silence and resulting ambiguity was unbearable.

The longness of Laura's body, which would eventually make her the more graceful, the more womanly of the two, gave her the appearance of a teenager not yet accustomed to her body. She even slouched, draining her movements of any femininity. But it was more than a physical uneasiness that circled her. The slight curve in her back and the protruding underbite were joined by an uneasiness that resulted from her moving from a small rural community to a large metropolis. Her mind was not ready for the changes in size and values. This tension was her charm. It was what drew Joe to her.

"Maybe," began Laura.

Joe peered out of the corner of his eyes. He had learned that, when it came to women, the most successful things happened peripherally.

"What?" asked Monica, overflowing with hope.

He listened to her. It was her laugh, simple as that. Or rather, it was the way her face lit up, a dull greasy light, unpretentious and sincere, that captured his heart. Hearing her speak made it obvious. Oh, later there would be a whole host of things that he would use as stock answers to that question: her tiny hands circled with rings; the way she took care of her little brother; the way she closed her eyes and clasped her hands behind his back when they made love, as if she were praying; her sneaking into his work and his admiring her shape before recognizing her, and on and on. But locked into his heart was that short laugh, that laugh that seemed to try to keep itself secret, that shy, nearly embarrassed laugh that made him sigh. But he couldn't. Not here.

"I don't know. It's just that... I don't know what you will say. Either of you," continued Laura carefully.

He continued watching them out of the corner of his eyes, his eyelids making small slits. He knew what he was witnessing. Here, before him, were the two girls who had said: *nothing.* When Monica was haplessly, unknowingly, passed among thick frat boys with the message, "If you're looking for an easy lay," and later, upon finding out, sat for three days without speaking; when Laura drove six hours every weekend that summer just for the chance of seeing Gabe, always ending up at Monica's summer apartment soul beaten, occasionally laid, and sadly hopeful; when they chronicled every insult, injury, joy, tear, ache, they said: *nothing.* These were the two who had held each other and said: *nothing will come between us.*

"It's just been so difficult since we got back from California. So I was thinking that maybe," began Laura, addressing Joe who was now looking down into his lap, "you would consider dating both of us. We both like you and you like us. I mean, if Monica would agree," she added hastily.

This was what he had hoped for, been waiting for, tried to plan for, but had never thought would actually happen.

After a moment's reflection, Monica added, "I could live with that. What do you think, Joe?"

It was the most pleasant moment of his life.

CALIFORNIA

The midsize rental car sped along the Santa Monica freeway.

"Where do you want to eat?" Laura asked, looking at her nails, which she filed studiously.

"I don't care," Joe said indifferently.

"Well, let's see," she said, peering out the passenger side window, hands and file falling into her lap. She tucked her long right leg beneath her and watched the many restaurants and businesses framed by the rows of palm trees. "It looks like we have plenty of options."

He scratched the back of his head although it did not itch.

"I said I don't care."

"Alright, let's see. How hungry are you?"

He did not respond for a moment.

"Yeah, I'm not *that* hungry, but I'm getting there," he finally said.

She smiled. They drove for a quarter of an hour without speaking.

"Last night was great," she said with a coy smile.

He looked at her blankly, not knowing what to say or how to feel. She didn't notice.

"Would you mind closing the window, darling?" asked Laura.

"What?" he asked, continuing to look straight ahead, although he had heard her.

"The window. It's blowing my hair all over and it's going to get all tangled."

He said nothing.

"Joe?"

He remained silent.

"Can't you put it in a ponytail or something?" he finally said, loudly.

"I guess so," she said. And then, "Is something wrong? You seem upset."

"I'm not upset."

"Are you sure?"

He turned to her, jaw clenched. "What did I just say?"

She shrugged and pulled her purse from the floor of the car and began digging through it, looking for an elastic ponytail holder, humming quietly. He sighed heavily, concentrating on staring directly ahead, noticing nothing except the cars in front of him, and the speed he was going (just over the speed limit). He tried not to notice his hunched-over girlfriend (why did I have to use *that* word when seducing her, he asked himself) rifling through her purse, plopping all sorts of items between them: a brush, wallet, several sets of keys, a pack of gum (which slipped through the break in their seats), a compact, a pocketsize Kleenex, and another nail file. He restrained himself from asking why she had several sets of keys. When it was clear she had not found a ponytail holder, his body tensed up like a coiled snake, waiting for her to speak, becoming tenser as she put her things away. She marveled at them as if she were seeing them for the first time, took a stick of gum, offered him one (a stern shake of the head), and finally turned to him, a look of satisfaction and completion in her smiling eyes, "Nope. Don't have one. Sweetie?"

He looked at the speedometer, a passing car, then back to the speedometer.

"Sweetie?"

"What?" he asked as he watched another passing car and the speedometer.

"The window."

"Fucking fine," he said, rolling his window up in an exaggerated display of effort.

"Sweetie, what's wrong?"

"It's just so goddamn hot," he said, then abruptly stopped. Then just as abruptly he started again, "Do you have to be so worried about your looks? I mean, I am here with you."

She sat back, stunned. She knew what he was saying.

"I just don't want my hair to get tangled. That's all," she said truthfully.

The strings that bind every couple were tightened severely in Joe and Laura at that moment. After several minutes of silence, guilt forced him to speak.

"So where do you want to eat? Looks like there are plenty of places around here. Any of these look good?"

"Sure."

"You like Italian, right? Let's go to that place over there. What do you say?"

"Looks fine."

"We don't have to go there if you don't want it. Look, there are plenty of other places. What about that place? You're not even looking."

"Whatever you pick is fine."

"No, it's not. Don't be that way."

"What way?"

"That way. The way you're being. That upset way."

"How do you want me to be?" she asked.

"Forget it."

"Okay," she said dismissively. He almost did.

"I'm sorry, okay. It's just… it's so hot. I'm sorry, okay?"

She looked at him and he could feel it. He could feel the words building behind her silence, words that would explode at him, repeating everything he had promised and how he had reneged on every single syllable. He wouldn't go through this, not today.

"That's it, we have to pull over."

"What?" she asked, pulled out of her hurt by alarm. It would take her a long time before she realized how he had cheated her out of her say and an even longer time before she realized that she could never forgive him for that. "Why? I'm sorry. I'm sorry."

Determination like censorship came over his face; he was no longer aware of her.

He gave the steering wheel a hard turn to the right, nearly hitting the car next to them. He was desperate to exit, but there was no off-ramp. His fury had the car on the right shoulder and nearly in the ditch by the time an exit presented itself. Laura pulled herself down into the seat and said nothing.

Exiting, Joe came to a stoplight, turned right onto a cross-road, and pulled immediately into a gas station; he was nearly out of the car as he slammed the car into park. Bolting out of the car, he rocketed around the pumps and out into the parking lot like a missile following the heat of a moving target. The people who saw him were sure he was drunk.

He finally spotted a phone booth. His step became fiercely focused. He entered the booth and slammed the door behind him so hard it opened up again. Laura sat in the car staring at him.

"Yes, I need to make a collect call."

"Area code and number please."

He groaned and let the phone slide from his ear down to his chest.

"Sir. Area code and number please."

He hung up the phone, exited the booth, stormed into the gas station, withdrew twenty dollars from the ATM, had the cashier break the twenty and came back to the phone booth. The dorm rooms were incapable of receiving collect calls. He finally got through.

"Hello," came the small, broken voice from the other side of the line. He nearly hung up.

"Hi," he said, his head lowered, nearly whispering. Even over the phone he couldn't stand the thought of her eyes looking at him.

There was an extended silence. He wasn't sure if she was angry or hurt, and he wouldn't know until he heard her speak, which explained her reluctance to do so.

"What are you doing?" he asked.

"Nothing," she said. He would swear her head was down, too, although for very different reasons. "I was just about to go for a walk. It's pretty nice out."

"That's cool. It's nice here, too." The words he spoke belied the emotion behind them.

"I know. I saw the weather for out there."

"Oh, you did. What have you been doing?"

"Not much. Getting caught up on homework mainly. That's all I did yesterday. Not too much fun, but I'm glad I'm done. I have biology completely done. Just have psychology and trigonometry left. I don't like trig at all. Kinda putting it off till last, I guess. How about you?"

"I don't know," he said, trailing off. "Went to dinner at a cool place last night. It was on a pier. It was kind of funny. We were a little short so I had to go back to the hotel to get more money while Laura waited, so I took a really long time just to piss the owners off and shit. And then when I came back, we owed like two-eleven, I pulled out two-ten from my left pocket and counted it out real slow and was like, 'I'm going to have to go back.' For the last penny. You should have seen their faces. It was sweet. Pure Morrison! Then, as they were losing it, I pulled the last penny out of my right pocket. It was awesome. Laura didn't love it too much, but I knew you'd appreciate it."

She laughed quietly and warmly but she couldn't hide the fact that she had had been crying.

"Are you there?" He knew she was, but he didn't know what else to say.

"What do you want me to say? You broke up with me to go to California for spring break with your ex-girlfriend. I know you had the trip planned before we were dating. I know it's complicated. It still hurts. I've been going crazy thinking about what you two have been doing."

"What was I supposed to do?" he asked in a whisper.

"Not this."

In her silence she turned from him; he could feel it. With the silence came a resistance, a turning away, the way a Venetian blind, with a single rotation of its handle, shuts out the sun completely. He had to act now or forever lose his chance of keeping her.

"We're having a miserable time."

"Good."

"Why would you say that? I'm trying to tell you ... I don't know, forget it."

"What?" she asked.

"Nothing. What does it matter? I'm just trying to tell you that I made a mistake. But apparently you don't care."

"I do care. I'm sorry. You don't know how terrible it's been back here alone, wondering what you two—"

"It's been terrible here, too, you know. Why do you think I am calling? Here I am in this beautiful place and all I can think about is you. How I want to be back with you. How I miss you so bad I've gone to the bus station to see if we can come back early. How I think I'm in love with you." He stopped abruptly as if his words were as much a revelation to him as he knew they would be for her.

She was openly crying now.

"You mean it? You're not just saying that, are you?"

"Do you think I would just say that? I thought I knew you, Monica. I thought you knew me."

"I do. I do. I love you too. I'm so crazy about you I don't know what to do with myself."

"Let's work everything out when I get back, okay? I promise everything will be okay. I better get going."

"Okay. I'll meet you at the bus station."

"You better not. I don't think Laura's going to want to see you. I will call you when I get back to school."

Joe hung up the phone and exited the phone booth, smiling. He walked back to the rental car. He and Laura drove for miles without speaking, uncomfortable, the obvious sitting before them like a child in a classroom with his hand stretched into the air waiting to be called on, for his question to be answered.

"That was Monica."

"I know."

He looked at her, surprised by her terseness. "It's not what you think," he said with a smile.

"What do I think, Joe?"

"You think I called to get back with her. That I wish I hadn't come here with you. All that crap."

"Crap? And yes, that is what I think."

"That's what I love about you. So nervous all the time when you have nothing to worry about. I'm here with *you*, Laura," he said with emphasis.

Cruising down the Santa Monica highway, a child's arm slowly lowered itself onto Joe's knee. It would be several miles before a smile of satisfaction would blossom on his face.

TOOLS

Class had been over for some time and Joe had been out walking the neighborhood. It was a habit that he had picked up when he first started college. Having just gone to his favorite used book store he would walk the sidewalks of lower-class suburbia deep in thought, the sidewalks allowing him to look just beyond his feet, the descending break in the curbs letting him know when, for those brief moments, he had to look up. After several hours of wandering, he looked up and it took him a few moments to realize where he was. Entering his dorm room, he didn't notice the object at his feet. He placed his keys on the dresser, slipped his shoes off, and stretched out on the loveseat.

A piece of paper that had been slid under his door caught his eyes. Lifting himself off the loveseat with his elbows and exaggerating the effort this took, he picked up the piece of paper. He was surprised when there was no message of love on it. In the middle was a voluminous hole, the edges charred from burning. Holding it up, he felt as though a deep, empty eye were peering at him. Unsure where this came from, he was about to set it on his dresser next to his keys when his door burst open, and Monica and Laura took their respective places on the bed and loveseat.

"What are you looking at?" asked Monica.

"Nothing," he said, setting the paper on his dresser discreetly. "I just got back."

"You're not going to believe what we just heard!" ejaculated Laura.

"Laura!" snapped Monica. "You don't even know if that's true. I don't know what's gotten into you lately."

After the dust of Monica's admonishment had settled, Laura continued.

"I was talking to Marcus at lunch today and he says that Matt was up all night crying."

Marcus, a terminal loner who adored Laura, had only one kidney, was ugly, and liked to get drunk and walk in the rain pitying himself because girls never liked him. Matt resided on the completely opposite side of the social spectrum: handsome, athletic, and desired by all the undergraduate women. He was not scholarly and looked up to Joe because he was.

"Still can't let go, huh?" Joe asked unsympathetically.

Monica shifted uncomfortably on the bed.

"Word is Matt's coming to you for information," Laura said definitively. After this, she sat back and awaited his response.

"Hmm. What could I have done? And now what to do? What to do?" said Joe, lowering himself to the bed.

"Nothing you could do. Nothing," said Monica, setting her hand tenderly on his shoulder. "There was nothing that could be done. When fate intervenes… Dammit, Laura, you just couldn't wait to open your big mouth!"

Joe was concerned for only a moment.

"Monica, I need you to go to Snyder's and pick up a sympathy card," he said with the cool of a general giving an order. She hesitated.

"What?" he asked, balking at being questioned.

"I don't know," she said, shrugging her shoulders slowly, her face pulled into an ugly grimace, "don't you think that's a little weird?"

"I'm not going to have you give it to him," he said, snapping. "I'm sorry. Come here sweetie," he said, taking her taking her into his arms for a moment. "I just need you to pick it out. I'll take of everything. Don't worry. Just trust me." She did, and she dutifully went off.

Laura looked skeptically at the door, at Monica's vanished presence, and at Joe's face, which was concentrating heartily. "You think he's not going to find out?"

He looked up slowly, "Oh, I wholly intend for him to find out."

"He looks up to you, you know. Not that you care. Don't you care?" she asked. "Of course you don't care. That's the business you're in: fucking with people." She was visibly disgusted. "Do you ever think about anyone other than yourself? The consequences of the things you do?"

"Is that what you think?" he asked, hurt.

"Joe, don't try that innocent thing. I know you too well. And yes, I do think that."

"I'm really sorry to hear that," he said turning away. "Your opinion means a lot to me."

"The hell it does. Then why? Why all this?"

He softened and took her hand. "Laura, come on," he said tracing concentric circles on her palm. She nearly swooned.

"Stop," she said meekly. "I know what you're doing."

"I'm not doing anything," he said, watching her intensely, circling with two fingers now, "I just want to do what's best for Matt. For you. For everyone. Don't you want to do that? Do what's best?"

She nodded, agreeing.

"If this is handled just right, everyone will understand," he said, letting go of her hand, which hovered in the air for a moment before falling into her lap. "Matt's not going to like what's going to happen to him. Now you said he's coming to me?"

"Yeah. He says you're the only one who understands. He's really upset. Crying a lot."

"Ok, you need to divert him from me for a little bit. I need it so that, by the time he talks to me, he'll be happy for me, that he sees it as the best thing for everyone involved, that Monica wasn't right for him, that kind of stuff."

"Why me?"

"Isn't it obvious?" he asked with a gesture of disbelief. "You've been in the same position, you can understand what he's going through. You're the one who can calm him down, create a bond with him. He'll get to vent all that ugly stuff with you."

"Why would I do that? Why shouldn't I let him nail you?" she said with months of bottled-up scorn.

"Think of all the pain you suffered. Don't you wish you could have vented? Especially to a sympathetic ear."

Regardless of the fact that it was coming from him, regardless of the fact that she was being manipulated, he was right: she wished she had. And he knew it.

"Once that's out of the way we'll move him on to Monica. He'll see her change of heart, that they have nothing in common. I'll talk to her about that later. And then he gets to me. By that time, everything has been resolved. We'll be like two soldiers. One has been defeated and one is the victor, but they bear no ill will against one another; in fact, they respect one another. He'll probably tell me that she's more compatible with me, slipping in a few things he didn't really like about her."

Laura sat confused and mad, but as always, willing to listen. When he was finished, she headed over to Matt's dorm room to begin her part in the plan that had been laid out for her. Waiting patiently to hear from Monica and Laura, Joe wrote. Later, he would make love to Monica. And much later, he would make his way down to Whitman Park to another girl.

He had nothing against Matt. In fact, he liked him. But he was an obstacle that had to be eliminated. He had certain feelings for Laura and different ones for Monica. It was too soon to tell with the new girl. But as he sat writing, he knew that all of this was of no consequence. That which transcended everything, and determined every action, was his desire to transgress laws and to put those transgressions into writing.

LAURA (OR *FUCK LOTTE*)

She reached into the deep pockets of her long green-brown army coat (which she adored and wore everywhere) and pulled out a pack of cigarettes. Continuing to search the pocket (which quickly became a pillaging) for a lighter without success, she searched the other. Still not finding it, she stopped walking, placed the pack of cigarettes beneath her right armpit (where it disappeared) and began digging in both pockets simultaneously. Finally finding the lighter in her right pocket (where her cigarettes had been), and grabbing the pack of cigarettes with her free hand, she pulled one out, lit it, and began to laugh. Why did I have to stop walking to concentrate harder, she thought to herself? It's like when you're driving, you always turn the radio down when a cop passes, as if the silence will save you. She resumed walking, amused at what she perceived as her species' lack of sophistication.

After a few minutes, she remembered her destination and her thoughts turned to him. It was all such an accident; a lovely accident, but an accident nonetheless. He had shown no physical attraction to her at all for weeks. All they did was talk! She could never have imagined such conversations. (Which wasn't saying much coming from Platteville, Wisconsin, population barely enough to provide patrons for two liquor stores, three churches, and two carpet stores.) Yet there they were, in the cafeteria with Matt, Marcus, and whoever else, it didn't matter. Their intimacy must have been apparent, for, the always alert, always roving Marcus, who had adored her from the moment he first met her, asked, "Are you guys going out?" Without hesitation Joe answered, "For a while now," and walked away holding her hand, her heart barely able to keep up with his never faltering steps. They left a destroyed Marcus to a three-day drinking binge.

Once outside, she was quiet. There was nothing in her upbringing to tell her how to respond, nothing within her limited radar to determine if he was putting on some sort of show, or if he was earnest. She needn't have wondered for long. Within thirty paces of Sorin Hall, he turned to her and kissed her. There was no question if she concurred, agreed with his methods; there wasn't even time for an expression of joy. He wasn't asking. And she had no choice but to go along with him. But she didn't want a choice. And he knew this.

Strangely enough (or so she told everyone in Minneapolis) she hadn't been attracted to him either. It went without saying that she longed to be his "girlfriend" (a term she loathed without being able to find an adequate substitute), but she was not like the other girls she had met since moving from Platteville a year ago. They all sought love (another term she loathed) with their eyes alone, picking out what or who would look best on them like earrings with an outfit. Yet she knew that eyes were poor interpreters of what the heart sees. He was different. He wasn't concerned with appearances or parties (there was always a sarcasm about his presence) or money. She was frightened by his decree that existence was meaningless. That man was free to choose. She was touched, if confused, when, nearly in tears, he would read long passages of *Nausea* to her. He refused to move out of the dorms after his first year like most students who longed for the independence an apartment provides. "Put it all on my bill," he would say. "Why should I worry when everything I need is here? I have a lifetime to worry about that crap. And even then is too soon. I need time to work. It also makes me thankful I'm not a painter," he said with a smile. "All I need is a pen, paper, and my head." At the memory of these words she sped up her steps.

Approaching his dorm, she checked her watch. It was early and she had stayed late. She didn't know if he was a morning person or someone who slept in; she was never allowed to stay and there was no explanation. Although she didn't understand, she respected him and never asked. Staring at the outside of the dormitory and up at his window, she sighed. She sat on the stairs and had another cigarette, fooling herself that three inches of rolled nicotine might make the sun rise faster and quell the aching in her heart.

"Jesus Christ," he moaned.

It wasn't possible. But of course it was. There was no way to deny the buzzing that filled his dorm room, his leaden, dragging head, or the fact that it was already morning. Then there was the duty that he had to adhere, no matter the cost, to his schooling, his relationships, everything. Ignoring what that awful buzzing was reminding him to do, he continued to lie without moving, the nasal voice of fate pushing its way through the tiny speakers of his clock radio.

He hated his alarm and rolled away from it. But his grandmother, a strict Catholic, who, until she got married, was an equally strict Lutheran, taught him never to hate anything. "Hate is an infection that changes you into that which you hate." He rolled onto his back.

"All right, all right," he said, sitting up and shutting it off. "But I do hate the *sound* of my alarm." About this there was no doubt. His grandmother would have to let this go.

He used to have it turned to the radio setting. It was not as jarring. But it was too subtle. Too often he found himself in between waking and sleep, singing along with songs before a too abrupt a change in song tempo woke him up. Or the words of the DJ worked themselves into his already occurring dreams. He couldn't shirk his fate, even for a few more minutes. There was too little time. As much as he hated the whine of the "alarm" setting, he knew getting up was the only authentic choice.

His job was simple. Every morning before class (not to mention between classes, after class, and in any spare moment), he set to paper everything significant that happened. This, he discovered, took time. And was exceedingly complex.

⌒〜

Stubbing the cigarette on the step, Laura stood and entered the dorm, the sun most definitely higher in the sky.

He eyed the door, first in disbelief, then, as the timid knocking continued, severely annoyed before turning his attention back to his frantic scribblings. He was well aware this would be of no use; the knocking did not cease. Besides, it was impossible not to answer a ringing phone, someone calling his name in a crowd, or, in this case, the knocking on his door. There was always some free-floating bit of inspiration that someone else hadn't identified, had let slip away: he would never let that happen. This isn't to say that he was enthusiastic about it. He put his pen down with a look of regret usually reserved for lovers, rose, and turned to the door.

"What?" he barked at the door in a fury of impatience.

Laura backed away from the door as if someone had physically swung a fist at her. She considered tiptoeing back to her dorm, but the hall was too long. She would be caught and there was nothing worse than leaving after disturbing someone; it was like not following through on a promise. She had to go in.

"It's me," she said quietly.

His eyes closed, he sighed, resigned.

"Come in, come in."

She opened the door slowly.

"I'm sorry, I couldn't sleep," she said, lying. "And I took a walk and I saw the light on in your room," she said leaning against the closed door, lying again.

97

"It's okay. Someone has been pranking me all night, pounding on my door," he said, also lying.

"Oh, that's too bad. I don't want to bother you. You look busy," she said, sitting down.

"Sit down, sit down."

"I can leave. I shouldn't have bothered you. I know how you hate that. I just wanted to see you." She started to stand up.

"No, no. Don't worry about it. It wasn't going anywhere anyway," he said with a groan. "Just a few little sections that don't want to do what I'm telling them. Words have a mind of their own. That's what makes it so exciting. Writing is like exploring. You always discover something. It's what keeps you going too." He stood up, collected bits of paper and the notepad and shoved them into his top desk drawer before sitting back down on his bed.

Looking up, she saw a piece of ripped notebook paper with the words FUCK LOTTE pinned to his bulletin board. "What does that mean?" she asked, pointing it.

"Fuck Lotte," he said easily, leaning back against the wall. "It's my credo, I guess. It's from a book by Thomas Mann, *LOTTE IN WEIMAR: The Beloved Returns.* And I guess I have some problems with it."

"Like what?"

"It's like an apology. In *Buddenbrooks* he used a lot of people he knew as models for his characters and got into a lot of trouble over it and in *Lotte* he's kind of saying sorry for that, like he shouldn't have done that. Total bullshit. I mean, is he sorry he wrote *Buddenbrooks?* You'd trade that away because some nobody got mad? Truth is never reassuring. A writer puts everything, including himself, on the chopping block every time he picks up the pen. Fuck Lotte."

"I agree. It can't be considered exploitive if it gets at something fundamental, something real."

"Exactly! Getting at truth is impersonal. You just have to lay it out there. Joyce said that he wanted to show the truth about Dublin in a style of 'unscrupulous meanness.'"

"But he loved Dublin," said Laura." All of his books are about it. And what good is art if it isn't honest? I am working on a piece about the relationship between me and my brother and there are times when I get a stomachache working on it. But I can't apologize for things that are true."

"That would be like apologizing for your life. And I can't think of anything more repulsive," said Joe.

"That doesn't mean I want him to read it, though," she said.

"Why? Because he'll be hurt by it? If the truth stings it's because you're not honest with yourself to begin with. You can't be responsible for that."

"He is my brother."

"I don't see how that matters," he said, perturbed.

"You and family," she said with a laugh. "I did have this idea. I'm not sure what you'll think. But I thought we should each write a story about how we met. I think it would be interesting to see how our perceptions on the same event would differ. It would also be cool to see how our styles differ. All that stuff."

"Like when Van Gogh and Gaughin painted each other," he said.

"Yes. I've been doing a series on all the people I know here. Little short pieces. Have you written about any of the gang?"

"You mean have I written about you?" he asked.

She turned away. "Maybe."

"Depends on how memorable you become," he said, kissing her. "Course I wouldn't want you to hold it against me."

"Why would I do that?" she asked, nervous.

"Ah, now you're thinking like a reader, not a writer. You know that writing only partially reflects the subject written about. That it more accurately reveals who the author is. Here," he said, going to the stack of books on his desk, picking up and paging through one of them. Finding the desired spot, he read, "'The projected creations of primitive men resemble the personifications constructed by creative writers; for the latter externalize in the form of separate individuals the opposing instinctual impulses struggling within them.' That is how I feel about writing. Writing to control the internal wars."

"Can I see that?" she asked, reaching out her hand.

As she paged through it, he said, "And that was only a foot-note."

"*Totem and Taboo*," she said, curious. "Can I borrow this?"

Pulling the book back from her and placing it back on the shelf above his desk, he offered, "We'll go up to Midway later. Best bookstore in town. I know they have it. They have a lot of Freud. I'll buy it for you."

She smiled, then frowned.

"What's wrong?'

"I don't know. Within six months of coming here I lost my virginity, dropped acid, and really discovered literature. I felt free. Like I had finally broken away from Platteville. From my parents. But I'm not free. I sentimentalize Plath. I mystify acid. Deep in my heart, I still think sex is dangerous. That I'm being a rebel doing something wrong when I have it. I still look at Gabe when he's around. And all I write about is home." After a moments silence she said, "I don't want him back."

"I know."

"What if I really can't get away from those things? What if I don't know how?" she said, sincerely scared.

Pointing to a large poster of Jim Morrison on the wall he sang, "'*Tell me where your freedom lies. Deliver me from reasons why you'd rather cry; I'd rather fly.*' It's all up to you. I was no different from you. I was raised Catholic. Went to a Catholic high school. I had never even tasted beer until the first house party I went to. And sex. I had barely kissed a girl. But now I'm a totally different, better, freer person. You just have to want it."

"I think I do. It's just hard losing that innocence."

"You haven't lost any innocence. People only say that, sentimentalize their childhood, to avoid dealing with the tough shit from that childhood. We may be seniors, but we're still young. We have plenty of time to get past all that crap. Let's go to Midway now. I mean, do you have anything else going on?"

"Yes, I mean no. Let's go," she said, heaving on her coat. "Will it be open this early?"

Looking at the clock on the wall, Joe said, "We'll get some breakfast first."

"You're going to have to meet my friend Monica. She's trapped, too."

"I would like that."

They rose and set out to get some breakfast and then headed for Midway bookstore.

SLEEP AND THE SITUATION

5

THE WALK TO THE DOOR

He wasn't in his dorm room five minutes before the inevitable knock came. He sighed. He knew how long that five minutes had been for her. He also knew that, in the time it took to cross the street, go up the stairs, and walk down the hall, she had convinced herself that she had given him enough time. Standing in silence and looking at his feet, he wished she'd leave. Couldn't he have a few minutes to mourn? Regardless of what he had to do, Monica was sweet and beautiful and he longed to hold her again. He had loved her and missed her. Laura had been easier to let go of. Never feeling as wanted as Monica, she just went away. And it was true; he cared more deeply for Monica. He sobered up quickly. Another sad truth was that Caroline knew this, but again, she'd think that the walk to his door had given him enough time to get over Monica. He should be passionately excited to see her. Looking at the blank and unforgiving door, he knew what Caroline was thinking even if she didn't: that the emptiness he was feeling at the loss of Monica would be replaced by having only her. "While the sun was out." It was as simple as opening the door.

Loss didn't work that way. If there was anything he knew, it was that. He also knew that she would put a stop to that logic before pushing it to its natural conclusion: if she could so easily take the place of Monica, then someone else could so easily supersede her. He didn't know why this was so. He managed a meager, "Come in."

"Hey, sweetie," she said, entering and rubbing his shoulder. "How'd it go?"

Despite her obvious attempt at empathy (eyes turned down, voice lowered, rubbing his shoulder), her glee spilled out of her entire body He didn't know what an implosion was, but he was pretty sure that she was headed in that direction. He had been right. Take out one, put in another. They always wanted that and then wondered why it never worked.

"Awful," he said harshly.

She lowered her eyes, this time disappointed. I'm being honest, he thought. He watched her placing herself in a position to be consoled. It would have been ridiculous if not for its sincerity. Ah, what's the point, he said to himself. "But things have to be done. As much as it hurt," he said making sure to stress the past tense, "I couldn't be happier now."

Given permission to express her joy (even at the expense of another's pain), her upturned eyes and smile gave witness to that ecstasy that knows no boundaries, and Joe couldn't resist. His eyes softened momentarily.

"I guess I should be all official about this," he said, taking her by the shoulders, looking at her square in the eyes, "Will you be my girl?" by which he meant *only girl*.

All the joy in her body popped its way out in a single syllable. "Yes."

At least they had avoided an implosion.

She looked over his shoulder and out the window. "Let's go for a walk."

"I have homework."

"Later?" she asked meekly.

"Absolutely," he said with great assurance. And with that, she left the room and he sank into his bed.

⌒〜

He was just happy she fell asleep so quickly. They got to the cabin late and he did everything to make her comfortable. After walking her into the cabin and setting her into the most comfortable chair (a hideously ugly red-vinyl easy chair) with a magazine, he jumped into action. He unpacked the car, bringing in their bags, the games, the food, the beer, the boom box; stocked the refrigerator, pulled the grill from the garage, undid the fold-up beds, none of which needed to be done that night. "You work hard," he said, when she felt guilty about not helping. "You deserve to relax and not worry." His caring moved and relaxed her. By the time he came to bed, it was only moments before she was asleep. Normally this would have bothered him, causing him insomnia.

All of his life, women fell asleep before he did, moments after lying down. The light needn't be off but a minute, sex finished but a moment, the last period added to the last sentence of the day's conversation, and they were gone. The light needn't even be off in some cases; entire parties could be twirling around them. He was always astonished that women could fall asleep sitting up, mocking the sleeping position. Some could fall asleep while driving. This was foreign to him. He could not release himself in that way.

When he was a little boy, he would stay at his Aunt Mary's nearly every weekend. He loved her and everything about being at her house, except for sleeping.

"Mary, are you asleep?" he asked from the darkness, the blanket, which was part of the strange, suffocating darkness around him, pulled up to his chin. It was too hot for the blanket and it made him feel closed in, but he was unwilling to give it up.

"No, I'm awake," came the reassuring voice of Aunt Mary from across the hall and deep in the master bedroom.

That was good. It should have relieved him. And it did, but only until he stopped talking. When her voice ceased, so did his solace. He lay trapped in his mind, trying to fall asleep by will alone, yet listening intently for any signs that his one life-jacket of hope was being pulled away from him by sleep. Only six, he didn't know that he should simply shut his eyes. He still believed that he fell asleep with his eyes open; that he awoke by actually opening his eyes was not a contradiction, so he lay staring.

"Are you still awake?" he asked. He hadn't heard the sound of sheets shifting for an eternity.

"Yes." The response had been slower, the voice weaker.

"You don't sound awake," he said, as if logic could keep one from sleep. This seemed only natural, as it worked on him.

"I am," said the voice, this time louder, the strained force-fulness ignored by him, for now. If the process of falling asleep was exhausting for him, it was no joyride for Aunt Mary either.

It was in that same darkness, in the seventh grade, that his fear revealed itself to him. Unable to sleep, he listened to the wind, passing trains, the occasional clap of a stranger's step on the sidewalk. He mind roamed through the thoughts and feelings that passed through his consciousness like colors. On the verge of sleep, he awoke violently. He lay perfectly still, afraid to open his eyes. As the blackness retreated behind doors and corners, he realized that the darkness—in his room, in the house, of the night pressing up against the windows—clung to the walls and extended its fingers into everything. He even felt the fingers of darkness in the ribs that supported his own body. "There is no God," he said when the sun finally rose.

This was years before college, before he discovered that there were entire movements in the arts based on his nighttime experiences, before he really began to write, before he understood those words he had spoken at sunrise, before he misunderstood that the ultimate goal of all his endeavors with women was freedom. That it was through them that he was to attempt to free himself from all conventions, traditions, rules, laws, and obligations.

He looked over to Monica: small and curled, she resembled a smile, an unconscious smile, reflecting the trust and faith she had in him. He was astonished. Even in sleep he was not this sure of things, much less of his understanding of another person. How could one be that confident, and in sleep? He slept in unforgiving, hot sheets that resisted every attempt at comfort. He felt the desperate need to wake her up, to talk with her, to make love to her.

He greatly appreciated all of her emotional gifts. Yet, they left him lacking. Nor was it about sex. I'm not that shallow, he thought. Although extremely gratifying, it was not the prize he sought. He could have done without it (and in fact had for long periods), but it was written into the contract and he understood that. This isn't to say that he always took the opportunity, which often worked in his favor. Not sleeping with a woman was easily construed as respect or sensitivity. And it was. He needed to believe that he was in love with them. Everything had to be real for him to fulfill this contract.

Nor was it about possessing. He got no comfort from the draw of a woman: the moment he knew he *could* have her, the moment when friend or virtual stranger was transformed into lover was exciting. But there was an excitement to a lot of things. Even the acquisition of the heart was only a step. These, he believed, were all precursors to his transgressions of some law and ultimately his freedom. Disregarding rules (or even seeking out rules precisely to break them) gave him the sense that he was more powerful than others and accountable to no one but himself. By transgressing laws he was able to create his own laws; this was freedom.

The truth was that a woman's presence offered no solace. Once asleep, she was a just another inert bit of terminal darkness, something he fought so frantically to keep out. She *was* a stranger. Not out of choice, but by design. He didn't understand that all attempts at connection were counterfeit. Or if not an illusion, at least exaggerated, the way children take map distances for actual miles. Laying deep in the hot bed, he watched her perfectly content form and did not understand her at all.

"Are you alright?" Monica asked when she awoke the next morning. "You tossed and turned all night. Did you sleep all right?"

"I slept fine. You?"

"Wonderfully."

⌣⌢

"Who needs a beer?" Joe asked as he reached the door. One—two—three— he counted to himself. "Chuck, you need one? Cool."

Entering the cabin, he was greeted by Monica coming out of the kitchen, beer in hand. She set her beer and two others on the table. She approached him, eyes bleary, filled with that sloppy love that alcohol brings to the surface. "Come over here," she said placing her hands firmly around his waist.

"I have to grab beers for everyone," he said, trying to wriggle himself free from her grasp, looking at the yard.

"I'm sure they can wait. Now come over here," she said, placing her hand on his face, pulling it toward her. She looked into his eyes. Everything she felt—love, lust, thankfulness, the need to make love, the instinct to fuck, to cry, to sway, to dance, to laugh—she saw reflected in his eyes. Everything was beautiful. He scratched his neck just beneath his collar. She smiled. God had aligned everything in the world for this one, perfect moment. She was married to this world, to this man, to herself in a way she had never been before. It needed expression, witness, consummation. She moved in to kiss him, a simple, soft meeting of their lovely lips. This was better than two rings, a priest, and a congregation. That was for others. This was for them. He backed away.

Her entire body reacted in shock: her arms pulled back, coming together just above her waist; she leaned her entire upper body to get a better look at the man who had become a stranger in that small gesture.

"What's going on?" she muttered, hurt.

"Nothing," he said, trying to pass her into the kitchen. He had wanted this scene to wait until tomorrow. He tried to fall back upon casualness.

"Fuck you! What's going on?"

"Why should anything be going on?" he said with a smile of disbelief.

"You've never pulled away from me." Tears began to pour down her cheeks. "I want to know now!"

Leaning in the doorway, Chuck said, "Are those beers—oh, sorry," and ducked out again. Quiet murmuring came in from the yard.

"See, the guys need their beer. Sweetie, I'm just drunk. There's nothing going on. Can't we talk later?"

"No! I want to talk now!"

At that moment Todd, their oldest mutual friend, came in, having been sent by common consent. Being someone who would never meddle (he cherished both of these people), he was physically uncomfortable. He made up for it with the biggest smile he could muster.

Monica rushed to him, throwing her tiny arms around his stocky frame, burying her face in his chest, sobbing. Todd looked to Joe in complete wonderment, his upturned hands asking him what the hell was going on. Joe simply sighed. Todd looked down to Monica.

"What's going on, sweet?"

"He won't kiss me!" she sobbed into his chest.

Again, Todd looked to Joe who simply looked to the ground.

"I tried to kiss him and he backed away."

"Is that all?" he asked, pulling her away from him in order to look her in the eyes. "Look at this guy! He's been out with the guys smoking cigars and he knows how much you hate that. He probably wanted to get something to cover that awful stench. Especially if he was going to kiss something as lovely as you!"

Turning her head she blinked at Joe in disbelief, hope still lingering inside of her.

"Is that true, Joe?"

He sighed heavily. "I was smoking cigars."

"I don't care. I want to kiss you."

She went to him, nearly charging him. Again he pulled away.

"See! See! He won't kiss me!" she screamed, sobbing, falling again into Todd's arms. "I want to know now! Tell me what's going on now!"

"Can't this wait until tomorrow?" Joe asked in a whisper, dreading her response.

"Oh God," thought Todd.

"No! No! No!" she sobbed.

"Just let me take care of something."

And with that Joe excused himself to the kitchen, returning with a handful of beers, picking up the two left by Monica on the table, bringing them out to the conspicuously hushed crowd outside, and encouraging them back to their game of bocce ball. He returned.

Still buried in Todd's massive chest, Monica peered out cautiously like a wounded animal. "I want to talk. I need to know."

He knew that there was no way that she would wait until tomorrow and no way she would take anything less than the truth, even if she already knew what it was or what its consequences would be.

"Okay."

He was saddened when she seemed relieved.

"Come on," he said, ushering them into the small bathroom (the only private place in the cabin) made smaller by one of the two folded-up rollaway beds crammed against the wall.

Wiping her eyes with toilet paper, she asked, "What's going on? Why won't you kiss me? Are you mad at me?"

He knew these questions were bullshit, a way of easing them into the harder, darker realities.

"No, no. Nothing like that."

"Then what?" she asked, throwing the toilet paper away.

111

He looked at her face, tender and broken. He had the urge to lie, to wait until they were back in the Cities. It would be so much easier away from this place, the booze, and all these people. But the journey to their end had already begun.

"We have to break up." He leaned against the tiny sink. "I can't articulate the reason." He knew of all the reasons that this one—the truth—would be the hardest to accept, even harder than what she would consider the truth: the other woman. There was no way to explain to her that it was not the other woman but the *demands* of this new woman that had brought about this scene.

"What do you mean?"

"You want to know why, but there is no why, not the kind you want. There is no other woman," Joe lied. Then telling the truth, he continued, "I still love you, I haven't changed…"

"I don't understand."

"Just what I said. What has tied us together is just gone. Over. Done. Whatever it was, it's just gone."

"I have to get out of here."

She burst out of the bathroom. The lightweight door nearly followed her. But, having nowhere to go, she was at a loss. She stormed out into the yard, up and down the dock, and finally back into the cabin and into the kitchen where she began wrapping the uneaten hamburgers in tinfoil and tossing them in the refrigerator. Next, she turned to the meager number of dishes and began filling up the sink, washing the few plates and utensils as the sink filled. By the time the sink was full, there was nothing left to wash and she drained it.

Then she rushed once again through the tiny cabin, through the back door and into the yard facing the lake, where everyone else was in the midst of their game, trying hard to leave her to her pain.

"Hello... hello," she beckoned. When she had everyone's uncomfortable attention, she continued, "I just want everyone to know that I've had a great time but that I have to leave you now. There are burgers in the fridge. If you want them later just heat them up in the microwave. Remember to put something over them or they'll splatter. Anyway, bye." And with that, she headed for the cabin to collect her things.

Still leaning on the sink when he heard Monica's declaration to leave, he straightened up and rushed out of the bathroom, only to run directly into Monica.

"What are you doing? You can't leave."

"I'm not talking to you," she said defiantly.

"You can't drive. You've had too much to drink. You'll kill yourself. And we drove together."

She was in the bedroom, throwing her things into her bag. He followed her in and grabbed her, turning her around.

"Don't touch me! You have no authority over me any longer!"

"The hell I don't!" he screamed. "Okay, okay. I don't have any authority over you. You're right. I'm sorry. Just please don't leave." He looked at her, standing there with her bag dangling from her limp arms in a pathetic display of independence and knew she wouldn't listen. "I'll stay on the couch. This room is yours. Okay? Okay?"

"I can't believe this," she said, pushing her hair out of her eyes. "I lost my best friend because of you. To think I was dumb enough to believe you didn't fuck her in California. I believed you for so long. And you waited, waited until I was so crazy about you that..."

She staggered out to his car, tossed her bag into the passenger side, fell into the driver's side, started the car, and threw it into gear. Joe stood just outside the back door of the cabin. Then, just as quickly, she shoved it back into park and yanked herself out of the car, staggering back to the solitary, unmoving Joe, and shouted, "I don't know how to get to the highway. You *have* to take me there."

"Okay, let me get Todd's keys and see if I can take his car."

He could have easily refused. The series of unmarked, intricate dirt roads made it probable that she never would find the highway, but it was equally probable that she would hit a tree or end up in a swamp. Soon she was following him.

Seeing the drifting car in the rearview mirror, he thought that her swerving seemed like the gentle swayings of a weeping willow in the wind (such was the delusional effect of his drunkenness). But she was drunk, he reminded himself, her bouncing head barely able to stay afloat; it was impossible to indulge in such things. He nearly pulled over to force her to stop. He even slowed the car, but he knew it was useless; now in his car, she would keep going. Passing him as the on-ramp to the highway approached, she rolled her window down and screamed, "I hate you!" as loud and angry and hurt as she could. He would never forget the look on her face.

He later found out that she drove only a few miles, pulled over, and fell asleep. This still distressed him. "She could have been raped."

The next morning, the phone rang. Everyone in the cabin knew who was on the other end. His head aching from booze and the hours he had spent crying, he rolled over and picked up the phone.

"Hello."

"It's me," came the meek voice on the other end. "I know I shouldn't be calling…"

"It's okay…" he reassured her.

"And I won't after this. I just need to ask you one thing."

"Okay."

"I know we broke up and everything, but can you remind me why? I can't remember?"

Joe sighed and began to recount what had been a truly awful day.

DEFEATED

He pulled the chair from his desk and sat defeated, yet unwilling to admit it. He stared off into the farthest corner of the room, at the moment neither sad about the love he had just lost nor joyful about the love he had just won, but conscious of the concessions he had allowed himself to make, concessions that were the result of a forced hand. This brought him the anger and resentment he was to feel for a long time, feelings he made sure he would not forget.

"I'll tell Monica."

Eyes that were expecting nothing but meetings in parks late at night were raised to new levels of surprise. Normally, this would have excited him greatly.

"Really? You mean it? Just you and me?" asked Caroline.

"Yes," said Joe.

"I'll be able to see you when the sun's out? Maybe we can have a picnic tomorrow, or just walk through the streets holding hands. I don't care. The sun will be out!"

"No."

Her heart sank because of what she thought was the inevitable: he had met someone else. He felt this.

"I can't tell her over the phone."

"That makes sense. That just means you're a big person. You'll just have to see her. One last time," she added with force and finality.

"I have no way of reaching her until Saturday."

"So you'll see her Saturday. I'll just see you after. We can meet at Ginko's and go from there. I don't care what we do. Anything is perfect."

"You don't understand. We have plans to go up north at the cabin. I have to go up there with her." She was about to speak, but he continued, "There's a whole bunch of us going up there, old friends, we haven't hung for a while. I won't be back until Sunday night. I can't call the whole thing off. Everyone has rearranged their schedules, taken time off work." He looked at his watch. "I have to start packing. I have to leave right away in the morning."

"So she'll be staying there overnight... next to you. You don't love her anymore, right? You love me?"

"I don't love her."

"You aren't going to make love to her?"

"Jesus, no," he said exasperated. "I have to get ready, okay?"

"Okay," she said, nearly crying. And as she reached the door she turned to him, "You have a cabin..." she began, caught in a fury of new feelings. "I have to go."

He said nothing, let her leave, and began to write down what had just occurred, starting with the words, "You have a cabin?" He looked up momentarily and continued, "her attempt to quell her emotions was harsh, like swallowing hard food that resisted going down."

CONCESSIONS

They all looked to the door. Someone tried to rush in, but had pushed the door before completely turning the doorknob. They waited. Caroline burst into the room. It was difficult to assess what she had been expecting, but it was not Monica and Joe on the bed and Laura on the loveseat. Looking almost dizzy, she muttered a few things about having to get back to her homework, apologized for interrupting and, as abruptly as she had entered, exited the room.

"That was a little odd," said Laura sardonically.

"Were you expecting her?" asked Monica.

"No," said Joe, shaking his head.

"She looked drunk," Monica said.

"Probably was," said Laura. "Her roommate said she's been coming in really late the past few weeks." She rolled her eyes in delight. Monica rolled hers in disgust.

"Well, I have a little homework myself and then I have to get to bed. I'm really beat."

Touching her hand to his cheek, Monica said, "You've been so tired lately. Don't work too hard, okay? You promise?"

"Yes. Yes. I promise," he said impatiently.

"Oh, leave him alone, Monica. He's a big boy."

Monica looked at him, her eyes soft. "Goodnight, sweetie."

"Night."

With that they were gone. The door had barely shut, their voices barely dying at the end of the hall when in burst Caroline, in no way resembling the confused apparition that had appeared only a short while ago.

"Weren't expecting them?" he said with a smile. She didn't answer. "You're here early. I still have some writing to finish, but I can meet you at the regular time." He rose to show her to the door. He wasn't looking at her; she wasn't looking at the door.

"I can't."

"What?" he asked, confused and angry, as if jerked off a track.

"I can't. I just feel awful. Every time I see her I get sick to my stomach. I can't even look at her. She's so nice. She even offered to help me with my 'boyfriend problems.' I'm going to tell her. I can't do this anymore. I thought I could, but I can't. I'm not like you. I have to tell her."

"Don't be stupid."

"I'm not being stupid."

"Of course you are. Just stop and think about it for a second. What did I tell you when we first started seeing each other? I told you how special you were and that I had to have you. I still feel that way. Don't you? Could you really end it?"

"No. I still feel that way. But I hate all this sneaking around. I just want to be yours alone," she said.

"I want that more than anything. It's like I told you before; I have to let her down gently. After her last boyfriend broke up with—"

"She tried to commit suicide. I know. How long will this take though?"

"Once summer comes—"

"Summer?" she asked, exasperated.

"I know that's a long time, but she'll have to move home and I won't see her as much. I can slowly break up with her then. She's very—"

"Fragile."

"Well, she is," he said sternly.

"What about me?"

"You knew the situation."

RILKE'S NUDGE

6

Caroline was not naive when she began seeing Joe. At least she didn't think she was. Raised by liberal parents, she was encouraged to gain experience of the world. By the time she finished high school, she had studied in Paris for a term, had good enough grades to start college classes her senior year, and had dated plenty of boys, most memorably a quiet religious boy who didn't like her smoking, objected to her swearing, and refused to kiss her. He thought it would be too tempting. He was probably right. She finally lost her virginity to a college piano player she met her senior year. Neither overwhelmed by sex nor left cold by it, she thought of herself as confident, experienced, in control, happy.

She had not been in love with any of the boys she dated or slept with. Moreover, she hadn't realized that she had never been in love until her freshman year when she began seeing Joe. She wasn't prepared for how bad about herself love made her feel; she felt she didn't deserve it. She thought of love constantly when she was with him. And when she felt herself in love with Joe, one memory always came to her.

Lying next to her on her dorm room bed, he would talk wildly about musicians, thinkers, writers: John Lennon, Mark

Twain, Henry David Thoreau, Robert Johnson. Each outburst was a combination of tribute, analysis, testimonial, and defense. Even his room reflected the intensity of his desire: he had no photographs of friends, family, or even living people, only his icons. He devoted the greatest amount of energy to Jim Morrison. The most trivial reason he could think of to speak about him was good enough. Everything about Morrison hypnotized Joe: his indifference, his hair ("the mane" he called it), his moodiness, his hatred of the establishment, the lizards, his poetry married to leather pants. Everything a young man could want, Jim Morrison possessed. Joe took his every lead from him: drinking instead of drug taking, growing his hair out, wearing only black and white, composing verse (which he already did but now it made sense); he even eschewed underwear, but only for a semester until he began to chafe.

His excitement electrified her. She found herself excited about people she had only vague notions about. Her bookshelves were soon lined with the tangible but unread proof of his personality, and she talked to friends with an expertise that was nothing but the confidence of love. She surrounded herself with him and with his words, his childlike energy, his naive attempt to tell her everything he knew right then and there. She was captured by what he said, yet she was equally hypnotized by what he wasn't saying. She knew that his excitement was an expression of appreciation for what those people had done for him. Propped up on his elbow, he lay on top of her and she knew she was in the shadow of something wonderful.

Without her noticing, he grew quiet. She didn't know when he had stopped talking. She had been staring at him without interruption, but he no longer spoke.

"I knew you were going to kiss me," she later said.

"You did not," he said. "How?"

"You were staring at my mouth."

"I was?" he asked, smiling.

She nodded. "You were nudged by Rilke," she said. "'Standing on my breasts' hills my feeling screamed—screams for wings or an end.' In that second before you moved, those lines were written on your face."

Looking at him now, searching for anything to wipe his nose with, she wondered how she could be looking at the same man. "Where did you go?" she wanted to scream. She wanted to understand that transformation that occurs when two people become intimate, that line that, when crossed, changes everything, that moment when two no longer skirt the perimeter but enter the waters of each other's hearts. There are only benefits reaped by this crossing: you learn, you laugh, you wash yourself of yourself in another's waters; the world seems only as big as the crook of your lover's arm. She had let him carve his face on her heart, only to have it rot like a jack-o-lantern. At night, she turn away confused and disappointed.

She recalled the first time she noticed a change. It didn't anger her then, but only caught her off guard like a dog realizing it is fenced in. They were out with friends and began arguing. Soon they were leaving, only to continue arguing in the parking lot.

"Well?" She hated when he wouldn't answer. But it was worse when she indulged his silence. "Fine. Fine. I'm overreacting, but Jesus, I just don't think I was wrong. You wouldn't act any different and you know it."

She stopped and turned around, expecting to see his blank face. To her surprise, Joe was at the end of the sidewalk, leaning against the wall of the bar, one hand on his chest. He was having trouble breathing. She ran to his side, slipping her tiny body under his arm in a vain attempt to support him.

"What's wrong? Are you okay?" she asked, her anger evaporated. She looked around for help, but the parking lot was empty. She turned toward the door, her chin barely able to rise above his arm. The sound of music throbbed ceaselessly from inside the bar. "Help! Somebody help! Can anybody hear me? I need help!" She paused, heaving, waiting for a response. She tried again, louder. Joe tugged on her from behind shaking his head.

"No," he gasped. "I'm fine. I'm fine."

"No, you're not, Joe. You're not."

"Yes, I am," he said quietly, his head still shaking.

They stood without moving. He still labored at breathing. She put her small, smooth hand over his heart.

"It'll be okay," she assured him, still scared to death. "Nothing to worry about. I'm not going anywhere. I'll take care of you. I love you." His breathing settled at the sound of her voice. Relaxed by the effect her tenderness had upon him, she whispered, "Remember that time right after we began seeing each other? We were at Lake Calhoun and we had a fight and you stormed off and when you came back you found that note I left you by our stuff—"

"I still have it," he interrupted, his voice unsteady.

"I remember seeing you coming down the path. I could tell you were barefoot right away," she said trying to look into his eyes. "You were walking like Charlie Chaplin. You sang *Bewitched* to me." She paused, caressing his thick brown hair. "It was the most beautiful night of my life."

Gazing up at his face, she was shocked to find him crying. Her grip on him tightened.

The next time she noticed the change was at the college bar that all their friends went to every weekend. For her, seeing the change was again like a dog passing that same fence, searching for some gap. They sat at a series of tables strung together like freight cars. People were coming in slowly, but Joe felt responsible for the table and getting everything ready for their friends. They always arrived an hour before anybody else, much to Caroline's chagrin.

"I told you no one would be here," said Caroline indifferently.

"Do we have to go through this?"

At 9:30, Keith, one of the last to arrive, entered, not alone as usual but with a woman. "This is Karen," he said to the tables, which, like the rest of the bar, were filled with people.

Joe saw a smallish, blond girl taking her place at the already crowded table. Her eyes were cold, her demeanor forced, a front of friendliness plastered over her body like an ad on a billboard. Joe turned his attention back to Keith and his friends.

"What's with Greg lately?" he offered to the table. He didn't like Greg, a regular at the bar they had met as they because regulars themselves. He was a tall, thin snowmobile salesman, whose greatest pride, and greatest injury to his pride, came from being a part of The Figure Follies. He took pride in doing what he loved the most—skating—but was crushed by not being tough enough to play hockey. Joe saw him across the bar sulking. Though he didn't like him, he needed watch him since Greg liked Caroline.

"Fuck if I know," retorted Brad quickly. "I wish he'd either figure it out or stop coming around. It's beastly the way he sulks like the rest of us don't have problems. I mean—"

"Beastly?" asked Jay in disbelief.

The table erupted in laughter. Brad grimaced, trying to hide his embarrassment. Although he was attending community college, he always felt bad that it was a GED and not a real high school diploma that got him there.

Keith, placing his elbow on the table, broke the jovial spirit of the group. "It's Amy. They haven't been getting along lately."

"Miss Alaska?" broke in Jay, loudly and gregariously. "How could anyone get along with her, much less fuck her? She never says a word. But you know she's in control."

"She looks retarded," said Caroline matter-of-factly.

"You know she does," said Keith with a smile.

"All I know is that I'd rather have two vertebrae removed from my back and blow myself then come home to that every day," said Brad.

The table roared.

"Gross," was all Caroline could say.

"Disgusting," hissed Karen, splitting the laughter like a lightning bolt, turning away from the table.

Eyes rolled. The laughter quieted, stretches of silence following. Karen, knowing the table had been silenced because of her, went up to the bar.

"What the fuck was that?" growled Jay.

"Who knows?" and "Who cares?" were the dominant responses.

Within a few minutes their conversation regained the momentum and predictability it had momentarily lost.

Joe, bored with the conversations he heard every Friday, found himself standing at the bar next to Karen, wondering why he had been so excited for this evening. Karen ordered a glass of red wine, he a beer.

When the bartender went to the back room, Joe was left standing next to Karen. He had his back to her but he knew she was there. There was no reason for either of them to still be standing at the bar. He knew that they were already engaged in a battle of wills. Whoever left the bar first was the loser.

After playing with his napkin, forcing down a pretzel (never before having known how difficult it was to eat when you weren't hungry), and beginning several conversation with Greg on the opposite side of the bar, who kept looking at Caroline, he thought, "Forget it." He knew he had to act.

He turned to his right fast, faster than he intended. She looked at him sharply, waiting for him to confront her. Instead, he walked to the cigarette machine and bought a pack. She couldn't know he didn't smoke. It didn't matter anyway; he had blinked first. Coming back to the bar, he grabbed his beer, walked back to the table, dropped the cigarettes in front of a confused Caroline, and sat beside her. A smug Karen followed shortly.

"Hey! Hey!" Jay yelled toward the door. Brad and Joe and everyone at the table turned their heads almost immediately.

"We've been waiting, you S.O.B." said Brad.

Jon walked in, his entire body as laid back as his smile. Although he had graduated their freshman year, he was part of their group. Everybody loved Jon. He was impossible not to like. People who only talked to him for minutes considered him a close friend. He wasn't terribly funny and he didn't tell a great story, but everyone wanted to be near him. He was happy with himself and had the rare ability to make you feel exactly the same way. That was what everyone loved. This overshadowed the tight-fitting shirt, the pants that never matched, the dried, cracking hands, and even his chronically bad breath, which he tried to mask with mint gum.

"Need anything, Johnny?" came a voice from out the bar. It was only one of many.

"A better job or a beer, whichever comes first."

Before his coat was off, a spot had been cleared at the table, a freshly poured beer placed in it. He wouldn't have to pay for a beer the entire night.

"What's with this place?" Karen asked Joe. "It's such a dump. I've never seen so many losers in one place. It's hard to keep a straight face. How do you keep a straight face?"

"Let's go," said Joe, rising, taking her arm, and directing her to the back hallway by the restrooms. He knew what could happen if anyone, even a woman, started shooting her mouth off. He looked at her leaning against the wall, her hands wrapped around the stem of the wine glass, a tiny smile offering itself to him.

"I don't know who you think you are," he began, angry.

She raised her shoulders slowly.

"You can't talk like that," he said, softening immediately. He was going to tell her that she was a little priss who deserved to be slapped. He was going to say that she wasn't anything special and why Keith would take an interest in her was beyond comprehension. That these were my friends and by insulting them she was insulting him. That maybe she should just get the fuck out. But all he felt was an overwhelming urge to kiss her, to sneak her out the back door and make love to her. Not at his place, or a hotel, or even in his car, but right there, in the bushes behind the bar.

"Is there anything else?" she asked. "You look like you have a lot more to say."

He continued to look at her.

"Kiss me," she said.

He wanted to kiss her. He even leaned in until he could feel the heat of her breath, her mouth preparing to be kissed. But he couldn't do it. Not to Caroline. And he didn't know why. "What the fuck?" he whispered under his breath. He left her in the hall and returned to Caroline's side.

⌒⌁

"Let's go," Joe said sternly in Caroline's ear while smiling and waving at everyone in the bar.

"Okay," she answered, surrendering to the inevitable. Caroline picked up her purse and jacket, although not fast enough for Joe.

"See you guys later," said Jon enthusiastically.

Joe nodded impatiently. Caroline wished she could be with Jon for a few minutes more.

Joe's impatience at having to say a whole list of goodbyes was a good indication of his personality. When he needed to leave, he halted anything he was doing and it all became immediately dead to him. Goodbyes served no purpose. Once his mind had been made up, he was already en route to whatever needed his attention.

Caroline, on the other hand, loved the buffet of social expectations. From the shower, to her careful consideration of clothing and handbags, to her time in front of the mirror, and the overall importance of being on display; it all meant more than any actual event. Goodbyes fell under this category. She knew that people looked their worst at the end of the night while she stubbornly persisted at looking her best. By saying goodbye to everyone, she left the impression of being fresh. By comparison, she would always be the most beautiful. Grab, hold hand, look into the eyes, then to the next person. Then, you're off!

They both smiled and exited the bar.

Walking ahead of Joe, Caroline barked, "What the hell is your problem? We were finally having a great time. Couldn't you try just once not to do this?"

His silences cut through her. She turned around venomously, "Could you just say it?" and slowly walked to the curb where Joe sat hunched over in the midst of a panic attack. "No one would believe me even if I told them. Big Bad Joe has panic attacks."

"Oh, shut up," he huffed angrily.

"I'm gonna go wait in the car."

He gave her a hurt, angry look.

She finally relented, "Are you okay?"

"I think so."

Her sympathy used to be genuine. Now it was required. Now it was a chore.

"Just breathe. You have to calm down. You know that."

"I know, I know," he said between harried breaths. "I just don't know. I don't know why."

"Something stressed you out. Now it's over. Now we can go." She began turning to walk away.

"I don't know why," he repeated. "Why did you do it?"

"Do what?" she asked innocently, walking toward their car.

"I didn't think you would do something like that to me," he said, still in the curb.

She had been drinking and, getting a little drunk, she had let her guard down and hadn't seen the signs. When he wanted to leave, she assumed that he was trying to get her into bed; she thought she had just avoided a fight; she wasn't against it. She rubbed his chest. He pulled away. She now knew this wasn't anywhere near over. He didn't want her and her desire was transformed into a frustrated, should-have-known anger.

"Sweetie, what?" she tried in a last ditch effort. If sex later was out, maybe sleep wasn't. "What, for God's sakes?" She was under the false impression an admission would put an end to whatever was bothering him.

"Don't get mad! I'm trying! God, I'm trying to tell you something that's difficult and you so don't fucking care. All your coddling is just to pacify me. I don't fucking need that!" Joe said.

"Just to pacify you? Is that what you think? Then go to hell! Who else would put up with this? No one I know."

"Oh, so you have to 'put up with me'? Is that it? I'm inconvenient to you? Well I'm sorry if the things that hurt me don't work for your schedule. Next time I'll make sure to check with you first," said Joe.

"Screw you. You know that's not what I meant—"

"That's sure as hell what it sounded like."

"Well, it's not," said Caroline.

"Then what exactly did you mean? Tell me exactly what you meant because I'd love to know. I sure as hell remember being there for you when you'd wake up crying in the middle of the night because you failed your French test. I remember being there when your mother humiliated you so badly you wouldn't leave your room for three days. Seems I remember a lot of things."

"Yeah? I also remember hearing about it every day for weeks. Who didn't you tell? You make me wish you'd never helped me to begin with. The cost is too damn high. I'd rather suffer alone," Caroline said.

"You got it," he snapped.

"I do anyway."

"What the hell does that mean?"

"Oh, did I touch a nerve?" she asked, her head protruding forward. After a moment she pulled back, "You're there for me. You're right. But you don't talk to me. Everyone thinks that I get the best of you but I don't. I get to read it in your stories like everyone else. I don't get to take things on my own terms or on terms that are just ours."

"You know I can't help that."

"I know."

She grabbed his chin, "What is wrong?" They both knew that this moment of tenderness was Caroline's attempt at ending this scene so that she could do the only thing she did with utter joy: go home, get in bed, and fall asleep.

He offered resistance to her small hand until she gave up and he turned away, tears rolling down his face. "Why did you have to do it?"

"Do what?" she asked flatly.

"All this time," he said in a brief soliloquy. "Maybe I don't get anything," he said, his words showing signs of resignation like sweat on a runner's brow. She was glad. Resignation was followed by self-pity, then melancholy, and then his self-pitying sleep. He was only a few maudlin reflections away from being finished.

"Why did you dance with that guy?"

"Can't we do this at home and not in the middle of a parking lot?"

"Tell me why you danced with him?"

She searched her memory, which in Joe's eyes confessed guilt. Any answer that wasn't instantaneous was just a method of rewriting history. In the beginning, she would ramble and later she would just lie to satisfy him (as truth wasn't what he desired), but now she was too tired; they were too tired; even the parking lot with its faded lights seemed too tired. She never wanted to know the truth about another man again.

"Greg, that's who. Greg with his ridiculously frosted blond hair. Everybody knows he's gay and that's why he's having problems with Amy. Did you see that stupid fucking hair? He even has a hair stylist," he laughed to himself.

"Adrian?"

His legs buckled. He began crying out of control. "You…" he could barely utter the words, "you know his stylist's name?" He was devastated. Watching him react was like watching someone smash a window with a hammer.

"He's a friend of Judy's. And I wasn't even dancing with Greg. I was dancing with Peggy and him. It was just for fun." She spoke as if reporting a story, handing him something objective. This was a clear sign to him she had done wrong.

He attempted to gain control over his crying.

"You did that move. Like you were going down on him."

"Going down on him? What are you talking about?"

"Right before you did it, your body prepared itself." He stopped once more, closing his eyes, visualizing her dancing with him—Greg. He continued crying. "The moment before, your body stopped, stopped for only an instant. You smiled." He was accusing her. He was looking for her to contradict him.

Caroline was so angry that she didn't know what to say. She had gotten used to the panic attacks, and had come to accept the self behind Joe's social self, but his turning on her, this had sideswiped her. She knew that she would have to change with him. She was furious to have to lose another part of herself.

"You're fucking crazy, do you know that?" she yelled. "It was him…"

"Greg," he said, clarifying, anger in eyes.

"Yes. I saw Greg do it to Peggy and so I did it. I only did it because I knew he was gay. Or thought he was. Maybe I didn't; who cares? He didn't even see me do it! His fucking back was turned! I felt like an idiot. I take this stupid chance and then I'm left to rot. And then I catch it from you. I wish he had seen me!"

"Took a chance? I'm glad you feel the need to take a chance with someone you're not dating." Behind him the music swelled as someone opened the door and slipped out of the bar. It was someone he saw every week but didn't know. He didn't even know his name.

"You guys still here? I thought I saw you leave a while ago."

"We did," mumbled Joe, trying to hide his swollen and red eyes.

Caroline did better, lifting her voice into its higher, playful range. "Oh, we always have a hard time leaving. Then we ran into Jimbo. How's Janis? I know she had that back surgery."

Joe groaned under his breath. Caroline pretended not to notice.

"She's a real trooper. I'm hoping to bring her by maybe in a few weeks." He paused momentarily. "Business picking up for you?" he asked Joe, mistaking him for Keith who had a small, struggling contracting business.

"Fine. Fine. Just fine. If I had a steady and reliable staff I could easily clear fifty thousand without even having to work, but as is …"

"Work ethic isn't what it was in our father's time."

"Amen."

Joe was enjoying lying and it was driving Caroline crazy. He could feel himself being drawn into a conversation of more depth. He felt rage rising again. He didn't want to talk to this guy. He desperately needed to make Caroline suffer for dancing with Greg.

"I can't remember if you guys met here or … ?"

"We go to the same college. We're on summer break right now but Joe couldn't resist a woman who spoke French. Isn't that right, sweetie?"

"Moi?" pointing to himself. "Definitely. How can you resist a woman you can't understand?"

After the man left, Caroline pushed herself out from under Joe. "Could you not try and be so obvious? No one needs to know what's going on with us."

"What about you and that fucking voice? The only time you use it anymore is when you want to give the impression of us as a happy couple. I'd rather be him watching us than me with you. No one knows how fucking miserable we are. Why did you have to dance with Greg?"

"I didn't do anything!" she screamed as loud as she could. "I didn't fucking do anything wrong! You think I even wanted to dance with him? You were too busy playing darts and smoking cigars, pretending to ignore me. To test me. To see what I would do. To see if I would come to you. Anyway, I failed, didn't I? I danced with the married fag."

"What about you? You run away the first chance you get. You pushed for us to be together, to see nobody else, and the minute that happened you did whatever you could to act like you were trapped. You pushed for this, not me!"

"So what are you saying? That you don't want to be with me?"

Their argument came to an instant halt. They would stay together; they were in love. Now she knew that she had fallen in love with a chimera. The person he had presented to her for nine months was gone and in its place was a vulnerable, weak man. He had lied to her and he would pay for it. The aftermath would become habit, an affection mixed with the waters of resentment until they could carry one another, if not to safety, then to quiet and sleep.

IF YOU LIVED HERE, YOU'D BE HOME BY NOW...

7

Lipman once heard that weight increases twentyfold on Jupiter. He didn't know if it was true, but it was a terrible thought, especially when regular earth exhaustion had set in, making life impossible. If he were able get away from his depression, he might see that the moods that engulfed him were as strong as Jupiter's orbital pull. But he could not. He was as helpless in resisting his depression as a rudderless boat is defenseless against the tides. To say that he rode it out would be inaccurate: these moods were not like storms, which came and went. There was no forecast of what was to come, with what intensity, and for what length. His grief sat inside of him like a massive bird, that stretched out its wings at its own will. It always had.

It was like sleeping. Ever since Lipman was a boy, he had slept tucked into himself, his body resembling a fist. He wondered about this idiosyncrasy. He told himself that he had a bad back to explain the reason for sleeping in such an uncomfortable position. But he knew he didn't have a bad back. He had never ventured to really understand why, had purposely avoided finding out. He had accepted it, like a manner of speech, a mole, a cowlick, like breathing, and went on sleeping like a fist.

This posture carried over into his waking hours. He was always poised in this position, pulled away from the world, preparing to be struck. Every decision required that he choose between his work and the Other, the nameless, faceless world he couldn't escape encountering. He did not know the difference between compromising and being compromised. Yet the more he tried to protect himself with humor, with success, with companionship, with actual solitude, something wriggled its way in, opening him up as wide as a bear trap.

Lipman believed that he was merely ashamed of his life but, in truth, he was ashamed of his suffering, which, so unaccepted by the people around him, he had buried long ago. It was his inability to experience suffering that caused him the greatest pain. When the massive bird beat its wings, he'd think, "I think I'm going to fucking kill myself."

Leaving his apartment, Lipman headed for the bar, never noticing spring racing through the brown yards. He entered and ordered a beer. Despite the laughter and the endless stream of conversation, the reality was that everyone was there to nurse some disappointment, to seek some solace away from or in the arms of somebody else who, without alcohol, would be repulsive. He became wearied and then hopeful when he saw Sean.

Sean was an old friend. But to say *old friend* was inaccurate. Lipman had worked with him shortly after his graduating college, a time when one pauses before one's adult life. For an education in the arts is a paradoxical thing. As an institution, a university's goal is to prepare each of its students for a career, making money, success—in short, everything parents want for their children. As a haven for the arts, its ends are the opposite.

At Hamline University, incoming freshman are asked to guess why there are walls around universities. (A strange question to ask, as Hamline has no such walls, although given it's location, it should.) *To keep others out? Protection?*

Aesthetics? To keep ideas in, they are told. Ideas need to be held in for the damage *they* can do. Lipman's first philosophy professor noted that, "Every college freshman is an atheist." College was a time when every student's preconceived ideas are thrown to the wind and replaced with ideas that, to the common man, are subversive and revolutionary.

For most, the time after college, before entering the workforce, is the equivalent of pulling one's foot off the accelerator without considering a change in destination. Even after starting his career, Lipman had remained in this same place. Whether this was a victory for the arts was impossible to say.

Lipman and Sean's work relationship had always been a blessing for them both. They shared interests in literature, drank too much, and were heartbroken. They frequently attempted to meet after work, but one of them always ended up canceling. Despite sincere intentions, they never met outside of work. They always sensed that a potentially great friendship had never quite developed. Their disappointment over this caused a resentment that led to the end of their near-friendship, as if they simply decided not to renew a contract.

They did meet years later, once, and purely by chance. Lipman had been having a drink with a rich, beautiful woman at a particularly shady bar. She had longed for a semblance of depravity to line her otherwise inoculated life and this place and Lipman provided it. She paid. Then she dumped him. He had seen it coming for months and he wasn't terribly hurt, but he needed another drink anyway. Well into Lipman's second beer Sean appeared, but Lipman, unsure of where they stood, simply pretended not to see him.

Looking at him now, Lipman was frozen between their past and his own personal situation, which he wished he could scream about. Sean still sat with a slight hunch that accentuated his pumpkinlike paunch. With his dark skin (he was of

137

half-Spanish decent), he still resembled a large kidney bean. Lipman hesitated, unsure if he should say anything. Before he could decide, Sean spotted him and, without a second's hesitation, he waved Lipman over.

"Words!" Sean exclaimed, using a nickname Lipman had long forgotten. "Man, what are you doing in this part of town?"

Lipman shrugged. "Nothing. Just having a beer."

"Me too. Just got off work—another killer twelve-hour day. Definitely needed somethin' and I guess this was it," he said, raising his glass as if to inspect his choice. It must have passed the inspection as he took a healthy pull. "Man, I haven't seen you forever. What have you been up to?"

"Not much, just working. Although," Lipman said only pausing momentarily, slowing himself down, "something has been troubling me."

This abrupt turn from the formal to the personal was typical of Lipman. Anytime he was with strangers (and Sean never moved beyond being a stranger) he felt the urge to confess. He felt uncomfortable with those he knew best. Whenever he shared anything with them, he felt as if they were trespassing. Even though with strangers he would end up feeling compromised, he needed a connection with someone who couldn't return that same connection.

"What's that?" asked Sean, sipping his beer, his voice echoing hollowly in his upturned glass.

"I'm so fucked up. I don't know. I guess I'm just unhappy."

"Unhappy?" Sean asked, his voice compassionate and warm. "About what? It's gotta be a lady if I know you," he said a familiar smile on his face.

"Kind of."

"I knew it. Good old Words has got himself in another predicament. I haven't seen you in how long? It's like we're

138

picking up right where we left off. You'll stew about it for a while, drink a little, and then you'll go off and write something brilliant."

"I don't know, Sean," Lipman said, uncomfortable with the compliment. "Sometimes you just want to end it, you know."

"Come on, Words, you know it's true. You've never written a bad word. Shit, it takes me one hundred drafts to get where your five get you."

"Thanks, I guess. But that's just it. I look around and I see people in churches, parents playing with their children, the guys where I work, dressed so perfect... and I don't know... it's not like that for me. I don't know how to do that. And when I do, it's so fucking wrong I can't stand it. Even the best things seem pretend."

"Come on, man, you know it's different when you're a writer. Observing eyes naturally isolate. I go through the same thing, at every job, with every girl, at every family function, everything I'm required to do. But you just have to accept it. Just make sure the writing is there, you know?"

"Why?" Lipman asked, exasperated. "I mean, if everything you report on feels two-dimensional, like you're living by proxy, what does it matter if the writing is there?"

"Because our job is to create something worthy of the ages. All you can concern yourself with is the writing, with the quality of the writing. Nothing else. As long as you are true to it, it will be true to you. And besides that, it will be true to the world. Imagine the ability to inspire others. That's a gift. It's beautiful."

"I'm not debating that the writing shouldn't be good. But if you are reporting on something hollow, doesn't it make the writing worthless, no matter the quality?"

"No, absolutely not. It is not our job to decide what we should or shouldn't write about or to make ethical judgments.

You just do it. Don't you remember all that crap we talked about, that there is creative genius and critical genius? Which do you want to be?" Sean asked, as if these were the only two choices anyone could have.

"That's too simplistic. It implies that we're not supposed to be responsible. And it's always the work, the work. What about living instead?"

"Maybe," Sean said, nodding his head seriously. "But, as I see it, you really don't have much choice. Neither of us do. You can either ride this thing out or quit writing—and you can't do that anyway. It will always come back: ideas, images, phrases. It's part of our makeup." Like Lipman, Sean had been writing for most of his life; it had been his obsession and dream, but never had it been something to question. "There's that great fairy tale," he continued.

Lipman sat back as Sean told him the story of the frog and the scorpion. He had heard it a hundred times before and despised it. The two creatures are on the bank of a river and are threatened by a fire. The only way to safety is to cross the river. The scorpion, who can't swim, asks the frog if he can ride on his back. The frog believes that if he complies, the scorpion will sting him. The scorpion points out that this would kill both of them. They set off. Halfway across, the scorpion stings the frog.

"'It's my nature' says the scorpion. It's the same with you, Words, and me. I don't know why you fight it. I mean, what's really going on? You knock a girl up or something?"

"No, it's nothing like that. It's not about a woman. Well, it is, but not like you think. I'm not like that anymore. I'm with one girl. But am I really with her?"

"Oh," Sean said with a nod. "Someone else caught your eye? Is that it? Always stay with the real thing. It may not be flashy, but love lasts. You have to remember that. God knows I've tried to tell you."

"No, no. There's no one else. All I know is that everything seems to have meaning."

"Jesus, Words, where the fuck are you coming from? First you tell me nothing has meaning, you see people doing their shit and it's not for you and now everything has meaning. Make up your mind."

Lipman sighed. "I *am* saying the same thing. All those people I was talking about, all the people here, everything they do seems imbued with meaning until I look at it. Nothing has any weight once I look at it."

"I'm not sure I get where you're going," Sean said. He thought it over as if he were running a hand over a new and strange object. "Wait, let me get us a pitcher." He made his way lazily to the bar, coming back with a pitcher. He refilled their glasses. "Now, please continue and let's see if I can follow where you're going with this stuff."

"Everything I look at is emptied of meaning, or the meaning I think it should have, the minute I look at it. It floats away like a balloon. I always thought my writing stopped that or at least slowed the process. It never made me part of the club that I wanted to be in but it seemed to anesthetize the wound a bit. But, like anything, the body... the patient comes out of it. I feel like I'm next. That soon I'll float away, too, and even that won't be real. I'm just chasing balloons, trying to pull them back down."

Sean gave him a confused look.

"I no longer recognize the meaning of things around me. When I try to describe how they are meaningful, I can't seem to find the words or even understand the relationships between people and events and everything else."

Sean's face changed instantly from compassion to disgust. (Although he opted to remember the balloon imagery. It was wonderful and he would use it.) "You're just brooding. You've always been like that," he said flatly, looking around uninterestedly. "You waste your energy on useless things. You're not talking about writing, existence by proxy, love, work, or whatever the hell you said. And when the hell have you ever stepped foot in a church? You're asking if existence has meaning and where writing fits in! At least be honest with yourself, with me. And at least have the intellectual honesty—the balls—to know that it doesn't matter. You're still here, you're still alive and capable of love whether or not the universe has any fucking meaning! There's still love!"

They were both silenced. Sean went up to the bar to order lottery tickets and a couple of shots. Lipman recalled a similar situation years back, in a similar type of bar, when, at his most heartbroken (a cultivated specialty of Sean's), Sean asked if his poetry was too sentimental. "You're like a Duke Ellington melody: sentimental but infused with the wisdom of experience," Lipman had said, lying. Looking at Sean, at the bar, perhaps he was right: not much had changed. Sean would never be a great writer.

"You didn't have to do that," Lipman said, reaching for his wallet as Sean set down the shots.

"Don't worry about it," he said, waving away Lipman's wallet.

"Do you remember reading Camus? I've been thinking about what he said, that suicide is the only philosophical issue."

"This is ridiculous."

"It's not!"

"Suicide? You want to talk about that?" Sean set his glass down and leaned forward intensely. "For God's sake, I just got off work."

"So? Haven't you thought about it? I mean really thought about it? When is a good time to talk about it?"

"Never, Words. He wasn't talking about actual suicide. He was referring to suicide only to reveal its absurdity. If you recall he also mentions Darwin and he says—"

"Galileo, actually."

"Fine, Galileo. And what he says is that when Galileo repudiated his own theories to the Church, which was obviously lip service, he was doing the right thing. Camus says that there is nothing really worth dying for."

"Not even love?" Lipman asked sarcastically.

"Life is too wondrous for that," Sean said ignoring Lipman. "Obviously, then, he's not going to turn around and tell people to consider actually doing that. He's being figurative."

"Oh yeah, I hear about that in the papers all the time, all the people that attempt figurative suicide. That the figurative suicide rate has sky rocked due to the recession. Very common."

"Jesus, you're too damn literal. For God's sake, you're a writer. By saying that suicide is the only issue, he's saying that there is no issue; that life is meaningless and it is a matter of whether you let this fact destroy you. That's the suicide he's talking about. And you're going to let this bullshit frame of mind destroy you? Suicide? Don't you realize what you sound like? You're in your thirties, for God's sake! Teenagers think about this shit. My sister went through the same thing. Wouldn't even come to her own birthday party. But you? Stuck in that angst we all left behind sophomore year? Yes, I've thought about it, so what? It's stupid."

"No, you're wrong. Heidegger says most of us do not have the courage to look death in the face. We say it's unhealthy to think about it, or that we only think about it when we're young and going through changes. We say that only a coward would kill himself. We do everything except really think about it."

"Heidegger was a nazi."

"Good argument, Sean."

"So I'm supposed to sit around and think about death? Boo-hoo."

"You *don't* think about. Instead you keep yourself busy thinking about money, about everything you don't really need. All the while the most important thing you have— *you*—is passing you by. Do you have any idea who you are or where you want to go or why you're here? Besides being a 'writer'? Things aren't justified because you write little stories about them. Why is that always the argument to end all arguments?"

"Talk all you want, because that's all you ever do."

"What does that mean?"

"It means that beneath all these words lies nothing, no follow-through, no action, just more words. Preach to someone else. Maybe I don't think as much as you, but I do things. Wasn't involvement in the world a big thing for Heidegger? Wasn't that his big phrase: *Being-In-The-World?* Bigger than contemplation? You're a damn child." And with that, Sean finished the remainder of his beer, downed his shot, and walked out.

Lipman sat, devastated.

After finishing his beer and the shot, he, too, rose, left the bar, and returned home.

⌒ᴧ

Pulling open the security door to his apartment, Lipman heard someone behind him ask, "Is this the open house?"

"No."

"Do you know where building 15 is?" the woman asked, looking at the number 13 over their heads.

"No." He was about to turn away when a sense of his own ignorance stopped him. "It's strange. This is 13 and that's 11," he said pointing to building to his right. "But that's 17," he said, pointing to the building to the left. "I've thought before about just walking through the entire complex to try to find it."

"So you don't know where it is?"

"I did try once, then it rained and I had to come back."

"Do you know where the manager's office is?"

He gave up the illusion that she was interested in what he was saying.

"Right around the corner."

She was already halfway down the sidewalk before she finished her thank you.

Lipman shut the door and went up to his apartment. How is it, he wondered, that I don't even know my own complex? I have lived here for seven years. He searched his apartment. He was astonished at the details he hadn't noticed or remembered, things that had no existence except when his eyes fell on them. It was as if his apartment were reborn each time he looked around, but as a horror rather than as miracle. No object linked itself to him. Nothing spoke to him in his language alone. If he were to walk out of this apartment, never to return, he would feel neither loss nor regret. And neither would the objects. That's what happens when you put your genius into your art and not your life, he thought bitterly.

Sitting down, he thought about Mr. Ebenheimer, his high school history teacher. He was a lonely man exiting middle age with nothing to show for it: no wife, no children, no house, no accomplishments to make him immortal. As a teacher, the only proof of his accomplishments were the fruits of someone else's.

Despite his own failed gifts, Mr. Ebenheimer occasionally lit up. This happened on those rare occasions when he spoke about World War II. He was never specific, but the tenor of his recollections told everybody that he had been a spy who had been taught to memorize his surroundings rapidity and accurately.

"Does anybody have Social Studies in Mrs. Brown's room?" he asked after an especially bad turnout on a quiz. He turned around and, with a stick of pink chalk, drew a large square. "I would like you to go into her classroom for exactly five minutes and memorize as many things as possible in that time." Mrs. Brown had only started that fall. Everything in the room was new.

When the class finished their assignment, Mr. Ebenheimer congratulated them on a fine job. "But it seems that you are missing several things." The class objected. Youth always doubts wisdom, though they want it with an almost blood lust. They wanted proof.

Mr. Ebenheimer approached the chalkboard and not only listed what seemed like hundreds of objects the class had missed, but indicated where the things were located in Mrs. Brown's room. Yet he didn't stop there. He was able to identify the color of the carpet, walls, and ceiling, and the number of windows and their distance from the door, things the class had completely ignored. The class, obviously impressed, humbled, and even excited, sat with an unforgiving eye. When allowed to check his accuracy, they found he had missed nothing and had gotten nothing wrong.

Looking around his apartment, Lipman was consumed by a grand sense of dissatisfaction. He closed his eyes. The only places that existed were those places he had written about, real or fictional. Their reality could not be doubted. Opening his eyes was like waking in a hotel.

The blind memorize furniture in order to navigate in their homes. Keeping each thing in its place is important to survival. The movement of one thing by even half a foot is catastrophic. Everything has its place and, in this way, a meaning. Lipman memorized in order to avoid catastrophe. All things had to be kept in place so that they wouldn't hinder him. Things had to exist in their place to be nonexistent.

He reached to the end table and picked up a wine glass containing a small pool of stale wine. He turned his wrist, inspecting it. He tried to find something unique about it, something supple in its curves, a trace of aristocracy in its material, even a nick in the lip to signify something. This search came up empty. Its curves were neither supple nor unique but entirely base. Practicality was its only purpose. It was made out of cheap, stock glass; its lip was dull and worn. It was, by every definition, his glass.

The phone rang. He made no movements but sat patiently waiting for this intrusion to cease. Three rings and then the answering machine. After the nauseating sound of his voice came the beep and then the sound of Leslie's voice:

"Hi, it's me. I know you're not ready to talk yet. You don't have to call. I can stay with Jody until… Anyway, I told Ken to put the house on hold. He said he could only hold it for a while. I'm not trying to pressure you. I just thought you should know. Anyway, I'm sorry that I'm not making sense. Sorry. I miss you."

His neighbors couldn't say exactly when Lipman pushed open his second-story bedroom window, but by 4:30 that morning, everything that he could fit through it—the lamp, his comforter, pillows, sheets, four wooden dresser drawers and all their contents, picture frames, rugs, emptied bookshelves, a second, taller lamp, and an antique mirror—he had thrown out of it. Someone finally called the police when the television, looking back up at Lipman with a cracked smile, hit the sidewalk with a hard, muffled crash.

INDIFFERENCE

8

Joe looked at the clock: **4:12.**

"Fuck."

He paced from the window to the closed bedroom door. Each side of the room repelled him, propelling him back to the other. Three steps was all it took. One, two, three, turn. One, two, three, turn. For twenty minutes he continued, until the thought of Caroline and Rick together stopped him cold. Then he started again. One, two, three, the window. Turn, one, two, three. The door. Back again. Twenty more minutes.

He turned the radio on. Noise. Incomprehensible. He turned it off.

Sitting on the arm of the couch, he tapped his foot furiously, staring at the clock. 4:43, 4:44, 4:45 ... until 5:00 when his housemates began arriving. 5:35. He clutched his stomach, threw open the door, and ran to the bathroom. His pants were barely down when it started pouring out of him. Three times this hour and twice the hour before. It would be worse now; six rooms and eighteen people. Somebody was always in the bathroom. The people. He was so sore he could barely wipe himself.

He looked out the window at Selby Avenue. Parked cars like tombstones littered the street. There were no people. To the right was the busier Snelling Avenue. The street Rick could be coming from. Cars growled with dissatisfaction. Everyone has a story. Watching the cars, Joe heard every story and they were all the same: a long list of regrets waiting for someone to attach to. Caroline carried her one regret, their relationship, to their doorstep every day.

He reached down to the television on the footlocker and turned it on. He couldn't concentrate. He turned it off again. Sitting on the couch, he grabbed a book, but shut it almost immediately. He saw his notebook and picked it up. All he could do was scribble faces with jagged lines and write the words, "I hate this," in thick, black letters. He stood up and did the only thing he could: pace.

He nearly knocked Caroline over when she came home from work—late. "Jesus. What are you doing?" she asked, pushing past him. Before he could begin with the questions about her day, about why she was late, about Rick, about where the fuck she thought she was going, she grabbed a towel. "Not now. I have to get ready." She headed for the bathroom, the sound of water soon following.

He bolted across the hall and into the kitchen. He opened the refrigerator, grabbed a beer that he knew wasn't his, and drained it on the spot, the refrigerator door still open. "What do I care? They all hate me." He tossed the empty into the trash, grabbed another, and headed back to the room he and Caroline shared, shutting the door behind him.

He looked back to the clock: 5:45.

There it was, the sound of a car turning from Snelling to Selby Avenue. "Already." He raced to the window and thrust his head and shoulders out. A red Escort passed lazily by. Maybe Rick wasn't coming. Maybe Joe should go into the bathroom and take her. "You smell like beer." That's what she'd say. Another car passed. He darted to the window. The Escort coming back. Rick would be leaving the store now, getting into his car and exiting the parking lot, the shape of his car pointing him here. Once on Snelling it was only a matter of four stoplights. If he made them all it would only be seven minutes. Now that he had entered their lives, it felt like he had always been there. Joe finished the beer and got another.

That same sick sound. "I won't give in," he said, racing to the window: a blue pickup, a green minivan, a rusted-out Camaro. Finally, the ugly, gray Mustang. Joe pulled back from the window. It was halfway down the block. Pulling back further, he saw it pass the house. He ran to the door, sped down the hallway and spiral staircase. He had watched the car for too long. He began to double back and headed for the back door. "Fuck. Fuck. Fuck," he said, catching himself, racing back up the staircase and to their room, setting the beer on the window ledge. Caroline would be mad that he was drinking this early—furious that he had stolen a beer.

The house echoed in silence as the water pipes were shut off. He had to get down there before Caroline came back to the room and before Rick had parked. If she knew what he was doing and, further, why he was doing it (because he feared and hated Rick and wanted him gone), she wouldn't come back for days. And he knew exactly where she'd be staying. Again, he sprinted down the hallway and staircase. He burst out the back door, and sat on the rotting wood bench, breathless, watching and listening. There was nothing.

Still panting, he heard Rick shuffling down the sidewalk. He closed his eyes. He was still breathing hard but not from running through the house and down the stairs. He had begun to hyperventilate. "Fuck, fuck." He tightened his eyes and concentrated.

"Hey Joe, what are you doing back here?"

Joe turned, slowly clearing his throat, acting as if he had just woken up, trying with all the strength he had not to reveal how hard his adrenalin was pumping. "Hey, Rick. Didn't hear you coming. What time is it?"

Rick extended a bare left arm. "Don't know. Never can get myself to wear a watch. Time just restricts me, you know? I don't want to be burdened. I just want to do things when they should be done. So, what are you doing back here?"

"Getting some sun."

"Back here?'

"Just hanging out, thinking."

"Cool. Save a few for me. Thoughts, that is. Is Caroline here?"

"I don't know. Maybe. I think so," he said.

"I found this sweet place for sushi and I've just been totally diggin' to take her there."

"Sounds good."

"You like sushi?" Rick asked.

"No."

"Well, it's definitely an acquired taste. Caroline tells me you're into literature. You know, she talks about you a lot. Really admires you. Where you're going with it?"

"I have a passing interest in the stuff."

"That's awesome. We should get together, just the two of us. Talk about the good stuff. Hash it out. We could learn from each other. What was she telling me the other night? Oh, yeah she told me all about some writer you like. He's mentioned in a song by the 10,000 Maniacs."

Joe rolled his eyes. "Jack Kerouac. What about him?"

"Caroline thought I would really get into his stuff. Said his style was a lot like how I think. She knows me so well. She's very perceptive."

Joe knew what was coming next and it made him want to throw up even more than he already did. Rick was going to ask to borrow a book. Joe hated lending books. What he hated more was that he had to. If he refused, Caroline would only have another reason to hate him and another reason to love Rick.

"Caroline said you'd probably be cool with me borrowing something by him. And don't worry, I won't bend the cover back. Caroline told me what can happen when people wreck your stuff. Whoa, you can get mad. I mean, it was a funny story. I just won't make the same mistake."

"Sure."

"Thanks," he said with a relaxed smile.

"Whatever."

"I'm gonna find her. She's probably waiting for me."

"No need to ask me."

Rick opened the screen door and entered the house. After listening for a safe number of steps, Joe turned around and stared deep into the unlit house, watching nothing but darkness and listening for anything.

ALWAYS VERLAINE

9

When the phone rang, he knew. They were calling him for a ride. He knew before he looked at the clock, before considering the possibility that it was for any of the fifteen other people who lived in the house, before he could get angry that it was two in the morning, that it was hot, that there wasn't air conditioning or even a fan, and that he hadn't slept, wondering what they were doing. He let it ring until someone picked it up and yelled, "Joe. Joe, pick up the phone."

He rolled over slowly. "Hello?"

"Joe, you have to come get us."

"Fuck you," he said, hanging up harshly. Almost immediately it rang again.

"Joe. We really need a ride."

He didn't answer for thirty dark seconds.

"Where are you?"

"I don't know. At an Amoco somewhere downtown."

He sighed. "Why isn't Caroline calling?"

"She's passed out across the street," said Rick.

Another long and dark thirty seconds passed. "I'm leaving now."

He got up off the floor, dressed, and headed for downtown Minneapolis. He got lost. His car overheated. Finally, an hour and a half later, he rolled into an Amoco for more water, only to find Rick sitting on the curb smoking a joint.

"That's nice," Joe said sarcastically, looking at Rick and to the dark lump that he knew was Caroline on the grass across the street.

After getting water, gas, and lifting Caroline into the backseat, they headed back to St. Paul with the radio off and the window open. Joe sat silently. Rick began and finished another joint.

"We were at some crazy party. People everywhere. They loved Caroline. Got her really fucked up though," he said, peering over the seat at her.

"Where's your car?" asked Joe angrily.

"I don't remember. Somewhere near Uptown I think. I'm not too worried about it."

Joe shook his head disgusted.

After ten minutes, Rick lit up another joint and talked and talked. "You're good. Your writing, I mean. Caroline showed me some of it. I was impressed."

Before Joe could feel the devastating effects of betrayal, anger, and defeat, Rick continued talking through a haze of smoke.

"*Verlaine exposed cruelty for what it is: an attempt to gain back ground we only imagine we've lost,*" he said reciting from memory. "That's good."

Joe said nothing for the rest of the ride. Instead, he kept a nervous eye on Caroline in the rearview mirror, afraid that if he thought too hard about what he was going to do, it would wake her. Amid protests of it being out of the way and it being late, he dropped Rick off at his place. With the exception of sleeping, Joe hadn't been alone with Caroline in weeks. Having her to himself was the only way for her to rediscover what he already knew: that they were meant for each other. This seemed a sure victory until, after they pulled into the driveway in front of the house, Caroline sat up, pushed the hair out of her eyes, and asked, "Where's Rick?"

Caroline got off the couch, opened the bedroom door, and went into the kitchen. Joe could hear the sucking sound of the refrigerator door being opened and Caroline rummaging around. It shut again with the same suck.

"I was thinking about high school today. Everyone was in such a hurry to grow up. Move out, get a place, drink, smoke, have sex," Joe said loudly.

"I was like that," Caroline responded. "I couldn't wait to move out. I hated my parents so much. I seriously moved out the day after graduation. Me and a girlfriend. Just packed up and took off. Of course, we had no money. We bought everything with credit cards. Six months later we had to go crawling back home. It took me seven months to pay that crap off. That was the worst year ever. And it only confirmed what my parents had always thought of me."

"So you were a bad girl."

"I thought I was," she said, coming back into their small room with a glass of soda.

"How old were you when you lost your virginity?"

"Eighteen. Why? You knew that," she said, taking a sip of soda.

"You weren't seventeen?"

"No."

"Because that's what Rick said last night while you were passed out."

"So what if I was seventeen?" she asked.

"So you were?" he asked back.

"Yes."

"Why didn't you tell me? Why did you lie? And why could you tell *him?*"

"Don't look so hurt. You would have flipped out if I would have told you the truth and you know it. You're always saying that girls have sex too young, before they're ready. I didn't need you to judge me."

"So you were seventeen? Fine, fine. Just don't lie to me anymore. I'm here for you. And if I judged you in the past I'm sorry. It won't happen again."

"It was dumb anyway. I was stupid and I felt flattered."

"I hope you don't sleep with everyone who flatters you, " he said before catching himself. "But you were young."

"Jill was asked out at work today," she said, changing the subject. "The guy asked her right where everyone could hear him. He could get fired for that. The worst part is how he did it. He told her that she had a 'great pooper.' And it worked. Oh, I can't wear this skirt to work anymore. Mr. Arndt said that from now on all skirts have to be below the knee. Don't you think that's a little sexist? I don't like having to go through all this for a lousy part-time job."

Joe didn't respond.

"Are you even listening to me? I don't know why I bother anymore."

"Who was that?"

"Mr. Arndt, my boss. I don't know why I even ..."

"No," he said with a forced easiness. "Who said that 'pooper' thing? That's funny," he said without smiling.

"Just a guy at work," she said dismissively. "I just don't know what to do about this skirt thing. It really bothers me."

"Who?" he asked insistently.

"Bob," she said.

"Bob who?"

"Bob Kantaris. He's been there a year and is going to Augsburg College. Is that enough information for you?"

"You dated him right before me, didn't you?"

"You know I did. I didn't lie to you about him."

She had only worked at T.J. Maxx for two weeks when Bob asked her out. He was never disrespectful and never talked about her when they broke up a month later. Nine months later, they still worked together and it was like nothing had ever happened.

"I don't want to talk about it. But that's all in the past. It made me stronger. Whatever kills me only makes me stronger, right?" she asked, attempting to quell Joe's rising anxiousness by quoting his favorite author, Nietzsche.

"Exactly! We all go through that shit. I know I did. Just like you. Suppose everyone does. Tough at the time. But you'd never change it. At least I wouldn't it. That's why I am who I am, I guess. You know?"

"I do. You're right."

He waited, letting the seeds he planted blossom.

"So you wouldn't change it if you could?" Joe asked.

"Of course I would. I wished it had never happened. But I can't change it now."

"So why did you let it happen then? Why did you lose your virginity at seventeen?"

"I was young, stupid," she said matter-of-factly.

He got up and went into the kitchen, taking a bag of popcorn from the shelf, placing it in the microwave, and punching a few musical touches of the keypad.

She looked at him fumbling in the kitchen and at the pile of papers stacked in the corner. She used to feel honored because of those papers, by his writing about her. What she didn't know then was that his life and work were inseparable, simultaneously creating one another, like Escher's hands that inversely do what the other does. What was real and what was fiction became indistinguishable. Those papers now made her hate him: in them something was a lie.

"You're amazing," he said. "I learn so much from you too. You're just unreal. The best. I'm so lucky to have you. Someone to really communicate with. Someone who listens and understands. There's no one I'd rather have as my lover. God, I love that word. Lover. You're my lover. Mine and mine alone," he paused. "Right?" Joe looked at the floor, his shoulders dropping. He didn't know what was happening to him. Since Rick came into his life, he felt as if he were perpetually drowning, the pathetic, desperate words he gasped the only way to hold on.

"Of course," she said impatiently.

"Are you sure?" he asked.

"*Yes!*" she hissed through her teeth.

"You don't sound sure."

"I am."

"Then why don't you sound sure? When people say things, you can tell if they're sure or not. And you don't sound sure."

"Is that popcorn yours?"

"Well, no, but you're my special girl and I wanted to make you something special. I'll replace it tomorrow," he said.

"With what money? You don't have a job."

While it was terrible that Rick and Caroline worked together eight hours every day now that it was summer, it was tragic that Joe worked only four stores down at Target. Coming back late one time too many after checking on Caroline and Rick (and making another ugly scene), he was fired. Since then, there had been many more ugly scenes in T.J. Maxx and no attempts at finding another job.

"Okay, maybe not exactly tomorrow, but soon," he said, pouring the popcorn into the bowl.

"They'll notice."

"Ahhh, who cares. Here, I'll write a note explaining that I grabbed it by mistake and that I'll replace it. Is that okay?" he asked, quickly scrambling for a piece of paper and pencil, scribbling a note and watching her most of the time.

"I guess," she said. "Don't put my name on it."

"I won't," he said erasing her name. "See what I mean? You're the best. Bob or no Bob. I have you now."

She said nothing but watched the television.

"Right?"

"What?" she asked.

"I said I have you now, Bob or no Bob. We're all that matters. The present and the future."

"Yeah," she muttered.

"It's like Sartre says, the past does not determine our present or future. We have to be strong enough to choose at all times. Most people just aren't strong enough to do that, that whole *condemned to be free* thing. Not us, though. Roaring into the future, nothing tying us down. Doesn't matter if he was a mistake." He caught his breath. "Are you sleeping with Rick?"

His voice ceased but not of its own accord. It just ran out, like film sputtering out of a projector. He looked at his hands as if this were the site of his silence and then to her. She said nothing. She just looked briefly out the window and tucked herself into the couch to sleep.

EVEN THE ETUDES

10

Lipman sat on a bench somewhere in the middle of the park. He watched the bliss of spring around him: walkers, joggers, speed walkers, mothers pushing strollers, elderly men on benches, couples with few words and simultaneous steps, teenagers dissatisfied with the sudden shortness of the trail.

"There you are," came a voice from the right. "I've been on the other side of the park for twenty minutes. Why would you sit here?"

Lipman looked up, "What do you mean?"

"What do I mean?" Roberts asked, slightly flabbergasted. "You sit on the wrong side of the park and then you pick the bench most obscured by…" He stopped and smiled. "What kind of toothpaste do you use?"

Lipman thought for a moment. "I don't know. Why?"

"No reason." Lipman had always been oblivious to the world. Roberts felt happy to see him. "Come on, let's go."

Lipman rose and they started down the trail.

"So what's going on?" asked Roberts gaily. He was being sentimental and he knew it, the way their steps felt quick,

163

tempered and in unison. They had walked this lake countless times, their conversations as unique as the lake was the same.

"I'm impotent."

To say that Roberts was taken off guard was an understatement. "Why are you telling me that?"

"Because something is wrong with me. I suppose you know that Leslie is living with her mom right now? I figured she'd call you but since I wasn't really talking to you either…"

"She thinks you don't want to marry her."

"I figured that's what she would think."

After a long silence Roberts asked, "Do you?"

"I don't know."

They came to a fork in the path. Without hesitation, they veered left.

"If you're doing all this because you can't get it up, Don… Leslie is the best girl you've ever been with."

"I know."

"And I think you owe her something—an explanation, a call, a letter, something."

"You don't understand. This used to happen all the time in the beginning. Whenever I was cheating on a girl or transgressing some law. And I know what it means."

"What it means? Impotence? Usually that you've drunk too much. At least in my experience."

A jogger passed them hurriedly.

"No, no. It would happen only one time. The first time. We would do the whole bit. We would flirt, confess our desire, drink—always after drinks when everything can be explained away—and pick a time and place to have sex. Or attempt to. Up until that moment, everything was smooth."

"Let me understand. You would get all hot for each other and not do it?"

"Rookie mistake. Rhythm is the key—knowing when to move in and when to pull back. If you make your move right away, you'll be grouped with every other guy who just wants to get laid. And that every girl tries to get away from. It's an easy mistake to make. But you'll never recover. It's better to just kiss. It shows you want them, but that they are worth waiting for. Nothing shows desire more than restraint."

"So what would happen?"

"We'd meet and be all over each other and then right at the worst moment, it would just die on me. It was like watching a flag being lowered." He waved at his crotch. "After that, everything would be fine for as long as I saw her."

"That hardly seems like impotence. More like cold feet. Or nerves."

"That's what I thought, in the beginning. Maybe I convinced myself of it. Told myself I was nervous because it was special; it was honest; I was in love. But deep down, I knew it was something else."

"I think you're overanalyzing yourself. Why couldn't you be just nervous? Or in love?"

"That's bullshit."

They considered and walked in silence. They passed a puddle, and two splashing ducks.

"You felt guilty, that's all. You can act out an idea, but people aren't ideas. And people still get hurt and you can't be immune from that. Not from someone you had feelings for, cared about, even loved. You felt guilty."

"Yes, but not in the way that you mean. I never felt guilty for the things I did. There was no reason. I believe believed that life was meaningless and that the only way to be free was to transcend the chains of society. I've known that since I was

165

a little boy. And the more society fought me, the stronger my resolve became. Do you think the fact that I am a writer is accidental? Writing is necessarily individualistic and violently opposed to rules, conformity, morality, and brotherhood. It is brutal and merciless and spares no one. That is its beauty. It isn't romantic bullshit. And the fact that you think that shows how strong those chains are. Being a writer means living that writing. Writing *is* rebellion."

"Great, but what does that have to do with your impotence?"

"Friendships, unions, marriages, family, any relationship that was sacred or taboo, I destroyed. My impotence was everything I fought against coming back to haunt me. It was a warning given at the point of transgression and, ultimately, the destruction of those things. Intellectually I couldn't be reached, but physically...."

"So you mean to say that you would become impotent at the moment you were seduced into accepting what you regard as mundane, uncreative, conventional? Namely, what anyone else would call a regular relationship with a regular girl?" asked Roberts.

"In a nutshell. But it was more than that, it was the morality behind those things."

"So you think that morality made you impotent?"

"I know it did. I was only able to conquer it once I *completely* let go of the moral convictions of my upbringing."

"That doesn't make sense. Maybe that is what happened before. Maybe morality was making a counterattack on your life. But why would it happen now? That contradicts what happened before. Now you're living within the very systems that you previously rejected, not tearing them down. You're engaged to Leslie, you have a great job; by every measure you're a regular guy living a regular, morally good life." Lipman cringed. "You're not cheating on her, are you?"

Lipman stopped in midstride, grabbed Roberts by the arm, and then let go, defeated by Roberts's words. They picked up their pace again. After a quarter mile, Lipman spoke.

"I am engaged to Leslie, I have a great job, and by every measure I am living a morally decent life. That's why it's happening now. After Leslie and I failed to have sex, she went to take a shower and I went into my study and did some automatic writing and guess what I wrote? '*I have put only my talent into my works. I have put all my genius into my life.*' Oscar Wilde."

"You think they're connected?"

"Of course they're connected! Don't you see? I am not living the way I should. I've sacrificed my art, my potential, and my personality in order to live like everyone else and I have no idea why. Maybe it was out of fear. I'm about to marry a woman who would be horrified by my deepest beliefs, and the horrible life I'm now living has made writing impossible; it's slowly killing me. Before it was my inability to transcend the moral convictions foisted upon me that was making me impotent. Now it is the reverse—it is my surrender to them— that is causing it. I am betraying myself and my beliefs."

"I don't understand how having a good job and a beautiful woman to spend your life with is so bad."

"It's not the *having* the job or *having* the wife or *having* the house. You think I wouldn't have those things in my life eventually? No, it's the *attitude* toward them that matters. You can't escape the world, but if you *believe* in its morals and hypocrisies, then you're done for. And I'm afraid that I'm coming to believe in it all."

"So what are you going to do?" asked Roberts.

"I haven't a clue."

They walked in a tense and awkward silence.

"She's beautiful; perfect."

"I know," said Roberts.

"I mean really perfect. I've never been with anyone like her. No one's ever made me feel the way I do when I'm with her. Pretty cliché, huh?"

"Probably."

"She can play Chopin. Even the etudes."

"Really?"

Again, silence descended upon them.

"She said something strange right after. That she couldn't compare to immortality."

"And she said this in response to your impotence? That is odd. How could a woman compare with immorality?"

"Immortality!" exclaimed Lipman "It doesn't matter." He immediately regained his composure and was himself again, the same guy who had appeared, to the best of Robert's memory, only a few months after they had met—reserved, heavy, even a bit gloomy.

"Even the etudes?" Roberts asked.

"Really."

"I never knew."

They neared the end of the trail.

ANGER

At the end of the unnecessarily wide aisle, one that could very easily allow three or four carts to progress simultaneously from freezer to freezer, Joe stood wrapped tight in black jeans and a thin, black turtleneck. It was too warm for what he was wearing, but he liked how he looked. He stood in stark contrast to the brightness of his surroundings: the white square tiles whose stacking design gave the impression that they were all running toward or away from something; the unblinking hangover-off-white fluorescents above; the rows of clear refrigerator doors, products backlit, that smoked when opened. He was very much like a black candle in the midst of day. He moved like it too.

He stood hunched over, examining the limp, shifting package of corn that he passed from left hand to right. He seemed to consider the package for some time, but was really only continuing the thinking he had begun earlier in the day; he tossed the corn in the cart thoughtlessly, just as he had the other nameless items, and headed just as thoughtlessly for the checkout.

He exited the store, got in his car, and headed for home. Sitting back against his seat, a light came over his face. It came suddenly, like a drop of water falling from somewhere unseen, surprising him. That's it, he thought, that's what is different. He was right. Everything had happened so quickly. First they were going to and then they weren't, the deadline to be out of the dorm putting pressure every decision Joe and Caroline tried to make. The thought of each moving home to different parts of the state was unthinkable. Three months was too long to be apart. True, it was just a room (a small, dumpy room in a house with ten or fifteen other people) but they'd be together and it was only until they could find their own place. It was settled, then. Quickly.

Needless to say, neither set of parents had taken it very well. In one of those final decisions that was final only until the next great idea materialized, Joe had told his mother that he would absolutely be coming home for the summer, giving her every reason he could think of but that he knew he would dismiss the moment he looked at Caroline. Joe's mother didn't like Caroline and was dead set against them living together. He was graduating and needed to look for a job. She also remembered too well the feeling she had had for a young man who had left her pregnant, alone, scared, and broke. Nothing like this would happen to her son. Joe's mother came home having expected him to have moved out of the dorm and back into their house, but it turned out to be his moving out, period. His thoughtless love and selfish smile were as wide as the chasm he was creating between them, his mother thought. She let him go without a word, which in his bliss he took as support. Later, he would discover her silence was punishment when she would not speak to him or lend him financial support.

Caroline's parents buried their anger in calm. She was their baby. As such, they did the only thing they could: blamed the maverick young man they had met only once. They said nothing when she moved in with Joe, but they never visited and they never once called.

In all that time the word "home" had never become part of Joe and Caroline's vocabulary. Like a receipt shoved in a pocket, they had stuffed themselves into their cramped room to hide from the scorn of their parents. The four walls became armor, the opposition they felt proving that they were doing the right thing. But now, driving away from the supermarket, Joe realized that it didn't matter if all they had was a single room, in a sickening house, surrounded by enemies. They had more than just protection: they had a home.

He pulled into the gravel driveway, catching his front bumper on the cement lip, and making an awful scraping noise. For the first time, he smiled knowingly. Shutting his car off, he got out, opened the backdoor, and reached in for his bag of groceries. Over his shoulder he could hear the screen door open and slam. He pulled himself out of the car to see who it was. He felt so happy that he even began an introductory, "Hey." Today was different. Good. No need for the short stare down that said all but "Fuck you," followed by the aristocratic turn and aggravated heave of a sigh he was accustomed to giving.

Joe turned expectantly, and saw Rick.

Once, when Joe was a kid of nine or ten, he was playing with his younger cousin on a tennis court. They were running around the perimeter of the three courts, not chasing each other or playing tag, just running and laughing, weaving in and out of the three courts, in and around nets held up by thin, very hard cords. Joe, running and laughing, his feet slapping the clay with loud reverberating echoes, misjudged the end of one net, turning too soon to come around to the other side. It was dusk and the net's suspension cord was barely visible. The cord caught him directly in the throat and Joe was knocked out immediately.

Seeing Rick felt almost exactly like that. Rick, smiling his flaky, dippy smile, some stupid green bandana around his neck like a hippy's golden retriever.

"Hey Joe, what d'ya got there?" Rick asked, sauntering up to Joe and his car, bending his body lazily to peek at what was inside.

Joe backed up, his body bent, loose and heavy, like a cat picked up by the scruff of its neck. "Caroline's not here." He nearly told him she got off of work in an hour, but he knew that Rick would be back in an hour if he did. He probably knew anyway.

"I know. She's not off 'til six. I just came to get a few things for her. She called me. No big deal. See," he said, holding in his hands her favorite lipstick, a folded-up piece of paper, and something he couldn't make out. "I'm bringing them to her and then we'll be back."

"You gotta stop coming around here," Joe said in an angry whisper.

"What?" asked Rick who had not heard the words but knew, from the tone of Joe's voice, their intention.

"Stop coming around here."

"Why?" he asked playfully.

"Are you really going to make me go through this?"

"Besides the fact that, unlike you, everyone in the house likes me and lets me crash here anytime and besides the fact that Caroline wants me here as she is tired of arguing with you, I like you, Joe."

"You have to stop seeing Caroline."

"Well, you know I'm not going to stop doing that," he said. "Caroline's an interesting girl with lots of possibilities that are simply not being met by you. She's funny and clever and open and has a lot to say about everything."

"You will stop seeing Caroline."

"We're planning a trip. Hitchhiking. All the way to Canada. Just her and me and our charms to keep us warm. Yes, we're going to do what you had planned to do together."

Shortly after Joe and Caroline began dating, and not coincidentally after Joe had finished *On the Road*, they had decided to take a hitchhiking trip to Canada. They wanted to experience the open road, taste life firsthand, and be free from all restraints. Fields with open night skies were just waiting to have poetry read to them and love made under them. Caroline knew someone who could get them acid, and marijuana was easily attainable almost anywhere. Anyway, you only had to be eighteen to drink in Canada. They had gone so far as to buy backpacks and a map. There was nothing more romantic. A trip like that would strengthen their bonds and bring them as close as any two people could be. That Caroline had told Rick about this when she and Joe had promised not to tell anyone—they were going to leave without notice— was awful. That he had been excised from his own trip, by his own girlfriend, was beyond words.

"You are not seeing Caroline."

"Yes, yours. She said that you had planned for the two of you to do this. To hit the open road. Take acid. Be totally free, I think she said. She said you said. Or something. Just see what's out there. It sounds like an idea you'd have, Joe. Or might have had at one time when you were looser," Rick said pushing Joe lightly on the shoulder. "Well, not now anyway."

"You are not seeing Caroline."

"Of course, those were the good old days when you were fun. Ready to give it all up: for poems, the road, freedom and Caroline. Don't forget Caroline. Does that sound about right? Young and fun. Not this piece of broken glass that you are now."

"Stop."

"So I'll see you in an hour," he said, preparing to go.

"You aren't listening. If you don't stop seeing Caroline, I will do something about it."

Rick leaned back on his heels.

"I'm not kidding, Rick."

"Sure you are, Joe," he said and began to walk by. Joe stopped him. Rick stepped back.

"I could tell you that Caroline will find out about this conversation, but I wouldn't do that, Joe."

"I know you'll tell her and she'll hate me, but I don't care. She does anyway. Just stop coming around here," Joe said with a sudden crescendo. He rushed Rick, grabbing his collar with both hands. Joe's hands were shaking. Rick did not react at all.

"This is your last time here, do you understand me?"

Rick said nothing.

"Do you?" Joe screamed.

"Sure I do, Joe."

Rick loosened himself from Joe's grip and trotted lazily away, Caroline's things in hand.

Joe reached back into his car and pulled out his groceries, the smell of paper bags and defeat clinging to him.

"God dammit," he said as he entered the house. He knew he only had an hour to compose himself before Caroline and Rick and regret and all the ugly things that had just happened would join him. "God dammit. God dammit."

He was shocked when, in an hour, Rick dropped Caroline off. He went to the window and watched Rick pulling away. Caroline came in and did a load of laundry while Joe tried to figure out how to keep her from going out with Rick.

In the end, Joe decided to simply ask her to stay with him tonight.

"Why?" she said dismissively, taking a shirt from the pile heaped on the floor, folding it and placing it in the small cardboard dresser in the closet just a few feet in front of her.

"You've gone out the last three nights—"

"I like going out," she said flippantly, in midfold.

"And in the last month it's been almost nonstop." He was sitting on the edge of the couch across from her, tense.

"You're exaggerating," she said, holding a shirt collar under her chin, bringing the sleeves into the shirt's middle with neat, robotic precision.

"I'm not. Why can't you just spend a night with me?"

She often responded to his words randomly, as if choosing candy from a box. To these she declined, instead looking down pensively at the pile of clothes in front of her. She cataloged how many shirts were left (seven), how many pairs of pants (eight; she was sure she was missing a pair), how many socks, and how many pairs of underwear. She noticed that she had large quantities of yellows and oranges and tried to pin some significance on this, but couldn't. What she did take note of in a more serious way was the need for more socks. She reached down and pulled out another shirt, tangerine, long-sleeved.

"I said, why can't you just spend one night with me?"

"I spend lots of days with you. I don't know why you complain so much. Since we've started dating, I've spent all my time with you. My grades went down because of all the time I spent with you. My relationship with my parents deteriorated because of all the time you insisted I spend with you."

"You're gonna blame all that on me?"

"I lost all my friends because of you. You lost all your friends because of you. Or us. Or whatever you want to say. I am not going to lose this one." She paused briefly, flattening the sleeve of the tangerine t-shirt and walking it to the closet with the others. "And you never want to do anything fun."

"What?" he asked in shock, his shoulders rising like the hood of a cobra but quickly dropping in defeat, his body falling slowly against a couch that absorbed him indifferently.

She held her hands out to him without looking: he couldn't argue with the truth.

"I know everything, anyway—everything you've done, everything you've wanted to do and will ever want to do, everything you will say and when we go somewhere everything you think—everything you think of anything, how you'll react to any possible situation. Everything. Everything. Everything. You're the least spontaneous thing on earth. When I'm with you, I'm so with you that I can't get away from you. And I'm sick of it. Sick. I'm sick of you."

There was a pronounced silence.

"Can't you not see him just one night?"

"Sure," she said with an easy shrug of her shoulders.

He was relieved. The couch seemed to take him in with greater ease. He was going to suggest they go out for coffee and talk like they used to, get reconnected, find that *them* that they put aside like a well-worn book so long ago. Maybe things weren't as lost as he had thought.

"But I'm not going to. I like hanging out with him."

Joe's head turned, not too fast, but like fate, without error. Then came anger.

"God dammit, you're not! I absolutely forbid it!" he yelled. "You're not leaving this house with him again!"

"Shut up!" she retorted, looking at him for the first time since they began talking, each syllable thickly emphasized like a second coat of paint slathered on a wall. "You will not yell at me! You will not embarrass me in front of all the people who live in this house! Just shut up! Shut up! Shut up!"

"Then don't go!" he screamed, holding the word "go" until his voice sounded parched.

"Shut up!" she screamed back. "Just shut up! Everyone doesn't have to know! Why do you have to do this? I hate you!"

So forceful were those last words that he was reduced to hysterics, falling from the couch onto his knees, hyperventilating, finally crawling toward her, tears held back only by the yelping desperateness plunging through his body.

"Don't say that! Oh God! Please. Please. I won't yell. I'm sorry. Please. Please," he said in a panicked whisper. "Just please don't go and please don't say that. You don't hate me. You don't. I know you don't. You love me. You love me, Caroline. Caroline. I love you. I love you more than I have ever loved anyone. Just like you love me. Just like you say. Oh God, please don't go. I'm drowning. Please."

Caroline reached down, selected another shirt, and continued folding her laundry.

"Get up," she said without looking at him. "You're embarrassing yourself. A God damned grown man rolling around on the floor like a child. A fucking infant. And you wonder. And stop hyperventilating. Jesus," she said in disgust.

"Okay. Okay. See, I'm getting up," he said standing up, fragile hope in his voice, his rising made awkward by his insistence on looking up, his steps equally awkward as he made his way backward to the couch. "Okay. Okay. I'm stopping. I'm stopping," he whimpered, gaining his composure once he took his eyes off her and stared at his feet. Finally he was able to mutter, still somewhat prematurely, "See, I stopped. I stopped. Just don't go okay? Okay?"

She said nothing. She was folding pants now. There was nothing but the room's silence and their breathing.

"Fine, go," he said with another quick turn. "You don't even care. Neither do I. I don't know why you even stay with me. Just go and have a fun time."

"I will," she answered immediately, as if she had only been waiting for him to say that. "I've told you that all night. Since I got home from work. Your little diversion was just that. Now go in the other room so I can change."

"I just don't understand why you're doing this. Can you just tell me that? Answer me that one question and I'll never ask another; I'll go."

"I don't know what you want," she said. "I do everything wrong. Whether it's choosing where we eat, or when we have sex, or what books I read, what I like, what I dislike. Music. Anything. When it's not up to your standards you make me feel cute. And if I exceed your expectations, you're not interested. When I try to be your confidant, I'm supposed to be your lover, when I try to be your friend, you need mothering, when I try to be your peer, I'm supposed to be your student. I never, ever get it right."

It was at this moment that Rick came into the room.

⌒ʌ

"Hey guys, what's going on?" he asked with an indulgent smirk on his face. "Mark let me in."

"Well, actually Rick, we were just—" Joe began.

"Nothing. Come in! Come in!" Caroline said excitedly, tossing whatever article of clothing she had in her hand to the floor in front of the closet. She pulled at her watch, untucking its face from the underbelly of her wrist. "You're early. I'm not ready at all."

Rick took a seat on the couch next to Joe, leaning deep into its cushions, his legs spread far apart, his head thrown back toward his right shoulder in mock speculation at the ceiling.

"Actually, we were kind of in the middle of something," said Joe.

"Yeah?" said Rick unconcerned. "What was that?"

"Oh nothing, nothing," stammered Caroline, waving her hands at Joe's words the way one does to disperse smoke.

"Caroline, I think we really need to finish our conversation."

Caroline and Rick both ignored him and continued talking to each other.

"Do you think Keri is stealing?" Caroline asked Rick. She rocking back on her heels, stood in front of Rick and resumed folding shirts, both as a means of focusing her devotion on him but also as a means of avoiding Joe's impenetrable and unrelenting stare.

"I happen to know she is," he said, a spark in his eye.

"Oh, how?" she asked.

His eyes, once more searching the room, avoided hers until the moment he had finished speaking, "Because I helped her."

"What?" she asked, nearly in a whisper.

He scratched at the top of his head, "Just a few bucks from the register to buy some... necessary things."

Joe knew he was talking about weed and wasn't impressed.

"Aren't you afraid of getting caught?" she asked, still in shock.

"Nah, we've got it all rigged. Nothing to worry about."

"How do you do it?" she asked, leaning closer to him. As he described their process of writing up voids for items they had not really sold, taking the money from the register, and pocketing it, she stood transfixed and asked to be let in on the deal. He told her maybe, maybe. Clearly she was eyeing the bait on the hook.

"Big deal," said Joe dismissively, "Stealing. There's a minor law to transgress."

No one heard him.

"Yeah, it's pretty cool. And the extra cash comes in real handy," said Rick, tapping the small bulge in the pocket of his vest. "And if they ever catch on, I have it double-rigged so that Keri will get nailed, not me."

"That's awesome. I want to hear more about it but right now I need to change."

Reluctantly, Joe rose, as did Rick, and went across the hall into the kitchen.

"So, what are you guys doing tonight?" Joe asked Rick over his shoulder as he walked into the belly of the kitchen, trying to ignore the humiliation of having to leave the room when his own girlfriend changed (a recent, awful rule Caroline had put into place). With Rick there, Joe could pretend he needed something; once there, he looked straight ahead and out the misshapen kitchen window.

"So what are you guys doing tonight? Party or...?"

The question itself was terrible and made Joe want to fling himself out of this window. What was even more awful was that it was the only question he could ask Rick; they had nothing else to talk about, nothing else in common except Joe's own girlfriend. His breathing became labored when he turned and lifted his head to the empty kitchen. Rick had not followed him out of the bedroom. He felt the instinct to rise and head for the suddenly very closed door but, before this reflex could claim him, his muscles relaxed and he fell back into the truth of the situation, the stiff, wooden lopsided kitchen chair. Rick had not been asked to leave. This pain was compounded (amazing that this was possible) by the thought of Joe's own eventual return into the room. The thought of having to look at Rick, to meet his eyes when he was allowed back into the room was unbearable. So he sat and waited for emptiness, with its cold hand, to lift his chin and for Caroline to call him like a loyal and abused pup back into its house.

But she never called. He looked at the yellowing clock on the wall. It had been more than twelve minutes. There was no question: she had changed. He had been left quite deliberately in this dingy kitchen to sit and wait. Walking across the small hallway to the closed door, he could hear them talking. He couldn't hear their words, but it didn't matter. From the tone of their voices, the pauses, the quiet, acknowledging laughs, he knew. It was the relaxed conversation of two people who needed no reason to be together and who found any activity charming. For a moment, it was nice.

He went back and sat at the kitchen table. Then he walked down the stairs and outside. He paced on the sidewalk in front of the house for five or six minutes, came back into the house, and stared up the stairs before climbing them and entering the room. He was careful not to burst in, knowing it would confess his suspicions. He opened the door, headed for the closet and pulled out a pair of socks that he didn't need, sat on the couch, and changed them. Caroline and Rick ignored him and continued talking.

"So where are you guys going tonight?" It took all of his power not to vomit.

"We don't really make plans," said Rick, his head swiveling on his tan neck. "We just go out and let things happen, you know? Let life take us where it wants. I don't like to make plans. Too permanent. Too middle class."

"So, what, you just drive around? Or is a car too middle class?"

"Sometimes we take a car, sometimes we let our feets take us."

"And tonight?" asked Joe.

"We're taking a car to a friend of Rick's in Plymouth, okay?" said Caroline sternly.

"Just curious. Sounds fun."

"It will be something," said Rick slowly.

"And Rick is going to stay here tonight," said Caroline.

"What? No, he's not," Joe said, standing up.

"It's going to be late and I don't want him to have to drive all the way home."

"It's always late. There's no room. We sleep on the fucking floor. Where is he going to sleep?"

"On the floor, too."

"What's the big deal, Joe?" asked Rick.

"Shut the hell up," Joe said, pointing sharply at him.

"Don't talk to him that way," said Caroline.

"He's not staying. I will drive the son of a bitch home. I will call him a cab and give him the money. He can walk. With his feet, I don't care what the motherfucker does. But he is under no circumstances staying here."

"Yes he is," she insisted. "And he's neither a son of a bitch nor a motherfucker, thank you," she said snidely.

Joe ignored her second defense of Rick. "Oh yeah. You sleep right between us. We'll take turns on you throughout the night. It'll be a big fucking party! Maybe some of the others in house would be interested!"

"Hey, back off," said Rick.

"I pay the rent," she countered.

Joe closed his eyes.

"I'll just sleep on the couch," said Rick.

"I told you to shut the fuck up."

"Joe, I swear, if you talk to him like that one more time—"

"You'll what?"

She faltered for a response.

"I hate you!" she screamed and began crying. She darted from the room, down the stairs, and outside.

The room filled with a sudden and dramatic void, as if Caroline had sucked all the sound out of the room with her. Joe sat deep in the couch, his right hand planted firmly on his forehead, his left on his knee. He sat very much like a man losing grip of a rope. Rick sat straight up.

"You know you're losing her to me, don't you?"

"Yeah," he said after a long time. "I do."

Joe placed his fingers over his cheek and mouth. They were the truest words that had been spoken since Rick had entered their lives.

"So leave," he said angrily.

A bemused, closed-lipped smile awoke on Rick's face.

"Leave?" he laughed.

"You won. I've done this before. I know how it works. The logistics of pulling a woman away. The game. The strategy. The timing. The ebb and tide. When to attack, when to pull away. All that. You have her. You have her and you know it. Taking her from me is just ceremony."

"Right," Rick said with a nod of his head. "And leaving her to you is an even greater victory, isn't that how that goes? Isn't that what you're going to say next? She'll always want me, never having had me? And I'll have the added bonus of knowing she'll torture you for it. No. I don't think so. Not this time. You're very clever. More clever than me. At one point probably a better gamesman than me. But you lost sight of the big picture. Always being on the attack makes you vulnerable to attack. You have no defenses. You sent her to me. I will take her. Aesthetics means so little to me. And it will destroy you, more than it is destroying you now. And I will enjoy it. I'll enjoy it as I'm fucking her. That kills you doesn't it? More than anything I'd imagine. More than even losing her. The thought of me, of another man, of the Other, fucking her—your woman. Maybe you're not so clever."

"You're doing it anyway, so what do I care," Joe said dismissively, flatly.

Rick squinted as if thinking intensely, then laughed with an indulgent smile, "You do try, don't you?"

Joe looked up at him but said nothing.

"You know, we haven't been together."

Joe looked up again, his eyes giving himself away.

"Not her, Joe. Me. I've kept her at bay. I'm just waiting for the right time. But don't worry, it's almost here. Not her," he said again.

"Well, that's good to hear," Joe said sarcastically.

Rick rose to leave.

"I do like you, Joe. Too bad about all this, we could've hung. Done a lot of damage together, I'm sure." He laughed.

"Yeah, too bad," muttered Joe.

Rick left, no doubt to find Caroline and go out for another in a series of celebratory evenings, leaving Joe to another in a series of evenings in front of the window that faced Selby and Snelling, pouncing at cars.

Joe looked at the empty doorway. He wanted to give it the finger, to throw the clock at it, to cry, to scream. It was useless. He looked at the very empty doorway.

RAGE

12

He must have been gone for some time. The definitiveness of silence had fallen over their room like dust settling on a dirt road after the passing of a speeding car. She yanked herself to her side, jerking the small clock off the boom box: 7:15. Lying back on the multi-layered comforters that served as a bed, the clock pulled to her chest, she relaxed. She wasn't late. He must have left early to look for a job. She sighed, the clock slipping to her side. Rushing to catch it, its face upturned comically to hers, she picked it up and placed back on the makeshift nightstand.

Pushing herself up from the floor, Caroline cautiously opened the door to her room and headed for the kitchen. It was empty. She listened carefully. Everyone was either gone or still sleeping. She relaxed and immediately her body gave the impression of shrinking several inches. She promptly started a pot of coffee, placed two slices of bread in the toaster where they would stiffly wait, and she headed for the shower.

Reaching into the bathtub, she turned the knobs, the water exploding out of the faucet as if it had been waiting all night for someone to talk to. As she pulled the tiny knob at the faucet's top, the shower started babbling instead. Pulling her t-shirt over her head, she felt a chill run over her naked body. She was about to step into the shower when she stopped. She was feeling different, good. Peeking out of the bathroom door, she smiled slyly. She stepped into the hallway and tiptoed down its walkway, her last steps shorter and quicker as she darted into her room.

She never dared walk around naked even if the windows were closed, no matter if anyone was home or not and certainly not in a house full of virtual strangers. Today, however, it felt all right. *He* had told her that she was beautiful. She quickly pulled the shade to the window to her right but left the one straight before her unsheathed. Gritting her teeth, she smiled and laughed nervously. Several times she approached the window and pulled back. She had to hurry before the hot water ran out and her toast got cold. Beautiful. She was beautiful. She turned and placed herself before the window. Naked, but with her hands covering her breasts, she stood admiring everything that admired her: the trees, the unseen birds, and the parked cars.

Lowering her arms from her breasts she inspected them, along with her stomach, arms, neck, face, and imagined *him* inspecting them. She thought to herself, *he thinks I am beautiful*, despite the commonplace objections she had lived with for as long as she could remember—*too short, too wide, too hippy, saggy breasts*. She smiled. *I can be pretty*.

She didn't have to look back at the clock, which was staring at her like a stern mother. Now she was going to be late. Playfully she stuck her tongue out at the clock and headed back to the bathroom.

Passing the full-length mirror on the back of the door, she was about to enter the shower when a quarter-size shadow on her outer thigh toward her butt caught her eye. She passed a careless hand over it and stepped into the icy water.

Once out of the shower, she wrapped one towel around her hair, grabbed a second, placed a leg on the toilet seat and began drying her legs, humming to herself. Pushing the outside of her leg forward, she once again saw the discoloration. Annoyed at having missed it, she whispered "Idiot" to herself and wiped at it with the towel. She was about to turn away; it didn't wipe clean. She scrubbed a little harder. She tried to see exactly what it was, but she couldn't get a straight look at it. Turning toward the mirror and arching her back, she got a clear look at it and fell into a slump. Quickly arching again only to slump once more, she rubbed her hand over it in disbelief. It had been a particularly violent fight. She had never seen Joe so angry and he had never touched her before.

Lowering herself backwards to the tub's lip, she sat and it all came back: the arguing, the accusations, the pushing. The realization struck her with its cold, indifferent hand and she began to cry. She had to get dressed, go to work, and pretend that she was the same person.

DUCKS

13

Lipman sat on top of the picnic table, his legs resting on the uneven, cracking bench that stared at him like a vicious smile. It was hot and the wind was impatient. Roberts leaned against a tree and watched as a girl jogged toward him. She looked him directly in the eyes. In the last few steps before she passed him, Roberts smiled. She didn't react. Once she disappeared behind some trees, he looked at Lipman.

"Did you see that?" he asked.

"What's that?" asked Lipman.

"That girl jogging. She was looking right at me and when I smiled at her she ignored me," he said, looking in her direction.

"Let's keep moving, all right?" Lipman asked, barely listening to Roberts.

Lipman stood up and they cut across the grass and to the walking path.

"I do that all the time," started Roberts. "I think some girl is looking at me, I react to her, and then I'm totally wrong. And I couldn't even pretend like I was looking at someone else. There's never anyone else around. I'm amazed at how often I mistake *my direction* for *me*. Am I that self-centered that everything must be about me? That if it's not happening to me, it can't be happening at all?"

"We naturally assume that things are about us. The mistake you're making is that you're forgetting that people are turned inward most of the time. When alone, people are on auto-pilot, their bodies taking care of them while their minds are a thousand miles away. That girl was probably thinking about what she has to do when she's done jogging, that she has to go to the grocery store. Something like that. Let's pick up the pace." They did.

"That's depressing," said Roberts, reflecting on Lipman's observations.

"I guess," Lipman said, impatiently.

"No, it is. Because those are the things I think about when I'm alone. What I have to do next. Where I have to go. It's never thinking about anything substantial. I just take the living for granted."

"Believe me, I know."

"I don't want to think about those things anyway. Anytime I do, I feel like I have no idea how I got to where I am. Every time I reflect on my life, I feel as if I've woken up in a strange place. Which way do you want to go?" he asked.

"Let's take the shorter way today."

They veered left.

"What's the hurry?" asked Roberts.

"No hurry."

"It just seems like..." started Roberts.

"Well, it's not," retorted Lipman. "You don't want to think about those things. You've always been that way. You start to delve into something and you stop before you can get any-thing out of it. Denial. I can't live that way. Anyway, anytime

I acknowledge a woman who doesn't see me, I turn away ashamed. Whenever I meet a woman's eye, or think I do, I play out a variation of an entire scenario in my head. I immediately want to be with her. I nearly go crazy waiting for our eyes to meet because it will all be there—our love, our life together. And it is filled with limitless possibility. Both of us disappearing into something done on impulse, not thought out. We'll run away together and never talk to anyone we know again. Not family or friends. No one. And lurking behind all of this fantasy is my life. The fiancée waiting for me to call, my job, my family, my friends, and the disappointment I feel about all of it. That nothing has lived up to the promise I felt my life had," said Lipman.

"That's normal. Beginnings are always the most exciting part of every relationship, from the first look to the first few months. Who doesn't love those first few months together? Getting to know those new things about someone, what she thinks about things, waiting for the first kiss, how amazing making love will be. Those feelings naturally go away with time. People break up and get divorced because they think the relationship is over when that excitement ebbs away. But it's not. It is when that first excitement is over that you are ready to make that transition into the deeper areas. Because it doesn't have the same flash as infatuation, most people give up. It's true whether you're talking about a woman or a new job—anything new. It's nothing to be ashamed of."

"But that insight is useless. I understand it and so do you but the disappointment is still there. And what makes me so ashamed is that, when I act on those things, I am admitting that the still-unextinguished hope has made a permanent place inside me. It confesses that I still believe that love can save. I haven't overcome that part of me that wants to be swept away, to be fooled, to believe in nonsense, to be ignorant. I hate those kinds of denials. I thought I wanted freedom. What I really want is absolute, unforgiving self-knowledge."

191

"It's probably the same thing. Don't feel ashamed for having hope. Maybe self-knowledge can indulge in those things while still knowing they are illusions."

"Come on. You know that isn't possible. The other night I happened into this bar. Happened," Lipman said with a self-deprecating laugh. "No one happens into a bar. I'm not sure what I was looking for, but I was looking for something. Eventually I saw what you always see in a bar: guys trying to pick up women. I watched a dark-haired man and a woman and their entire conversation bothered me. I wasn't sure why. But I started writing it down, word for word. Here, I have it," he said, pulling several folded pieces of paper out of his pocket. He pointed to a bench and they sat down. "I've modified it a bit, adding narration, but the dialogue is verbatim."

"Let's hear it," said Roberts, leaning back and closing his eyes.

"Up to you to break this time," he said, tipping the cue to her.

"I'll try," she said, snatching the cue playfully away, taking up his challenge and throwing her hair over her shoulder.

She bent over provocatively and after careful consideration, sent the white ball sailing toward the obedient still colored balls. They exploded in all directions, none of them finding a hole. Taking his turn, the young man said nothing, sinking two balls before missing one.

"What are you doing tonight?" he asked.

"What?" she asked, even though she had heard him, eyeing the far end of the table.

"You said you like being outside and it is nice out."

"I don't know."

"I'd try to help you think of something, but I have some things I need to take care of. You know how it is."

"Oh, you have things to do, do you?" she said, straightening herself after sinking the bright red ball.

"I might catch a movie. I don't know. It's pretty cool here," he said, picking up the pool cue.

"I could drink, play pool, hang out with you."

Watching the couple from the bar, Charles recognized the big risk the young man had just taken. It was not only in the words but in the change of voice, the lack of eye contact, the playfulness he so easily adopted.

Lipman went to the next page and began reading again.

"If you don't have anything to do, would you like to hang out?" he suggested.

"I don't know," she said. " I could spend a quiet evening with a book. But you never know. I mean, you don't seem too insane," she said, looking at him.

"Too insane or too intense?" he asked, making a move for the inside pocket of his coat and a cigarette.

"I guess I'll have to find out."

With that, it began. He wasn't going to catch a movie and she wasn't going to have a quiet evening with a book. As he placed four quarters into the machine and as she went to the bar for change and beer, Charles turned away with a sense of disgust. Those lines, the man's approach, it was all familiar. And if measured in wholly scientific terms, he was that young man only a few years ago. The thought was horrifying, more so for the fact that, in some strange way, he still was that man.

"Thanks for the game."

"No problem."

"Let's blow outta here," he said.

"What do you like to do?" she asked.

"Lots of things."

Lipman folded up the papers. There was a silence.

"It's good," said Roberts, opening his eyes and sitting up. "On the one hand, the dialogue suggests you are unhappy with romantic love, that the pool-playing motif shows that you are sick of the game of love. But maybe you want to suggest that he wants to show his true self to a woman and not dazzle her or confuse her or even lie to her with his date persona, what we all put up in place of the real thing. I guess you're talking about how love can be a denial of self, of reality. Or I'm guessing that's where you are headed with it?"

"Something like that. Here," he said handing the papers to him. "I don't need it." Roberts reluctantly took the papers and placed them carefully into his pocket. They got up and began walking.

"Why are you giving me this?" he asked. "The other day you told me that you couldn't write, yet what you read seems fine. You are writing."

"Yes, but I can't keep it."

"Why? You told me that you couldn't write, but you are writing. You told me that your job, Leslie, that everything is a problem. That your attitude toward those things, your belief in what they stand for, their view of morality that they support, is killing you. But you are writing and that part of you gets reflected in the work, so what is the problem?"

"That's the problem. The life I am living has poisoned me. Every time I write something that is true and real I feel a tremendous sense of guilt. Like I'm committing a sin, that I'm seeing the world as ugly and devoid of hope, ignoring the good in it. Intellectually, I know that's not true but my gut clenches up so tight that I have to stop writing to make it go away," he said, growing increasingly agitated with every word. "It's all words with me anyway. Ideas, theories. I've never lived an unselfconscious moment in my life. I live in order to write it down. Writing is recording. But recording what? Reflections? Other people's lives? I need to *do* something."

"Do what? What is there to do? Just live. What do you want?" Roberts asked. Getting no response, he simply walked in silence. He was surprised when he found himself several paces ahead of Lipman. He was even more surprised when, looking over his shoulder, he found Lipman bent over, hands on thighs, attempting unsuccessfully to catch his breath.

"Don, are you alright?"

He nodded yes.

"Why don't we sit down for a minute?"

Again, Lipman nodded and slowly they found their way to the edge of the lake and a downed tree. For a long time, Lipman avoided eye contact with Roberts, muttering a series of thank you's and I'm okay's under his breath. Roberts sat quietly, pretending to look past Lipman and at the grandstand at the other end of the lake; in fact, he was staring intensely at Lipman, watching his sad, defeated eyes.

"Look."

The sound of Lipman's voice startled Roberts. Lipman was pointing to a spot a few feet from shore where a plain brown mother duck had just entered the water followed by several of her ducklings.

"See how they just follow her wherever she goes? If she goes right, so do they. When she goes left, without reason, they follow, no questions asked. All around the lake they do this, all day, every day. It's as if there's an invisible string connecting them, keeping them all together," he said.

They watched the ducks in silence. Lipman was correct; their course was not charted but spontaneous, relying solely on the whims and wisdom of the mother. They glided single file along the shore, following her like soldiers, their course swiftly and severely altered to the center of the lake when a jogger—the girl Roberts had seen earlier—approached the lake's edge, their nervous paddling relaxing once there.

"Our problems and regrets are the same as those ducklings," said Lipman.

"I suppose you're right. We give birth to our troubles the same as that mother duck gave birth to her ducklings. We own them," Roberts added quietly.

"Except that those ducklings eventually find their own way. Not troubles. They stick with you for your whole life."

Lipman looked deep into Roberts's eyes. "Why don't you start walking? I'll catch up to you in a minute."

"I'm in no hurry."

Eventually Roberts stood up and walked away, while Lipman watched the ducks paddle aimlessly, but as if choreographed, around the lake.

BEGGING

14

Although the sound of the microwave door slamming woke them up abruptly, sleep hung in the room; Joe's eyes opened wide, and he placed his arm around Caroline who struggled under its weight. He began kissing her.

"What are you doing?" she asked, pulling away.

"I want you."

She looked at the clock. "I have to get ready for work."

"I thought you didn't have to work today."

"Well, I do."

"Last night was nice," whispered Joe with a smile, tightening his grip on her. "Like it used to be. Everything else was far away: the money worries, our parents, everything. I had a great idea for tonight. Do you want to hear it? I thought we could go over by school and walk those great neighborhoods. You know, like we did when we first started going out? You remember that? We did that all the time. And we would pick our favorite house, our favorite car, our favorite lawn, all that stuff. We haven't done that in so long." He waited to see what she thought.

Caroline looked at the clock, "I work until six."

"That's cool. We can do it after. It doesn't get dark until late."

"I'll need to shower, change clothes, and eat," she said.

"Okay. So we'll go after that," he said, beaming.

She finally submitted.

"Great. Great," he said, sitting up. "Oh," he said quietly. "Don't forget to pay the rent. And don't worry, I have a couple of interviews today. I'll be able to pay you back soon."

"Rise and shine, my favorite little sleepers," came a voice outside their door. Before they could respond, the door opened. Rick, wearing black pants, a blue muscle-T, a bandana pushing back the wildly sprouting hair from his face, a fresh cup of coffee in an oversized mug in his hands, walked in.

"You're here awfully early, aren't you?" asked Joe.

"I knew Caroline worked early today and I thought I would give her a ride."

Caroline smiled at him. "Can I have some of that?"

"It is for you," he said, handing the mug to her, her face disappearing behind it as she took a careful sip. "And I knew your car's been on the fritz as of late," he said to Joe.

Joe had heard a terrible clanking sound but, knowing nothing about cars, he had simply played his radio louder when he drove; he knew this was a case of poor judgment, but he had no money.

"It's not that bad," he scoffed.

After Caroline showered and she and Rick were preparing to leave, they noticed Joe was dressed and ready to leave as well.

"What are you doing?" asked Caroline disdainfully.

"I thought I'd ride along."

The three of them departed. They were two or three blocks from T.J. Maxx when Rick abruptly turned onto one of the side streets and pulled the car over. "I need to talk to Caroline alone. So we're going to get out of the car and you're going to wait here."

Before he had a chance to respond, Rick and Caroline had exited the car and were sitting behind it on the curb. Joe couldn't hear anything they were saying and he didn't dare turn and look out the rear window. For several minutes he sat, his feet tapping the floor of the car, his hands slapping his thighs, trying unsuccessfully to catch his breath.

"I'm right fucking here." But before he could reach for the door handle, he stopped. What would he say? They're just talking. Escape is so easy. They would just be talking and he would be mad for no reason. But Joe had felt a change between Caroline and him. They were going to go out, after work, and it was going to be like it was. He just needed to trust in her, in them. And she would be furious if he got out. He tried unsuccessfully to find Rick and Caroline in the side and rear-view mirrors.

The doors opened. "Sorry, friend," said Rick, lowering himself lazily into the car. "Took a bit longer than I thought. But it's important to get things right. Wouldn't you agree?" he asked as he started the car.

"She's late," was all he could say.

Caroline looked out the window blankly.

"Only by a few minutes."

"Twenty," Joe said, looking out the window.

Rick pulled up in front of T.J. Maxx. Joe got out of the car and let Caroline out. "What were you guys talking about?" he whispered over her shoulder, but she was already gone. He got back in the car.

"Boy, it's already hot and so early in the morning," said Rick, wiping his forehead directly beneath his bandana. "You have nothing to worry about, Joe, we were just..."

"I'm not worried," blurted out Joe angrily.

The car crossed Snelling.

"Where are you going?" asked Joe. "You should have turned left. Why are you going this way?"

"Relax, I know a quieter way. Don't worry so much, Joe. Someday you're gonna give yourself a heart attack."

After crossing Snelling, Rick followed the frontage road onto the quiet suburban streets, and then promptly turned into a driveway, stopped the car, and got out.

"What are you doing? Where are you going?" asked Joe through the open driver's side window.

"This is where I live."

Joe opened the car door and looked at him over the roof of the car. "So what? I still need a ride. My house is five miles from here."

"It sure is hot," was all he said before entering the house. The front door closed. The house was a stranger, impenetrable.

Joe wiped the sweat from his brow and looked down at his jeans and long-sleeve shirt. "Jesus Christ. You need to take me home. Please. This is nowhere near my house. Come on, it's so far. You can't do this to me. Please."

He looked at the faceless house.

"Come back out here. Please."

Lowering his head he shut the car door and began the long, hot walk back to his house.

When he got there, he found a note:

Joe

Rick and I are going to Canada. Don't know when we'll be back.

Caroline

P.S. Don't freak out

ALL ROUTES
LEAD HERE

15

Their bodies did not move in unison; the young man's hips rose and fell with the determinism of a wave controlled by forces he couldn't identify, while hers lay bonestill, unresponsive to the way his body, with its unending ebb and flow, mistook hers for the moon. At last, her patience ran out.

"Are you almost finished?" she asked coldly, her voice striking a discordant note in the barely audible rocking of his breathing.

He paused, astonished. "What?"

"Well, don't stop, for God's sake!" she seethed, startling his body back into its mechanical motion, his face still frozen in shock.

In a matter of minutes he was finished, lying in a pool of confusion and pleasure, while she dressed and headed for her car. She didn't care if he thought her a bitch. He wanted her for one reason and he got it. For him to be offended by her behavior was just hypocrisy or bad conscience. She had time for neither.

The car sped along the empty two-lane road. Driving automatically, Buster Keaton-faced, she lit a cigarette, its nervous fumes rising and exiting through the small crack at the top of the window. Soon she reached the city limits and passed breathlessly on, continuing toward Charlie's.

The trailer park she lived in approached on her right side; it had a large billboard in the shape of a trailer with working headlights that read: *All Routes Lead Here.* Within moments, the trailers appeared. Large, mammoth squares of darkness. They sat unnaturally close to one another. This, she knew, was a trick of the dark, to make things seem closer to one another than they were. She had been in the dark with a lot of men and no matter how close their bodies seemed, she had never been close to any of them. Not that the men cared. Everyone she knew accepted a physical union as something deeper. Feeling a pinch, she adjusted her bra strap and cursed it under her breath. As she passed them she saw the tall, swaying grass and cattails that she had seen the first time she came this direction. Now she remembered the route number.

Pulling into the parking lot, she exited her car, tossing her cigarette to the ground, and dashed into Charlie's with a crash. The bartender dropped a glass, a couple at a table looked up, and a man at the end of the bar burped under his breath. Looking around at the bar that she had come to for the last four months, she was disgusted with herself. She had first come there to escape herself and now this escape, too, had become a numbing habit. Doubling back, she exited the bar swiftly. But once in the parking lot, she stopped. Where was she going to go now? What would be any different anywhere else? She hated herself and that she couldn't cast this off as simply as walking out of a bar. She walked across the parking lot to the church and sat on its large cold steps as if in the lower jaw of a large stone beast. Looking back at Charlie's as if at her fate, she stood up and went back in.

"What's this?" asked Caroline as she approached her regular place at the bar.

"A beer," answered the bartender, walking away.

"Why did you bring it?" she called after him, leaning away from it as if it were contaminated.

"That's what you always have," he said stepping back to her.

"But I didn't order it."

The couple at the table watched.

"That's what you usually have."

"That's not the point," she said pushing it away. "Just forget it."

Her beer glass stared wantonly at her as she exited.

"That's the price for good service," the well-dressed man at the table said with a laugh. The bartender closed his eyes in frustration and emptied her glass into the sink beneath the bar.

After driving halfway out of town, she came to the place with the tall grass. Then she turned the car around, drove back, parked, and reentered the bar. She felt the same disgust come over her and, for the first time, she admitted to herself that she didn't know what to do. She sat.

Eventually she found herself listening to the couple behind her. They were talking about a recent trip to Italy, specifically about their journey to a Civita, a place she had never heard of. Its obscurity seemed to be the point: they considered themselves travelers, not tourists. Her spirits lifted as she thought of joining their conversation. Her brother had been to Europe and had a similar traveling philosophy. She had listened to his stories for days on end. She could steal his stories, make his experiences hers; she could become him. Her spirits fell just as fast when she saw them leaving. Everyone else knew her and no one new would ever find their way here again.

When the door opened, Caroline looked up in anticipation.

"Hey, Dennis," said the bartender lazily.

Caroline slumped and watched as Dennis, a regular, held up a finger to the bartender and made his way to the phone. Realizing that he didn't have any change, he came back mildly frustrated and sat next to her. He was halfway through his beer before he acknowledged her. This was the same entrance Dan made when she first met him.

"Hey, Caroline. How are you?"

This was the only thing she remembered Dennis saying to her in the brief time he was there. Instead of replying, she decided on a plan of action; she'd call Dan the minute Dennis left. She did this, and Dan entered the bar just when she told him to come. Caroline was sitting at the bar, talking to no one, and nursing a beer. Dan headed for the phone, stood by it a minute, and finally sat next to Caroline. He was halfway through his beer before he acknowledged her.

"So you want me to say the stuff exactly?" he asked under his breath, leaning toward her without looking at her.

"Yes."

"I didn't realize how late it was," he started.

"From the beginning."

He waited a few moments before saying, "Hello."

"Hi."

"I'll have another beer."

She frowned, defeated. Perhaps she had been wrong. She looked at him. When he didn't acknowledge her glance, she peered hopelessly into her empty glass. When the bartender tried to take it she balked, "I'm not done with this!" After staring at the puddle of beer in the bottom of the glass, she looked to the stranger once more. Perhaps he hadn't felt her watching him before. Or perhaps he had been too afraid to appear forward. Again, he failed to respond.

"Not very polite," she finally muttered.

"What's that?" he asked staring at the back wall.

"Most men would offer a girl a drink."

"You seem quite finished." He turned toward her. "Or at least you seemed quite finished when I sat down." When he still refused to order her a beer, she did so herself. She was tired of every meeting with a man being part of some game she had no recollection of wanting to play, being told why she was playing or how she could win. But worse than that, she was tired of herself.

16

He could hear the click of the last lights. **Caroline** appeared out of the imposing darkness. Walking to the closet, she slipped her pants off, then her shirt. Unhooking her bra, she placed her right arm over her breasts as she walked into the bathroom. She always did this, as if her breasts would fall away if she didn't.

Dan was lying still, pretending not to watch.

When she returned from the bathroom, she was wearing an extra long t-shirt that extended to her knees. She climbed into bed next to Dan. Lying on her right side, she stared at the wall. Sleep was just something else that offered no reward. She closed her eyes; she knew that he was waiting. Lying on his side and turned toward her, his whole body was tensely poised in the form of a question mark. She turned toward him.

"Long day, huh?" he asked immediately.

"Yeah. I've got to get up early."

"Oh." There was an extended pause. "Me, too. We should probably go to sleep."

The exchange was economical, a simple transaction of words. All that was left was to give the obligatory kiss and turn to sleep. She was wise enough not to be relieved. She knew that each second of silence gave him the momentum he needed to ask her to have sex with him.

He flopped awkwardly toward the nightstand and clock and back again. "'Course it's only a little after eleven. What time do you have to get up?"

"Seven-thirty." She had no strength to lie to him.

"Eleven-thirty to seven-thirty… that's eight hours. That's a lot."

"Yes."

He placed his hand on her hip. Her body tightened.

"Do you wanna… ?"

He moved in to kiss her. With a start, she quickly pushed him away.

"Fine, fine. But only if you brush your teeth first. You smell like beef Romanoff."

He rose, tripping on the way to the bathroom, struggled to find the bathroom light, and brushed his teeth for the second time that night. Caroline lay on her back, waiting impatiently. She heard the water tighten to a halt.

Despite her annoyance, he returned happy. Slipping into the bed next to her, he placed his hand immediately on her hip. He kissed her arm. Then her neck. Propped on his elbow, he let his his mouth find hers. Eventually she kissed him back. He positioned himself on top of her but she would not embrace him and he slid off. He kissed her mouth a while longer, and then tried again. This time they fell together. Shortly after, she pulled her t-shirt off. It would only be a matter of minutes before she would be allowed to fall asleep.

She didn't understand why she hated making love to Dan. It hadn't been like that before. She never felt love for him, but it had still been enjoyable. He would do whatever she said, no matter how belittling or humiliating. It wasn't sex itself that bothered her, but Dan's desire for sex. All men wanted sex. He only wanted what all men wanted. The need for sex bonded all men together and, being connected, they all became inextricably bound to Joe, the only one she had loved and hated. Caroline and Dan had acted out their first meeting, retiring to Dan's for the evening with the understanding that she would not stay after they made love. What made this night different was that after tomorrow, Caroline would leave and never come back.

DEFECTION

17

They were ushered into the house the way all people are ushered into a family's home for the holidays. Their coats were taken, regrets about not seeing them enough were given, drinks were offered, and they were led into the living room. They joined Leslie's sisters, Jody and Lisa, and their boyfriends, Eric and Tom, who were all sitting in silence. It was always uncomfortable talking to them and, since this was the first time Lipman had seen Leslie in the better part of a year, it was that much worse. He didn't know what her family knew about their situation, but from the silence, he assumed that they must know everything.

As the atmosphere thawed, giving way to a stilted but steady conversation, Lipman thought about what had made him call Leslie after so long. The truth was, he really didn't know. Maybe it was because Leslie's sisters had always been harsh to her and that if she showed up without him—without her fiancée—they would have sat, boyfriends in hand, and destroyed her. Maybe it was because he missed her. Maybe he didn't want to see his own family. Whatever it was, they were called into dinner.

The food was passed around in competing funnels of motion. Arms moved mechanically. Clanks and silences.

Leslie's mother, Sherry, looked around, inspecting the scene. It would only be a few moments before she began. Like most families, this one had a dictator. Without a doubt, Sherry was in charge; she dominated the conversation and was never wrong.

"They're on him again," said Sherry, resigned.

"Who?" asked Tom.

Lisa gave him a quick, disapproving look that, because she was always giving disapproving looks, went unseen. She didn't like what anybody said or when they said it. She made a profession out of being unhappy. What Tom saw in her, nobody, including her mother, knew. "Who else?" she sighed, answering for him, as she always did, looking to her mother and frowning. Tom only looked up briefly.

"Governor Ventura. The goddamn Republicans have hated him from the beginning and the Democrats hate him because they think he stole their votes. It doesn't seem to matter how important his election is for third parties around the country. Or that he had no lobbyists to give him money. He has nothing to answer to except his own integrity."

"Do we have to talk about this?" Lisa pleaded, not eating. Being a vegetarian, she wouldn't eat a traditional Thanksgiving dinner. This being her house, Sherry would make nothing but a traditional Thanksgiving dinner.

"I agree," said Leslie. "Politics at the dinner table is always a bad idea."

"But that's what we always talk about," said Jody quietly.

"It's just like Clinton," Sherry said, bringing up her own favorite politician, while technically talking about something else. "Not only did he lower the deficit, he got rid of it and still he had a million detractors."

"That's not correct," said Larry, Sherry's husband.

Larry had essentially slipped into nonexistence years ago, when he underwhelmed his way out of his marriage and out of his children's lives. If initially forced out of participating in his family's life by the women in his household, his retreat eventually became by design. It was easier to let them do what they wanted than to fight everything. And in fact, his shadow-like existence had given him special authority. Anyone who speaks infrequently is given special attention when they do speak. His side of the table, which for days and years did not exist, could be pulled into relevance by mere syllables.

Everyone waited. He finished chewing and swallowing. His slowness was intentional, a reaffirmation of his power and revenge on his pushy family.

"He did not make the deficit disappear," he said, raising his eyes to Sherry's already-objecting face. "The deficit simply went down during his administration. A lot of what happened during his administration had its foundation in Bush's and, more significantly, in Reagan's administration. Not everything that happens during a president's administration can be directly attributed to him. Clinton simply knew how to take advantage of those things that were already latently there."

Lipman seized this opportunity, attempting to pick up where Larry had stopped. "Yes. Yes. You can only give a person credit for those policies he personally enacted, policies that may not see their fruition until another administration takes over."

He looked to Larry for affirmation, but none was coming. The women said nothing either, but continued eating, except for Lisa, who sat looking bitter, resenting the fact that they were still talking about politics. It was always this way, in this family or his own. People were always ready to accuse others of stepping on their toes even if they were agreeing with them. He shifted back into his seat.

"Oh, hooey," said Sherry, dismissing him with a wave of the hand. It was characteristic of Sherry to annihilate arguments and dismiss people in this manner.

"We were at Don's Uncle Jim's yesterday," began Leslie. They had gone there to pick up a set of chairs they had been promised for their house. It was the first time Lipman had seen Leslie again. They took the chairs only to stop his Uncle Jim's pestering. No one in Don's family knew the situation between Leslie and Lipman. Now Lipman realized that no one in Leslie's family knew, either.

"Why?" asked Jody abruptly.

"To pick up a set of table and chairs."

"Where does he live?" asked Lisa

"In Bloomington," said Leslie.

"That's kind of a drive," began one sister.

"And with the condition of your car," continued the other.

"We took Don's car," she said definitively. "Anyway, they're really Suzie's—"

"Suzie? Who's that? Another one of Don's relatives?" asked Jody, puzzled. "I thought you said you were going to his Uncle Jim's?"

"We were. Suzie is Don's mother and Jim is her sister's husband. Anyway, he was going to sell them so Suzie bought them for us."

"Why is *she* buying them?"

"And *giving* them to you?"

Being snobs, Lisa and Jody jumped at any sense that their sister needed money. It wasn't that they would help; they wanted to make her feel bad. Leslie sighed and wanted to cry.

"Uncle Jim and his wife Monica are buying a new set and remembered that we really liked their old set. Suzie wanted to

get us something special and so she's buying them for us."
Leslie was happy to complete an entire sentence.

"How's the house coming? Shouldn't you have closed by
now?" interrupted Sherry.

"There are just a few holdups," offered Leslie.

"Like what?"

"I have some credit issues," said Lipman. He didn't have to
fear any further questions since Lisa did what she always did.
Completely ignoring the conversation that Leslie had begun,
she started her own with her sister.

"Do you remember when Deb went to buy her car?" Lisa
asked. Debbie was an old friend of Lisa and Jody. They had
gone to school with Debbie; she had come along on their
family vacations and had enjoyed looking down on the rest of
the world with them.

"Oh yes," Jody said empathetically. "The trouble she went
through. She's not the brightest girl in the world. What did
her mother say? It was very funny. Something about her being
a lollipop?"

"Jody, you couldn't tell a joke if your life depended on it.
What she said," Lisa said, turning to the table as if letting
them in on a secret, "was that salesmen stuck to her if she
were a lollipop."

"That was it," said Jody with a silent laugh.

"No, dear," Sherry said very quietly with authority.

"Yes, it is," Lisa and Jody said.

"What you have to understand, Don, is that Deb isn't real
good with money."

"Or men," chimed in Jody.

"Or men, yes," agreed Sherry with a knowing laugh. "So
after several fiascos with cars..."

"And men," said Lisa.

Lisa and Jody and Sherry laughed smugly at their own wit.

"And men," continued Sherry. "Her mother asked her, 'Does your head turn into a giant lollipop the minute you walk into a car dealership?'"

They all laughed, very satisfied with themselves.

Lipman sat back, looking past it all. Underneath the table, he gave Leslie's hand a quick, tender squeeze.

"I think you're forgetting something," said Lipman.

"What's that, dear?" asked Sherry.

"Leslie never got to finish her story," he said.

The table's momentum, fueled by Lisa, Jody, and Sherry, screeched to a stop. It was as if something terrible had just entered the orbit of their self-satisfaction. Again. As they looked at him, he remembered the first time he had dinner in this house. That night, before he and Leslie had left, he stopped in the bathroom.

"He's actually smart," said one sister to the other. At that time, he couldn't tell their voices apart. At that time he didn't realize that it didn't matter.

He had stood in disbelief. Those words weren't addressing his intelligence. Stating them simply an excuse to express astonishment, contempt, and jealousy. Why? Why would anyone want to be with her? How was it possible that anyone could love their sister? In that moment, he had not only understood their family and his position in it but came to understand all families.

As Leslie began to finish her story, Lipman got up and went to the refrigerator. He needed nothing but release. After staring into the light for an appropriate amount of time, he returned to his seat.

Listening to the conversation orbiting around him and seeing the love return to Leslie's eyes, he was baffled by the phenomena of family. For all of his twenty-seven years he had gone to his Uncle Eddie's house for Thanksgiving and Christmas and Easter and now would spend his twenty-eighth here. It seemed natural enough; the Lipman family always got together and he was soon to be part of it. But looking around, talking about things he didn't like, conforming to ceremonies he didn't believe in, he sighed; he came *only* because he was bound to. Whether by tradition, blood, law, or circumstance; it didn't really matter. They were all the same, a kind of quiet slavery. Every year he dreaded going to his Uncle Eddie's and every year he would dread coming here, dread that was always, in some way, justified by his alienation from them. He had nothing in common with any of them and disliked most of them. Families consist of people who, if you weren't related to them, you'd hate, he thought.

"How is that teaching thing going, Don?" asked Sherry. She had no idea he had given up teaching and had been in admissions for some time. "What is it that you teach, psychology?"

"Philosophy."

"Any favorites?" she asked.

"Too many to name. Nietzsche, Sartre, Kant, Plato."

"Philosophy always sounds interesting, but it doesn't have any practical applications," said Sherry.

"Actually, Plato defined a lot of the Western tradition, including the way we still think today. A lot of people don't realize how much of Christianity comes from Plato," he said unconvincingly, really wanting to tell her that she was right.

Sherry looked at him for a long time.

"Wasn't Plato a homosexual?"

Lipman refused to answer.

"Larry, Larry," Sherry called until he very slowly looked up. As Lipman made his way to the patio where the beer was, he heard her ask, "Wasn't Plato gay? Weren't all the Greeks gay? Disgusting."

It always turned out that he had nothing to say at any family gathering. He'd always have to pretend. He'd be a Democrat with Leslie's family, a Republican with his own; he'd like sports, or say he was a Christian. In his youth he regularly made these concessions, but no longer. Being accepted and being made a jackass amounted to the same thing. He would no longer betray himself. At first he spoke about things he cared about, but soon learned to just keep quiet. The pattern always seemed the same: everyone was encouraged to give their views no matter how ignorant, forcing them on others without the fear of being contradicted. And they wouldn't be contradicted. Dissenters were not granted the luxury of free speech. They all thought the same thoughts. Everyone except him. It was obvious to him now that he called Leslie in a last-ditch effort to reconcile solely out of guilt.

"Don's in admissions, Mom," said Leslie, as Lipman returned from the patio.

Soon they were talking about the upcoming wedding and Lipman left the table once again.

"You're not using that awful girl Stacy to do the girls' hair?" he could hear Sherry ask Leslie.

Walking into the den, he observed that even the dog ignored him. He sighed and walked through. He ended up in the dimly lit living room, where coats were piled on the couch. It was the most silent of the silent rooms he had been in this evening. White Christmas lights, wrapped around the artificial tree, blinked on and off every few seconds. He stood in the room's center, alone and silent.

For a long time he simply stood there. After a few minutes, he began to scan the room disinterestedly. Everything in the house was as it always had been and always would be. The upright piano stood to his far right, where Leslie's spoiled cousin, John, would play Chopin preludes to demonstrate that he was self-taught; no one seemed to notice that he had no feel for the music. Then the hutch and the Christmas tree, tucked away into the corner, dark then light, and quiet like a man rolled into an overcoat. When his eyes reached the couch, he noticed the concentrated darkness of the antique coffee table standing before it. He continued looking around, utterly disengaged.

He heard the sound of approaching footsteps. They were fat and impatient. He turned around but couldn't see anything until the Christmas lights blinked on again. When they did, he saw Eric standing in front of him. Eric, who hadn't seen Lipman, started and took a few seconds before speaking.

"I guess I'm not the only one who wanted to be alone."

"Yeah."

"I'll hear about it later. I'll just say I was in the bathroom. She won't believe me, but what can she say?"

They stood in silence.

Eric continued nervously. "The dinners get to be too much for me. These family affairs always overwhelm me. I try to avoid them as much as possible. It kind of backfires, though. I don't see any of these people for months and then here they all are eating, laughing, asking me questions—always the same ones, too, and then with you and Leslie getting married—it doesn't help. I mean, I know it's not your fault, but seeing as Lori and I have been together so much longer, they naturally want to know when we will, you know? Our engagement is more a business thing, though. It's hard to explain. We both can have things on the side as long as it's kept quiet and neither of us asks questions. Ah, hell. I hate these things. Each one of these people has a life story more boring than the person before them. It's worse at my family's. All those lousy kids running around screaming. Hell, my brother Michael even brings his damn dog. And it always seems that we gain three or four people a year from marriages or boyfriends or best friends. I mean, don't these people have anything else to do? Don't they have their own family's? I can't keep track of their names. As a matter of fact, I don't even try to; I'll never see them again anyway, so who cares, right? At least not till the next holiday."

Lipman nodded indifferently and, although he showed no signs of interest and even turned away, Eric continued talking.

"At least the turkey was good, though. That's one thing you can always count on, good grub. At least you have that to look forward to."

Lipman glanced toward the couch and again at the coffee table. He now noticed that there was something on it.

"I mean, how often do you get a free meal? I'm usually the one picking up the check, if you know what I mean. Lisa sure sees to that."

As the Christmas lights blinked on, he was able to make out a pile of books. On the top of the pile, the name *Kant*, spelled in gold letters, shone. And then it was gone. Why they had a book by Kant or whose it was, he couldn't possibly guess.

"Sure, I may do all right for myself and even Lisa does, but that doesn't mean I'm below a free meal now and again. Especially the way Lisa spends." He laughed, satisfied with his candor. "Danger of these women, you know!"

Again the lights came on and again the gold letters flashed. Lipman was mesmerized.

"And boy, what stuffing. Her cook may be from Vietnam or Laos but, man, that ain't no third-world cooking."

Kant

"I bet you didn't know she has her food catered. She usually doesn't let people know her little secrets until they're in, but seeing as you're in, there's no harm in telling you."

Kant

"Sherry's all about presentation. As long as everything looks all right, then everything is all right. I remember once the toilet overflowed during one of her big dinner parties. Whew! You've never seen someone blow their top like she did. I think it was one of Leslie's exes. Oh, I hope you don't mind me saying that. I know some guys get weird about that kind of stuff."

Kant

"I didn't think you were like that. Anyway, you'll be fine. She likes you. I think everyone does. I know your politics drive Sherry a little nuts, but she needs a little sand in her oyster once in a while and my time for that passed a long time ago."

Kant

"Anyway, how about you? You holding up? I know it can be hard around this time of year. Especially with the ladies we chose to be with. Or with the ladies that chose us. Ha. Just kidding. Love is like everything else: a pain in the ass. No, no. You know I'm joking. Just give and take. A lot of give. God, I can't stop. Too much wine. Too much of their expensive wine. I should stop. God knows I won't. Not with them supplying."

Kant

"Anyway, I heard you were a shoe-in for director of admissions. I know how political that stuff is. You must be playing the game right. Get 'em right where you want 'em and then soak 'em for as much money as possible. Perfect timing with you and Leslie and everything."

Kant

Lipman lifted his face for the first time and looked at Eric, who was now smoking.

Kant

Lipman looked at the book, which looked back. "I'm done with that."

The lights went off and the book was gone. Lipman walked out of the room.

LOVE WITH A VENGEANCE

18

ERIN: GIRLFRIEND OF CHUCK, FRIEND OF ALLISON

Each time Joe stayed, he awoke before her. He looked at her mouth and wondered how it must've looked the night before as she said in the dark, "Take me," and whether it looked the same when she said those words to Chuck or if it revealed its disingenuousness. Turning away from her, his glance emitting the wrath of retribution, he took pleasure in looking at the picture of a window she had drawn, in pencil, on the wall; he liked the plant sitting on the ledge, blowing slightly from what must be the cool morning breeze. In her letter she had told him how her skill in drawing had improved. She didn't have to add, "because of you," to her letter for him to know that this was true.

"What are you doing?" asked Erin, eyes barely open, as Joe struggled silently to put his clothes on.

Pulling up his jeans, he whispered, "Leaving before Chuck gets here." Squinting at the clock next to the bed, he said, "Graveyard shift is over. Not to mention I have to get to work soon."

After the devastating blow he took when Caroline left him for Rick, Joe kept to himself the rest of his senior year, graduating with honors and several writing awards. He spent the next several years working for a temp service, traveling throughout Europe, eventually going back to school for his teaching license. At the age of twenty-three, Joe was now a student teacher, and looking to go back to school for his Master's; maybe he'd teach writing to college kids.

"Come back to bed," she said, patting the comforter.

"You know I'd love to, but I really have to go."

"Don't worry about him so much. I have him all taken care of. Anyway, he's not coming home this morning. So why don't you come back here and wake me up properly?"

He paused in anticipation before unbuttoning his pants, sliding them to his feet, and stepping clumsily out of them. "Really? Not coming home today? How lucky for us."

Crawling into the bed, he found her beneath the covers and stroked her arm and hip like a wave. "How lucky for us," he repeated, kissing her neck. "I'm tired of him. I always have to leave right when things get going again."

"You don't have to worry about that today," she said, climbing on top of him, pulling off her t-shirt. "I called him last night and told him not to come home today." She slid down and began kissing his chest.

"What do you mean you called him?" he asked, opening his eyes.

"I don't know if it was all the beer or the cologne you were wearing, but I couldn't wake up and have you gone again."

"I didn't know he knew about me," he said.

"I may be a lot of things, but I am not a liar. Now enough talking, you. We have more pressing things to worry about," she said, making her way further down, slipping his underwear off.

"He doesn't care that I'm here? That we've been together?"

"I told him from the beginning that this is my life. If he doesn't like the way I live it, he doesn't have to be a part of it."

"And he's okay with that?"

"He doesn't have much choice," she said, mounting him. "Oh, he's not a jealous person, but he should be," she said, letting out a quiet moan.

She was nearly asleep when she heard Joe getting dressed again.

"Where are you going? I'm not seeing Chuck until tonight. We have all day."

Joe ran his hands through his hair, "To get you some breakfast."

"Wake me up when you get back."

Joe got into his car. He didn't come back and he never saw her again.

NANCY: JOE'S COWORKER; RANDI: HIGH SCHOOL STUDENT

Joe and Nancy huddled around the small table in a forgotten corner of the tempered, upscale restaurant, speaking in soft obbligato tones. They were only a few paces from the entrance, and the chaos of the outside world seemed on the verge of pushing its way in; their attentive eyes, focused on one another, cast a protective circle around them.

"You can imagine how surprised I was to get your call. Don't get me wrong; I'm having a great time, but you've never shown any interest in me before," Nancy said.

"You knew how I felt long before I did anything about it. I had to be careful. If anyone knew I liked you, much less went out with you, we'd both be fired," Joe said.

She reached across the table and took his hand. "I'm glad you took the chance."

Over his shoulder, Nancy saw Brad, Jimmy, and most significantly, Randi, a high school student in Joe's first student-teaching class who, although not stupid, had failed her entire last term and summer school, walk in. Randi's makeup work had extended into the fall and would most likely put her graduation off until the spring, a full year after she should have graduated. Joe knew that she was like most young women; she loved older men. Their affair had been short, intense, and had left her terribly bitter toward him, as she believed that he loved her. Joe also saw the group, his eyes boomeranging from Randi (already preparing her fake ID for the waiter) to Nancy (a teacher at the same school Randi was attending). Nancy pulled her hand away, sliding her chair over.

"Joe, holy Christ, I was just talking about you!" Brad exclaimed, turning to Jimmy and Randi.

"Hey, Brad. Good to see you," Joe said, extending a confident hand to greet him.

"Ah hell, that ain't gonna be good enough, Joe," Brad said, pulling Joe from his seat and embracing him. Settling arrogantly back into his seat, Joe placed his arm around Nancy. Brad eyes widened, "Girlfriend?"

"We work together. I was having dinner with a friend when I ran into Joe and thought I'd say hi," offered Nancy with an uncomfortable smile, attempting unsuccessfully to shrug Joe's arm off of her.

"An extreme pleasure to meet you. Mind if we join you?" Brad asked, already squeezing his way behind Joe's chair.

"There's not enough room," she said, panicked. "Four-person table. You and your friends won't all fit," she said, pointing to Randi and Jimmy who were still waiting to sit down.

"Actually, Brad, we were hoping to be alone."

"Another time then, and I mean it. I don't see you as much as I'd like. You guys enjoy yourselves. Although I know you will." He made his way a few tables back with Jimmy and Randi.

"Brad's an old friend," said Joe, removing his arm from around Nancy.

"How does he know that girl?"

"I don't know, why?" asked Joe, lying. Joe had set Randi up with Brad, another student-teacher from a different school, after he broke up with her.

"She's a student."

"Well, then, we better be very careful," he said kissing her on the cheek, her eyes glued on Randi. Looking down at her watch, she said, "I really have to go."

"Now, don't let one student horrify you. She's an adult and she certainly doesn't care what two other adults do on their own time."

"She's barely an adult. You don't know what this girl is like. I really have to go."

"That's a great idea. I know just the place."

"I would love to, Joe, but my babysitter expected me about an hour ago." She looked at her watch again. "The plight of the single mother."

"Come on," he pleaded. "Can't you stay out just another hour? Your babysitter will be thanking you. The longer she stays, the more she makes, right? I'll even pay for her."

"I really can't. She's really great and great babysitters are hard to find. I don't want to lose her."

"I understand," he said, sinking back into his chair.

"Call me and we'll go out again. Somewhere else."

"I don't have your number."

"Oh shit, how much do I owe?"

"Just go. I'll take care of the bill."

"Call me. Really."

With that, she was gone.

Joe sat nursing a beer. He waited until Randi headed for the bathroom. He followed her, taking her by the arm before she could go in. "Are you even going to let me explain?"

"Explain what?" she asked, yanking her arm from his hand, furious. "Don't touch me!" He stood in front of the door. "That you're already fucking someone else? That you blew me off for *Mrs. Schmidt?* And then you have the balls to take her to *our* place?"

"It's not like it looks. And this is not a date. I swear."

Joe didn't know what it was that made him so attractive to women of so many different ages and backgrounds. Sometimes he thought it was his intelligence, other times, his sensitivity. In reality, he didn't care. He couldn't comprehend that his ability to be whoever these women needed, that his moving in so many social circles in a way so unusual for a relatively recent college graduate, pointed to an utter lack of self and fear of nothingness. He had no idea that, through responding to these women, he was searching for himself and trying to fill the lack of meaning he discerned in the world.

"I saw all I needed to see," she said, attempting to push past him.

"No, wait," he said, pulling her out of the doorway. "I've missed you."

"Bullshit."

"Really! That's why she left and I didn't go with her. The minute I saw you, I knew I had made a big mistake."

"Why should I believe you?"

"Why would I lie? If I were just looking to get laid I would have gone with her."

She looked at him for a long time. "You really sent her home because of me?"

"Let me buy you a drink," he said, leading her away from Jimmy and Brad and to the darkest part of the restaurant's bar. There he recounted the mistakes he had made with her and how he would never make them again.

Reentering the restaurant, Nancy looked at the now-empty table where she and Joe had been sitting. She was about to leave when she saw him, arm around Randi, in the back of the bar. In the ensuing chaos of voices, accusations, and threats, all that Joe could say, in the quietest of whispers, was, "Don't do this." Eventually he was alone, drunk, and glaring at the hotel key he had pulled from his pocket and laid on the table.

ALLISON: FRIEND OF ERIN'S, WIFE OF CHRIS, MOTHER OF DANIEL AND DEACON, CHAIRWOMAN OF THE LOCAL PTA

"Hey, what are you doing back here by yourself?"

In an extraordinary stroke of luck, there stood Allison, a short Indian woman with a slanted forehead, badly damaged hair, and a rough sense of humor. He was certain she had stepped right out of a song from the Stones' *Beggar's Banquet.* He clumsily shoved the hotel key into his pocket. "Just having myself a little relief. How about you?"

"Just finished a final and needed a little relief myself. Mind if I join you?"

"Please," he said, pushing the chair next to him out with his foot.

"Should we go?" she asked, two hours and seven drinks later, with a nod of the head.

"Absolutely. Let me just use the bathroom."

Exiting the bathroom moments later, he made his way down the long t-shaped hallway. Coming to its end, he turned to the left and heard a voice on his right, a voice he recognized as Allison's. Her words were spoken quickly and quietly like an animal poking its head out of the ground and retreating immediately. She signaled to him desperately. Even her gestures were rapid, as if given any duration they would be heard.

"I have to go pay before we can go. Is something wrong?" Joe said.

She shrugged her shoulders, as if suddenly she had no idea why they were alone, in a hallway outside of a bathroom, instead of anywhere else on earth. He lifted his face and looked down at her, urging her to speak.

"I wish it had been me," she said.

It was obvious she needed to be say something. Allison was in love with Joe and everyone, including Joe, knew it. Nevertheless, for the better part of six months Allison had to watch as Joe pursued Erin, her heart breaking when he finally succeeded in winning Erin's heart and body. She promised herself that, if by some miracle, he was to ever desire her, she would never forgive him for his affair with Erin. Little did she realize that this was a promise contingent on its content never being fulfilled.

He placed his arms around her waist. "It is."

Despite her sudden happiness, she pulled away, defying the gravity of her desire.

"I don't want to be second choice."

He sighed, and smiled, "Believe me, you're not."

"I've wanted to be with you for months but all you cared about was Erin. Sometimes I would leave and you wouldn't even say goodbye. Do you know what it's like to be mad about someone who doesn't even notice you?"

He tried to interrupt her.

"I mean, why? Why now and not three months ago? If I'm second choice, I can't."

"Listen. Please. You never were second choice. I wanted you immediately but I couldn't approach you. I don't think you understand. Erin and I were never involved. I was just helping her through a rough time. But she was so fragile that if I would have let on about my feelings for you, things really would have gotten even worse for her. I had to act indifferent. I'm so sorry. Believe me, it was killing me too."

She softened immediately and he took her hand to kiss it. He frowned, "You're married?"

She pulled her hand away hastily, her face nearly bubbling over with regret.

"That doesn't change how I feel about you," he quietly clarified.

"Really?" she asked. The hope that had been a crack beneath a closed door was suddenly open.

He grabbed her face. "Really," he said kissing her swiftly. She gripped him tightly and kissed him more passionately than she had ever kissed anyone. He stopped her abruptly. "Let's get out of here. I'm sick of this place. I hope your husband hasn't given you a curfew."

"Not tonight. He took the kids out."

He smiled deliciously and exited the bar, Allison tucked into his embrace. Looking down at her, he knew they resembled the *Freewheeling Bob Dylan* album cover. He smiled and pulled her in tight. It was his favorite image of a man and a woman. Pressing forward, turned from the world, faces nearly touching, the warmth of their smiles and the unspoken promise they had made with their kiss the only nourishment they needed.

"My car is right over here. You can just follow me."

"Okay," she said following his arm and extended finger. When she turned back, she found a long, heartmelting kiss waiting for her.

As he pulled out of the parking lot and onto the street, he lifted his face to the rearview mirror, eyeing her decidedly. She was diligently following him, lane for lane and turn for turn. He could see her catch his eyes the moment he peered into his rearview mirror and smile. Once on the highway, she again shadowed him: retaining the same speed, matching his acceleration, braking simultaneously, changing lanes when he did, even putting on her blinker at the same time and for the same duration. The only difference was that a darkness had fallen across her face, leaving a empty silhouette made all the more strange to him by the fact that he knew her entire being was focused, like a laser, on his eyes reflected in the small oval of light that was his rearview mirror.

He drove automatically. His mind followed, mapping out what he knew so well. From the bar to the car, down the road, and to the hotel where champagne, the bed, and freedom awaited him.

Then she was gone.

She was still behind him but she was gone from his mind. He knew what was coming and tried to deny it. But it was never denied. She was gone. A strange rumbling replaced her. It began subtly in the deep center of his stomach where some people claim the soul resides. He barely noticed, attributing the feeling simple, affordable explanations: hunger pains or gas. Soon, however, it grew into an engulfing shivering. He reached for the window buttons to raise the windows but the windows were all tightly closed. He turned on the heat but was soon nauseous and had to turn it off again. She was gone.

The trembling in his body traveled up and outward, from his ribs to chest, until his hands and fingers shook. He nearly went off the road. Making tight fists around the steering wheel, he focused on the lines on the road, gripping with his eyes the consistent, sanity-ensuring line on the side of the road.

Soon air was rushing uncontrollably up his throat. With a jerk of his head, a dribble of vomit leaked out the corners of his mouth. He wiped it away. He felt more coming and slowed the car. Allison followed suit. A stifled whimper attempted to escape past his chattering teeth. He floored the accelerator, as did Allison. His entire body was shaking. He no longer could hold back the cries and murmurs and yelps. It took several black minutes before the sounds organized themselves to resemble what is called laughter. Several more miles passed before he yielded.

"Ha ha!" he blurted out in that moment of surrender, pointing past the windshield into the blackness in front of him, his demonic laughter colored with slivers of mockery. His eyes narrowed indulgently, "Son of a bitch! Ha, ha!"

Pointing repeatedly into the blackness, he laughed, one hand trembling over the steering wheel, leading him back and forth between the lanes of the highway, the other shaking in accusation toward that phantom judge.

"Ha, ha, ha!" he addressing it with scornful laughter, the tip of his finger pressed firmly against the windshield.

Sliding his hand to the armrest, he opened all the windows at once, the wind screaming at him. "There it is! There it is!" he screeched, suddenly pulling back wildly, finding the two white headlights in his rearview mirror, pointing with his thumb over his shoulder. "What about those?" he asked, referring to the glaring and surprisingly ethereal ropes of light attaching his car to hers. "She's following me! I can free her and she knows that! From her husband, from the job she hates, from her family! I don't have to believe for it to be true! For there to be meaning! Philosophy can explain it all! Ha! Ha! Ha!" He focused back on the lidless blackness in front of him.

"I'll prove it! I'll prove it!" he screamed even more desperately. He rounded a corner and changed lanes abruptly, placing a car between his car and hers. She changed lanes, her car immediately peeking nervously around the car between them. "See! See! I told you!" he cackled at the unblinking night. "Watch! Watch!" His erratic driving was too much for her. Soon she was in the passing lane forcing her way between his car and the stranger's.

He looked away from the darkness and peered into his rearview mirror, at the lights, at the small, silhouetted head, at her car following his. "They always follow. They always do. See? See? Meaning. Meaning. I told you. I told you." He laughed more quietly now, settling tensely back into his seat, exhausted, when the urge to cry fell upon him so swiftly and forcefully that the effort to stifle it contracted his chest and he gasped as sweetly and high as a little girl. Each streetlight illuminated the deep blue anger in his eyes, an anger that faded when he finally spoke again. "I'm lying, aren't I? I'm lying." The car slowed.

The darkness refused to answer him. Just as it always did.

IDEAFUCK

Joe picked up the clock on the nightstand, it's cord taut, fighting him: 12:27. He set it back down and resumed pacing the small hotel room, which was permeated by the scent of dried sweat and cologne.

Sitting on the edge of the bed, he yawned, closed his eyes, and opened them again quickly. A car approached. He sat up expectantly, straightened his tie, blinked exaggeratedly, and began the transformation from the person he was when alone to the person he was with women. Walking to the window, Joe cursed when a middle-aged man made his way hastily to the building's entrance.

Leaning on the table next to the window, he watched as another car approached. He glared at its darkened windshield, trying to transform whomever it was into Allison. The stiff muscles of his face relaxed, defeated, when a fat woman in an orange sundress got out.

He opened the door to his room, and stood in the hallway listening. There was nothing. Letting the door slowly close behind him, he dashed down the hallway to the elevator. He waited only seconds before heading down the hallway to find the stairwell. He stumbled into a dead end, confused. "Dammit," he said, nearly running past the elevator, which still hadn't come, to the other end of the hallway. As he pushed open the door to the stairs, he could hear the ding of the elevator, its doors opening.

As he burst through the stairwell door to the lobby, the woman behind the desk stood up, startled, and asked loudly, "Is there something I can help you with?"

Joe looked out the front doors of the hotel and into the empty parking lot. He could see a grocery store across the street. He could see an elderly man ambling mindlessly through the aisles; a young woman, obviously drunk, pushing a cart filled with potato chips and several cans of something; and a couple to the far left who stood holding hands, talking. He watched them with a sense of longing and regret and impatience. He thought that maybe she was waiting in her car in the parking lot. "I just wanted to know if I could get some extra pillows."

When the clock in his room read 1:43, Joe exited his room again, cursing, slammed the door, and marched to the phone booth in the hotel's lobby. He didn't want the caller I.D. on her phone to register the hotel's name (in case her husband answered). When it didn't work, he stormed back to his room and dialed her number on the room's phone. He was at first excited and then furious when she answered.

"Where are you?" he yelled. "Where did you go? I've been waiting for over an hour. No, I didn't say AmericInn. The AmericInn? I'm at the Northland Inn. I clearly said the Northland Inn. How long were you going to let me sit here? I don't know, call my house and leave a message. I did try your cell phone. You didn't answer. I don't care if your husband answers. You left me just hanging here. What have you been doing? You fell asleep? Jesus Christ!" He shifted the phone from ear to ear and with it, his tone. "You have no idea how great it was that you came tonight. I would've died. It's still early. Come meet me now. I need to see you," he pleaded, lowering himself to the edge of the bed. "I ordered some champagne for us. If you want, we can order a late dinner too. Come on. Then we'll order a pizza. Come on. I promise you'll have a good time. What? I can't hear you. What? Your kids? I thought your husband… Come on. You know you want to." In a fury, he stood up, "I am not going to be stood up by a little bitch like you. Fuck you and your kids," he said, slamming the phone down. AmericInn, he thought. What a piece of white trash. As he turned his head, the clock grabbed him. He dropped his head. It was past bar time.

At that moment, there was a hesitant knock at the door.

"What?" he yelled.

"Ah, it's the champagne you ordered," came a meek voice.

"Fuck," Joe said as he opened the door. "Here, just set it anywhere. I suppose you want a tip, too?" he asked sarcastically. "I'm sorry. Here," he said.

"Thank you," said the man, discreetly placing the money in his pocket.

"It's just women, you know? I was supposed to meet a woman here and she stood me up. That's who that was for," he said, pointing to the bucket, the champagne sticking out of it like a sinking ship.

"I can take it back if you want."

"Don't worry about it. Thanks, though. It's my own fault, I guess. She's married."

"That can be tough," said the man still standing by the bucket and champagne. "My parents got separated when I was seven and divorced when I was eight."

"She's not separated. At least not yet. I'm working on it. Not that I care. Maybe I should be done with women."

"You must love her a lot if you want her to leave her husband."

"Not even a little, friend. You have a girl? You been with her a long time?"

"Three years," the man replied.

"That's a good haul. Then it's the same with me as it is with you and her. You're not in love. You stay out of fear. Because you have a history. How can you leave her? After all the work you've put into her? You have too much pride in your work to do anything about it. Even if the work is shoddy."

"Then why are you seeing her?"

"You want to share the champagne with me? It's kind of lonely up here alone."

"I have to get back to work," he said, heading for the door.

"I'm kinda lonely," he said. "You have work to do at this time of night? There can't be anything to do. What is there to do? Just one glass."

"I really can't, sir."

"I understand. But you're going to make me drink my share and Caroline's."

"You're sure she's not coming?"

"Wow, that was odd," said Joe.

"What's that, sir?"

"Caroline is a girl I dated in college. That was years ago. Why would I think about her right now? Actually I'm waiting for…" he paused, reached into his wallet and pulled out another five-dollar bill. "Thanks for the champagne."

THE ACCUSATION

From his room they could see the backside of the building directly across from theirs. On it was a large sign that posted the temperature and the time, intermittently reading 11:48 and 72, and the awning of a small bar named Al's, inscribed with the message *You're here, so why not?* He had first approached her because he heard her speaking Spanish to the owners of the hotel, and wanted to see if she would ask the maid, who only spoke Spanish, if she would bring him an extra blanket.

She agreed, and in between their responses he managed to ask her if she was free and if she wanted to get a drink. He told her that it was his first night in Minneapolis. He had gotten a brief glimpse of her room and, based on the amount of stuff she had, guessed either that she had been there for some time or that she was going to be there for some time; and knowing that a person likes nothing more than to be needed, and that traveling can be lonely, he asked her if she would mind showing him around.

Halfway through the second bottle of wine, she began telling stories about the civil war that plagued her country. The alcohol brought her reminiscences to life as if he had been there, his imagination and memories of B-movies filling in the rest. He held on to the significant details for future use. Although his greatest desire was to tell her how attracted to her he was, he knew that the timing of this revelation was more important than the sincerity of it.

She told him about her best friend and her mother, who had to stand between a large bookshelf and a wall all night in order to avoid being captured or shot. Shortly after that event, her mother had decided for her that she would go to a university in the United States where her father, an American, lived. As he was out of town on business and she couldn't move into the dorms for a month, she was stuck in this hotel.

She had interrupted the story several times in order to push her hair out of her eyes. When she reached behind her to grab a clip to hold it back, he looked at her and said, "Leave your hair down."

The message of those words was unmistakable. And yet, he knew he was being clever. He knew that those words were innocent enough and yet could express the hidden desire he felt without committing it to a literal expression of actual desire. If she wasn't interested, which was entirely possible— perhaps she, too, was simply looking for relief from loneliness—she could respond as if it were meant as an actual compliment. He, in turn, could easily pretend that that was his intention. And in the course of a few awkward words and a few incomplete sentences, they could both act as if nothing had happened all the while knowing that something indeed had happened, even if no signature of an action could be pointed to in a ledger.

Yes, those words were perfect. He was so sure of his plan that he never stopped to ask himself how these words would ever leave his mouth, or why he would ever lead a conversation in the direction of her or her hair or even of Minneapolis at all.

How naive his friends were when they thought the affairs he engaged in hurt only the woman. He wondered about Allison, and Erin and Caroline (and all of them) on the other side of town (or the other side of the world) when one of them would say, in their simple and beautiful way, "our phone conversations aren't very nice." Yet all of this was so far away and he knew that this woman from El Salvador wouldn't ask why he wanted her hair down or if he had a lover or ever doubt what he meant.

"We're almost out of wine again," Joe said, lifting the bottle to his mouth, finishing the last of its contents and looking it over, pretending to have knowledge of wine. And after enjoying his knowledgeable appearance, he tossed the bottle into the tin wastebasket, noticing that the apple he ate some hours earlier had turned brown. She frowned. "You get it," she said.

He looked out into the night. The balcony was small and dirty and barely had room for the two chairs that they sat on. She had had to bring the chair from her room back to Joe's balcony. They laughed at how each room was allowed only one chair and how the management must've known that one chair would never be used. No one wanted to sit by himself in a hotel room. Maybe that was the point.

There was also something safe about the balcony. The fact that it stood away from the bed and seemed to float above the city, giving the impression that they were nowhere. He found comfort knowing that nothing can happen if you're nowhere. Even when they would move, had to move, wanted to move in to the bed, in to the realm of flesh, they would still be nowhere. Wasn't that, in fact, what all of this was about?

Weren't the looks, the wine, the chairs, and the words all part of a dance performed on a high wire? Sometimes the steps are simple, straightforward. You mean exactly what you say: that the wine is dry, the chairs uneven and uncomfortable, and that she looks better with her hair down. And at other times, one is like a virtuoso, dipping a leg down into thin air, into innuendo, and nearly falling as if into desire, but always pulling back and setting it squarely onto the wire again. Weren't they all leaning toward and hoping to fall past implication, into not only desire but bed? Perhaps the thrill that comes with the danger was what they wanted. Perhaps both of them knew that the moment one surrenders, like planets obeying the silent and invisible pull of gravity, implication and desire cease and everything becomes heavy.

He lifted his hand up to his mouth and pretended to take a long, healthy drink from an invisible bottle of wine and, when finished, looked over to her, his expression both clownish and vacant. As she prepared to leave, he pulled a wad of money from his pocket and handed it to her, his glance falling on the tin wastebasket and the brown apple. He thought it strange that the apple didn't turn brown until bitten into, until its secrets were exposed. Were his eyes turning brown? And was his skin, that which was supposed to protect and hide him, as thin as the apple's. Could it be punctured as easily, say by an act of clumsiness, by the gentlest of pressures applied by an outside force?

And as she reached the door she turned and asked, "Why me?" This was the one question that women always asked and that sent him into a frenzy of anxiety. Why her and not someone else? There was no reason. But to admit that would mean admitting that there was no reason for anything and that all his energy spent on conquering women and his life was meaningless too. He rose, approached her, and began kissing her. He was like the person attempting suicide who, deciding he is not dying fast enough, puts the blade down and, kneeling one leg at a time, begins doing push-ups. He never once opened his eyes to look at the phone that rang or the apple in the tin wastebasket or at her, before or after. When she eventually took the money from his disregarded pants, he failed to hear her when she asked, "Why do I have to get the wine? Do you want red or white?"

WILLIAM FAULKNER'S HANDKERCHIEF

19

She was not alive. Sitting at her desk, Caroline faced the window, the only window in the front office. She hadn't really slept for weeks; at least she didn't think she had. There had been a moment earlier in the day when she caught herself waking up, opening her eyes from a sleep she didn't remember slipping into. She couldn't be sure if she had napped briefly or slept longer. She stared at the curtained window, that smothered the room in gray and protected it from the street lamp outside. It was nonetheless the brightest part of the room. She couldn't help being drawn to it. She knew that this dark blue, barely lit curtain was a physical manifestation of her soul: dark, unforgiving. It was what reminded her that she was alive. She hated this window.

She was nearly dead and merely participated in the motions of being alive: waking, dressing, working, eating, undressing, sleeping, and repeating the sequence until the essence of her existence had been abandoned. She was dead and no one noticed. When she flashed smiles at people as they passed her desk, as they stopped to talk with her, when they said goodbye, her lips peeled back in a garish, disingenuous gesture; she had no idea where these smiles came from. Perhaps the residue of another life. But she knew that when these smiles finally ceased, she could commit herself more seriously to suicide. And thus to be reminded by that curtained window that she was still somehow alive ...

Leaning forward in her chair, she heard the reedy voice of George Downs. She had slept with George six months ago and since then he wouldn't leave her alone.

"How are you, Caroline? Still giving me the silent treatment? I told you that Stacy and I had a history and I just slipped. It hasn't happened since and won't ever again." He looked down at her. "You are stubborn. But I'm patient. We have too much of a connection to throw it away over a small mistake. Still nothing? God, you're a bitch. A bitch and a lousy fuck." Immediately he regretted that he had said that.

"Listen, I'm sorry. I really like you and I want to make it up to you. Why don't you let me make it up to you by taking you out for dinner tonight? Figlio's. My treat."

"Go away."

He was about to leave when he stopped. "I don't know what happened to you, Caroline. You used to be so much fun. So full of life. You're a totally different person from the one I went out with."

He paused forcefully and collected his thoughts. In front of her eyes, George was transformed. Gone was the calculating womanizer. He straightened his body, his face earnest, his expression like a loose stone being set. "I play chess every night. I love dissecting the game. Finding its hidden secrets, pinpointing each piece's relationships to the others. You can learn a lot about your place in life by playing chess. But you—you've cleared the board of all its pieces. Well, that's not exactly true. That's where I had you wrong. No, you've cleared the board of everything except the kings. And there you and your opposing king face the world, without the ability to do anything. Most of us aren't concerned with winning or losing. Not really. We just want to keep moving. You're concerned neither with winning nor surrendering, but with just standing there, two kings who know there are no moves, staring each other down. Who is the other king, Caroline?" The momentum of his words made him feel he needed to continue, but he had exhausted himself. "Hell, I don't know. You know where my desk is if you change your mind about dinner."

Standing up, Caroline looked George in the eyes with an intensity he hadn't seen before. "I quit."

Pushing rudely past him towards the women's room, Caroline knocked over a typewriter and its stand, its crash like an audible exclamation point. George suddenly found everyone staring at him. He raised his shoulders in confusion, throwing a laugh of disbelief into the office like a pebble hitting no one. He looked toward the bathroom and walked back to his desk deep in the office. "What a bitch." With this, he was back to his old, spectacular self.

Once out of sight, Caroline began to run, bursting through the bathroom door, sweating and confused. She was on the verge of fainting. Even now, only the tiniest hook of lucidity kept her from slipping into unconsciousness. She faltered to the paper towel dispenser and yanked on the little gray handle over and over, watching a long, brown tongue spit itself out. Tearing it harshly, she ran into the closest stall, placed the paper towel sloppily beneath her knees and violently threw up for twenty minutes.

Her head on the rim of the toilet, she groped along the wall, looking for toilet paper. Lifting her head, she wiped her nose and mouth with the balled up mass and saw the wrinkled and torn paper towel beneath her. "Where did this come from?" she mumbled, tugging at it until a piece tore off into her hand. Bringing the paper towel to her sore and puffy eyes, she realized, slowly and painfully, what she had done.

William Faulkner knelt on a silk handkerchief whenever he vomited in a public restroom. No matter how drunk he was or how urgently he needed to vomit, he laid it gently on the floor and lowered himself upon it. As Caroline exhaled and the rotten smell of defeat filled the air, she remembered William Faulkner and his indestructibility. No matter how intense his suffering or how altered his condition, he was able to hold onto a part of himself.

Lowering her head back onto the toilet seat, she surrendered to the tears she had denied for so long. In that tiny action, William Faulkner affirmed who he was. She cried harder. She didn't really know about William Faulkner and she didn't really know herself. Joe had told her about Faulkner's habit late one night. It wasn't a favorite anecdote of his and he never told it again. It was just some fact he knew. In grasping that strip of coarse paper towel, she was clutching at Joe. She stayed hidden in the stall until everyone had left and, after brushing the remnants of vomit out of her teeth with her finger, Caroline left her office, got in her car, and began to drive.

The traffic was heavy. As Caroline watched the people in the passing cars, she knew that everyone in the world was unhappy. Drivers sent up cries of opposition in long, strained, impatient horn blasts, knowing that an empty lane of traffic was happiness. She would not be disingenuous with her unhappiness any longer. After seven hours of driving, Caroline pulled into a small town, checked into one of its two miniscule hotels, and then found a bar at the other end of town.

She entered the bar and ordered a Vodka Cloudy, a remembrance of the last time she had felt possibility in her life. She watched a man and woman sitting down the bar from her. They were old, poorly dressed, and looked like they smelled. They didn't speak or watch the television above them. They sat, taking occasional sips from their respective drinks. She looked them over for some hint of familiarity, some signal that told the careful observer that this man and woman were lovers, the most intimate of friends, that the deepest of bonds was there waiting to be discovered, two people who said everything that needed to be said by merely being near one another. She found nothing.

"Are you lost?" asked the bartender.

She shook her head.

"Are you waiting for someone?"

"Not really."

The bartender looked around uneasily. There was something about this strangely quiet woman that made him uncomfortable.

"Drink okay?" he asked before walking to the end of the bar. Unsettled but intensely curious, he came back to her. "I don't mean to be shoving my nose into your affairs." He stopped. She said nothing. "It's just that I can't figure out what someone like you would be doing here."

"What's your name?" she asked condescendingly.

"Frank. Frank Lenning," he said proudly, straightening up slightly.

She knew that Frank Lenning had never been beyond the city limits of this tiny town.

"Need another?"

She agreed, even though she had barely started the first.

He hurried to make her another drink. It was clear that he wanted to impress her. It was also clear that he had no idea how to do this. His gaze darted like a frightened rabbit's through the bar in a vain hope that something would inspire him. Nothing did. Instead, he concentrated on making her drink. This was, at best, a stalwart attempt. Caroline watched as he filled the glass with ice, charged water, and a splash of coke, and then felt nothing but glee when the vodka bottle slipped from his impatient hands and onto the floor.

"Son-of-a-bitch."

He was unable to make eye contact. His frantic actions betrayed an overpowering embarrassment. She unabashedly observed the clumsy misgivings of his body, the sweat on his brow. He wasn't simple enough to act as if nothing had happened, and rather than clean it up properly, he rapidly picked up the large pieces of glass, tossed them in the trash, and finished making her drink.

"Damn vodka bottles. They make them so thin, it's hard to get a grip on them." His eagerness to put an end to his embarrassment only succeeded in lengthening it. His every step set off the crunching laughter of glass. He pretended not to notice the evidence of his clumsiness but he couldn't. Every movement set off the incessant chatter of the broken glass. "Now who did you say you were here to see? Waiting for, that is?"

Crunch, crunch.

"No one."

"Oh, yes. I asked you that already."

Snicker, snicker.

He stopped moving. This only worked momentarily, as he found that even shifting his weight caused shards to continue laughing.

"A little more vodka."

"If I'm good for anything, it's that." He tried to slow himself down. He even tried to pour slowly. He frowned, humiliated, at the glass at his feet.

As he was pouring the vodka, Caroline noticed that his left hand was disfigured, probably from severe arthritis. It appeared as if he couldn't move the fingers at all. She watched it carefully and made sure that he saw her watching it. He set the bottle down and examined his hand before her, turning it this way and that, as if a secret lurked behind each curved deformity. "I know it's ugly," he said sorrowfully.

"Let me see it," she demanded.

He held it up.

"No, let me touch it."

"I'd rather not. It's a bit peculiar."

"Arthritis?"

"I don't know. Woke up one morning and there it was, looking at me all Scrooge-like. Worked fine my whole life. It was like it suddenly decided it wasn't worth it. It was finished. I just had to get used to it."

"You're a cripple," she said, thinking, "All men are cripples."

"Let me touch it," she insisted.

He lowered his head. He did not want to talk about his hand or about being a cripple. But in his desire to impress her, he was willing to make light of his weakness. He searched the bar with his eyes. Caroline took a sip from her drink, waiting. "Here," Frank said softly, holding a pen in his good hand, a weak smile on his face. "Watch carefully." He held his crippled hand at eye level and brought the pen to its palm. He gave a quick, nervous look to Caroline. As the pen touched the center of his palm, his hand closed swiftly around it. "Try and pull it out," he said mechanically.

Caroline set her drink back on the bar, leaned forward, and gave the pen a few quick tugs, "It isn't going anywhere." She sat back without saying anything more. Frank tried to pull the pen from his hand but its clutch was too tight. Rather than magnify his foolishness any further, he lowered his hand.

For the next few hours she said nothing, occasionally looking at his crippled hand. When closing came, he was afraid to tell her.

"I'm sorry to have to do this, but it's closing time. I wouldn't make anything of it but I can't afford to lose my liquor license. In my book, a man, er, anyone should be able to drink as long as they want."

She exited the bar. He was surprised when he found her waiting for him forty-five minutes later as he was locking up.

"Are you okay?"

She nodded yes.

"Do you need a ride back to your hotel?"

She got into his beat-up truck and studied him as he drove. Pulling into the hotel's parking lot, he began his closing monologue. "I just want you to know that I am just making sure you get home safely," but she was already up the stairs, motioning him to follow.

He entered the hotel room to find that she had changed clothes and was pouring them drinks.

For most of the night, he talked first, telling her of his uneventful life. This took just over an hour. By appropriating incidents out of Troy Anderson's life (one of his regulars), he was able to stretch his story to two hours. The next day he figured that she knew as much about operating a bar as he did. He found talking to her exhausting. She sat straight up in her chair, sipping her drink, telling him, "Continue," anytime he stopped. He did. Sometime after five o'clock he was utterly bored with himself and simply too fatigued to continue.

"I really need to get a couple hours of sleep before I have to get back to the bar."

"Why don't you kiss me?"

He looked at her in amazement. Nothing could have prepared him for this question.

They kissed.

Soon they were making love.

Perhaps she was doing this as revenge against all the men that had used and degraded her. She didn't even know.

He struggled clumsily on top of her as she leaned against the headboard, almost sitting up. Her body gave no indication of pleasure. She lay there, simply allowing him to make love to her. More than once he stopped, only to have her push his hips back into motion. "Continue."

Throughout their lovemaking, Caroline noticed that Frank kept his crippled hand tucked safely behind his back. She now laughed. He stopped. She urged him to continue, but he wouldn't. He refused to look at her. She could sense that he was going to get off of her. Looking at his right side, she seized his wrist. He resisted only momentarily. She brought his crippled hand to her face. It was horrific and beautiful. She lowered it to her breast, staring at it intently. He looked at her in panic but he knew that he had no choice.

He turned his head slightly but continued to watch. The moment the center of his palm touched her soft, pink nipple, his hand clasped her breast as fast and tight and fierce as if it were a snake. She let out a dry moan but otherwise gave no reaction.

It wasn't until he was halfway home that he realized he had climaxed at that precise moment.

Caroline looked up at the window. She stood, naked, and peered out. She realized that her room looked down upon the roof of the room beneath. Opening the window, she climbed out and down onto the pebble-covered roof and sat, arms wrapped tightly around her knees.

The air was crisp. A light wind danced with the night. It dashed with the quick then slow movements of a child basking in its own unpredictability. As she shifted, it seemed to become aware of her, moving more forcefully in the deep midnight and beckoning her. She refused, laying her head down on her knees.

A train's whistle blew in the distance. Caroline lifted her head from her knees and stared into the darkness. Within seconds, a train roared past. By the internal lights, which shone relentlessly, and the rows of seats swallowed in its belly, she knew it was a passenger train. Yet, it was empty. The interior lights were shining on nothing, and all the seats faced forward with blank, sorrowful expressions. It sped by like tamed lightning. Caroline watched as it passed, the light melancholy and bursting with regret, the pounding of the train in stark contrast to the terminal silence of the emptiness within it.

She crawled frantically to the edge of the roof, cutting her knees on pieces of broken glass and rocks, her eyes identifying every row of seats. Car after car empty passed. She stood up waiting in anticipation; for what, she did not know. And then it happened, so quickly that she nearly missed it. She saw in the last car, halfway back, a man sitting wearing a coat, reading a paper, unaware of her pleading eyes. Then he and the train were gone. For several seconds after, the air resonated. In it she could hear the faded, muted voice of regret being pulled behind the train.

She lay down on the glass and rocks, staying there until the sun came up.

ARISTOTLE'S EGG

20

He looked at the clock hanging at the back of the classroom and then down at his notes; he was barely halfway through the lecture. As he continued, he added in his head how much longer he had left to how long he had to drive. He took into account the fact that she was always early and she was always eager. Adding this together, he realized that there was only one solution.

"I will cut you a deal," he said confidently, with a carefree mischievous smile. "You guys have really worked hard for the last few weeks and most of you have everything turned in. So I am willing to let you go early if you promise to read chapters eight and nine. That is what we have left to do, and do all the questions listed in your syllabus."

The minute he broached the topic of early dismissal, notebooks were closing, books were being tactfully shoved into book bags.

"How does that sound?"

Barb smiled and tried not to be obvious.

It was a no-brainer. Any chance to be released from class early created an exuberance in the air that the discussion of literature could never match. They knew that they had to cover certain material on order to pass their classes and graduate high school. Nevertheless, their ears waited for those words that signaled their release.

"And remember what Rilke said at the end of that poem: you must change your life."

They were all out the door in under two minutes.

Joe collected his things hastily and zoomed out the door past Barb, who was hanging out by the pop machine, without so much as a look. This did not alarm her. She merely placed her coins in the machine and pressed the 7up button.

Tossing his bag in the back seat of his car, its contents spilling all over the floor, he started the car, threw it into drive, and headed for Perkins. Looking at the clock on the dashboard, he floored the accelerator. He knew that she was already there and most certainly on her third or fourth cup of coffee, convinced that, like every man she had ever known, he had rejected her.

⌒◟

Barb sat at Steve's Bar and Grill sipping a coke. She wanted a beer, but was too scared to try her fake ID here until Joe got there. (The bartender always eyed her suspiciously.) She was patient and the first twenty minutes did not bother her. He may have got tied up at the school. He might be taking his time so that it would appear that he had nothing better to do. Anyway, in the past he had arrived as late as a half hour. When she had been there an hour and was shaking from the six cokes she had drunk, she was worried and certain that she had made a mistake.

Taking the napkin from beneath her glass, she made a list on the left side of the napkin: Coke, 7up, Pepsi, anything diet. On the right side, opposite each soda she wrote Moony's,

Steve's Bar and Grill, Bennigan's, his apartment. She had gone to the right place; 7up meant Steve's. This was their signal. Maybe he hadn't seen which soda she had picked; maybe he was sitting at another bar thinking that she had stood him up. Her heart pounding, she raced to the phone at the end of the bar and dialed his number, beginning her message with a desperate, "I'm sorry. I'm sorry."

A FURIOUS HISTORY

"It's me!" Maggie said into the small box. Up in his apartment, the fuzzy broken-up voice pushed its way through the intercom. Even in its muffled, distorted form, it aroused undeniable excitement.

Without a word, Joe pressed the buzzer, turned to the door, and unlocked it.

He soon heard the jingle of keys from down the hall followed quickly by a gentle knock on the door.

"Yeah," he yelled blankly at the door. There was a hesitation; the door did not move. "Come in," he insisted. This time the door opened, albeit cautiously.

"Hello?"

"Yeah, come in," he said. "I could hear you trotting down the hall."

She smiled.

The entryway was cramped. A bookshelf blocked the door. Carrying a small bag and wearing a large, heavy coat, Maggie found it difficult to maneuver; her enthusiasm for him, however, could not be swayed and she managed to call out, "Hi, cutie! What are you doing?" Her face, peeking into the living room of the small apartment, searched for him, barely able to contain its overflowing affection.

"Not much. Just reading. Looking for a passage, actually. For something I'm writing. I have everything Marquez wrote sitting in front of me but I can't find it. I'm sure it's laughing at me. It's driving me nuts."

She was directed to the ground by the sound of his voice. There Joe sat, in the middle of the living room, shirtless, legs crossed, absorbed in a large, hardcover book, several more surrounding him like little children being read to.

"I tried to get here sooner but it was impossible," she said, the strap of her bag sliding off her shoulder, dropping the bag to the crook of her elbow; she yanked it viciously up again.

He finished, piled the books on top of each other, leaned back, and turned his attention momentarily to her. "Oh, well, I'll find it later."

Joe had met Maggie at a theater where they were both seeing a movie alone when, as they were both leaving, Joe shouted, "That was terrible." He discovered that this dark, curly haired woman with the hauntingly sad eyes, ten years his senior, who never left home without an overstuffed and heavy bag (the contents of which was never clear), was unhappily married, raising two children who weren't hers and, because of some financial setbacks, was living with her parents. They went for coffee that night. Their affair started shortly thereafter.

"Do you want me to leave?"

"No, no, no. I'll find it later. What were you saying when you came in? I'm sorry."

The bag slipped to her elbow once more; she grunted quietly. For the first time, he noticed she was still standing just outside of the entryway.

"You can set your bag down," he said. Then looking around, "Anywhere. And come in, for God's sake. There, set it right behind you," he said, motioning to the bookshelf behind her. She turned around, removing the bag from her shoulder and leaned it up against the bookshelf. As she stood up, she noticed a black hairclip on the second shelf. It was not hers. It stopped her.

"I would have gotten here sooner," she began slowly. "But everyone was riding my case as usual. Where am I going? When am I coming home? My dad even asked me if I was seeing someone." She took a seat next to him on the floor. "Actually, he said that he knows I am. He went to the library to find me the day we went to dinner. Even though my car was there he went in and, of course, I wasn't there. Then he started grilling me about where I was. It was awful. I said I was with Holly at the lakes. He called her to confirm my story. I'm just lucky she backed me up."

"I'm guessing that your mom got involved after that?" Joe asked.

"She started crying, asking me how I could do this to Kyle. That Kyle is so wonderful. She said that if I leave Kyle, that—" She stopped cold and began to cry.

"What?"

She shook her head, unable at first to utter the words that were written all over her face. "She said that if we get divorced, that Kyle will be welcome in their house, but I won't." She sobbed harder. "How can she do that? I'm her daughter. You're right. You've been right about everything. That family is about obligation. Control. Not love. I'm so glad I met you. What would I do without you?"

Maggie had told Joe about her mother one night when they met at the Guthrie Theater. Her mother was an actress whose biggest role was a leading part in *The Goodbye Girl*. During intermission they began talking while in line for drinks. They walked through Loring Park after the show, where Joe learned that Maggie had always felt under the shadow of her domineering mother who had recently decided that, although the

259

Lord had blessed her daughter with looks superior to her own, he wasted this beauty on a talentless mistake. Walking with Joe showed Maggie that a man could be interested in her and the things she had to say.

Joe pulled away. "When are you going to stop this?" he asked harshly.

"Stop what?" she said wiping her eyes.

"All these bullshit games you're playing with yourself." Before she could speak, he glared at her. "You need to change your life, Maggie."

"I want to be happy. I'll leave him. I promise."

He leaned in and kissed her. Soon they were kissing passionately. All of the words that he had spoken were translated into the movements of their bodies. She didn't have the words that he had, but every idea he spoke she felt in her body, and with joy and longing and regret at the life she had lived so far, she jumped on top of him. And he, in return, lay back, ecstatic, and let her devour him.

"Give me one second," she said, pulling herself off him abruptly, excusing herself awkwardly to the bathroom.

"What are you doing?" he asked, loudly. "I'm so ready for you."

"I have to brush my teeth."

"Your breath is fine. Come in here."

She finished brushing her teeth.

"Was that really necessary?" he asked, pulling her to him.

"I'm sorry. He, Kyle," she said softly, ashamed, "won't make love to me if I don't brush my teeth. It's just an old, dumb habit."

She resumed where she had left off.

"You didn't seem into it. Did I do something wrong?" Maggie asked after.

"I was just tired."

Joe and Maggie walked along the river in Stillwater. Although the sun was out, the temperature was still well below freezing.

"I didn't think you'd actually come. I thought you'd cancel," said Joe, holding tightly onto Maggie's hand.

"Why?" she asked, smiling.

"Shit, I can barely get you to go to dinner, much less out of town for the night."

"I've thought a lot about the things we've talked about and decided to really consider your advice. Don't roll your eyes. This is a big decision I'm considering."

"You don't believe a word I say," he said with a wry smile.

"What are you talking about?" she asked, pulling her hand away from his. "I'm here, aren't I?"

"I'm not doubting your sincerity. I know you get excited about the things we talk about. But that's when you're with me. The minute you get home, you turn into the same push-over you were when I met you, incapable of making a deci-sion, dominated by your mother, and tormented by guilt at being with me. And Holly went out of town tonight. That's where you are tonight."

Slowly she took his hand again. "I'm trying. I am grateful for all the books and ideas and conversations. They've really changed my life," she said sweetly, quietly.

"Don't patronize me. All those things mean nothing if you don't put them into practice. What good is knowing how to fly a plane if you have no intention of ever flying one? You're considering living a life that someone else thinks you should live. That's the real crime, not this insignificant infidelity that you torture yourself over."

She turned and kissed him on the cheek.

"I told you not to patronize me. Not with sentimentality. It's the most false thing you could ever put your faith in. I'm not here to supply you with a treasured memory."

"I'm just trying to show you what you mean to me. I never thought my life would be happy again. I didn't even realize that I hadn't felt happiness until I met you. That's not false."

They stopped and kissed. They approached a bridge and they began to cross it, stopping in the middle. They looked at the river, at the leafless trees, the barren shores. Surrounded by a silence particular to the Minnesota countryside, Joe looked deep into space. "We must have the courage to face the fact that we are going to die. Heidegger wrote that. I think he's right. It's the most profound thing I've ever read."

Maggie stood silent, thinking about his words.

"Is that why you're so intense all the time?"

He did not answer.

"I don't know. I think that's kind of a bad way to look at things. I don't want to walk around thinking about my eventual death every day. I'd be more a nervous wreck than I am already," she said.

"It is the only anecdote to complacency," he said, still looking deep into space.

"It's not that easy for other people, Joe. You have no idea what kind of work goes into a divorce. Not to mention the money. I can't afford a lawyer. At least not a good one. Kyle has friends who are lawyers and they'll have plenty on me before this is over. Not to mention the fact that my parents support him, not me. And you've never met my mother. She's has more influence over my life than anyone. I can't just step away from that kind of thing."

"Don't waste your time," he said turning to her. A light snow had begun to fall and flakes clung to her curly hair. "That's all you have in this life. Waste is the only sin I know."

"Then we're all sinners, Joe," she said, kissing his unmoving lips. "Doesn't my being here say something about me and that I'm willing to sin against my marriage, my stepchildren, and my parents just to be with you?"

For the first time, it did. Joe started to change how he felt about his life and the women he spent it with, although clinging to his old way of thinking, he was unsure in what way. "Tomorrow you'll go back to a man you don't love. Tomorrow you'll be living your life with a man who doesn't respect you."

"Yes, he does, he just doesn't know how to show it. His upbringing was tough. I don't want to talk about it. It's hard enough to live it, much less talk about it."

They crossed the bridge and began walking on the other side of the river.

"The chicken or the egg?" he asked. "Which came first?"

"I don't know," she said, thinking about it. "This is dumb."

"Indulge me."

"The egg, I guess."

"You know what Aristotle says? The chicken. You know why? Because the egg is only a potential chicken whereas the chicken is actually a chicken. Imagine we're on a first date. You don't really know me and halfway through the date I tell you that I have the potential to be a warm, giving person but that right now I am an asshole whose only aim is to sleep with you. Would you go on a second date with me? Or even finish the first? Of course not. But you will go home to an uncaring husband every night. Why is it we accept in camouflage what we would never accept unveiled? It's not even camouflage. It's wearing fatigues in the city. It hides nothing. Yet we pretend. Why spend your life with potential? You're an amazing person. You just don't know it. You're ashamed of who you are."

"You're right, I fall apart at home. If I try and stand up for myself I always get, 'Have you taken your pills? Take your pills. You'll calm down once you have your pills.' Any feelings I express are just Mags being crazy or Mags being needy or needing her medicine or Mags being selfish. And I don't think that's fair. And what's sad, what you've shown me is sad, is that I bought into it for so long. Sometimes I just think I'm going to lose my mind. All of us in that house."

"That's why you're here," he said.

"Oh! Remember how I told you he stopped wanting to sleep with me," she said, lowering her voice at the words *sleep with me*, "and how it's been like seven months? How I always felt like it was my fault? Well, the other night we're having it out and then, out of nowhere, he tells me that I don't put out anymore."

"I'd have to disagree with that," he said with a smile.

She took him by the arm with her free hand and smiled back.

"Be prepared for that," he said. "It's easier that way. Turn it around. Dodge responsibility. If he's already doing that it's only going to get worse. You will be blamed for everything. You're the one leaving and it's always the one who takes action who will be the target. And why not? It will be easy to point at you, right? It takes strength to act. No one likes it and you're often left alone."

"But you'll be there when I leave."

He looked at her with a challenging, defiant look.

After a moment, she said playfully, "I've decided what I'm going to call my autobiography."

"You're writing your autobiography?" he asked.

"Well, no. Not yet. Guess. Wait, I'll tell you. Are you ready? *Aristotle on Marriage or How to Turn that Egg of a Husband into a Chicken of an Ex*," she said slowly, carefully. She grinned the moment she was done speaking.

"I love it," he said, laughing.

And he did.

She stopped them and looked into his eyes, "Let's go back to the hotel, Joe."

"I have something for you," he said, stepping away from her, digging into the deep pockets of his winter jacket. He pulled out a worn copy of *The Gay Science* and handed it to her. "This book changed my life." Joe had planned to give her this book on this trip. He always gave this book as a gift. He liked how it reflected on him. Yet, for the first time he wanted a woman to have this book for its contents and how it had changed his life, not as a reminder of the time she had felt genuine freedom by being with him. At this thought, he was ashamed. He was ashamed at how he used to laugh, thinking of this book on some woman's bookshelf mocking her inability to free herself, or how this book would take Joe's place after he left, a manual on transgressing society's values that these women would never appreciate.

Soon they were back in the hotel.

"Go ahead. Brush your teeth. I can wait," he said, annoyed.

"I don't need to," she said, smiling.

For the first time in his life, Joe cried after making love to a woman.

"I know it's not much, but it's mine," Maggie said, shrugging her shoulders modestly. Then with a sense of forgotten pride she repeated, "It's mine."

He knew how much fear, courage, uncertainty and hope were in those few words. He hugged her for a long time. There wasn't much to look at. She had no furniture except an old spare-bedroom mattress; she had some clothes and a television. The only lights in the apartment had been there when she moved in; the kitchen light, the hallway light, and the bathroom and bedroom lights. Like distant friends, they all did their best to reach the living room, bending around walls, straining giving the whole place a less abandoned, shadowy feel. The meek, soft light of candles circling them like new and present friends only enhanced this feel.

He pulled the long Subway sandwiches out of the equally long plastic bags, handed one to Maggie, and unwrapped his own. The mustard was strong. They must have been hungry; they ate half of their sandwiches before either said a word.

"These are very good."

"Yes, they are," he confirmed.

"I don't usually have these, but they're really filling and inexpensive."

"And right around the corner from here."

"That's good to know," she said, letting the silence recapture the apartment. "It's so quiet in here that I can't sleep unless I have the television on. I didn't realize how used to noise I was. I know I complained about it all the time. I didn't realize how comforting it was."

"You'll get used to it. Especially after you get your own stuff in here."

"I didn't realize how much stuff Kyle and I bought together. When we first got married we didn't have much either. We had to buy as we went along. With every new job or promotion we were able to get more and better stuff until our house became a little testament to our life."

"That'll be the fun part," he said, finishing his sub and wiping his mouth with a napkin. "Making this a testament to your freedom."

"Can you stay tonight? It's so empty and quiet."

"I can't, sweet. I have stuff I gotta do," he said. "In a few days everything will be done and I'll be here so much you'll get tired of me."

"You can't change your plans? Just for tonight? You can have the weekend. I'll see Holly and—"

"I really can't. I made these plans weeks ago," he said quietly. He had discovered that ending things with the other women he was seeing was difficult, but he was determined to make things rights with Maggie.

"You haven't told me that you loved me in a long time."

Joe had put his arm around her, "If you only knew how much I do."

⌣〜

Resting uneasily in the driver's seat, Maggie stared at the large windows in front of her, at the people in booths sitting across from one another, eating. She marveled that, when observed objectively, they looked as unnatural as she felt when she sat with a man. Two months ago she would have wanted to cry. She would have ventured home, taking the longest route possible, driving below the speed limit, and gone straight to bed without being able to sleep, with Kyle lying next to her, snoring. After meeting Joe that all changed. After being with him, the sight of a couple brought on a sense of immense hope. Looking at these couples now, she thought they all seemed tired and speechless. Only the people sitting alone, eyes focused on the food, seemed, if not content, then at least not exhausted. But sitting in a restaurant alone was *so* alone.

In a start she turned the key in the ignition. But before she could shift the car into reverse, she had already turned it off again, her windshield quickly becoming covered by snow, and the inside of her car darkening.

"What's wrong with me?" Maggie asked. "Just do it. Just go in. This time is no different than any other."

⌒ⱽ

Entering the restaurant, he quickly found Maggie sitting in a booth at the very back, a pot of coffee, a cup, and a book sitting in front of her. Slouched at her side was the always-overstuffed bag. It was good to see her. She looked apprehensive. "Oh, God," he thought, "she thought I wasn't going to show. I've been distant lately. I need to make it up to her. Especially since she was just served divorce papers by Kyle."

"Hey, what's going on?" he asked enthusiastically. "You look cute. I'll take a cup as well," he said to the waiter, who brought one over right away.

"Not much," she said, sipping her coffee, leaning back easily into the booth.

"I see you're still reading the book I gave you," he said, eyeing it, pleased. "I told you one reading would never be enough. It's one of those you'll read for your entire life. I'm really sorry about what happened today. He shouldn't have had that done at your work. He has no class. Are you holding up all right? I'm sorry I'm late. I got here as fast as I could. I'm going to make it up to you. I already know what we can do this weekend. There's a showing of Picasso's pencil drawings at the Minneapolis Institute of Arts that I think you would just love. Have you ever seen that stuff of his?"

She shook her head no.

"Good. Good. I think you'll just love it. Really gives insight into his work."

"I don't know. Maybe."

"Unless you have something else you want to do. I'm open."

"I can't stay very late tonight."

"Really? Why?"

"I have a lot of stuff going on at work that I had to take home," she said unenthusiastically.

"That's too bad. I've been doing some thinking and I've kind of been AWOL lately and I want to make it up to you. I'm going to help you move that stuff out of your parents' house. I don't care what they think or if Kyle will be there. Screw them all. If they can't handle it, then too bad."

"I don't think so."

"Okay, what's going on?" he asked, his voice dropping in tone.

"I can't do this anymore. It's too hard," she said, swallowing with difficulty and pushing her cup away.

"I know things are hard right now but we'll get through it. Just look how far you've come already. I'm here for you. You know that. I know the last few weeks have been tough and I really, really apologize. I've had a lot going on but I'm back.

For good," he said, trying to take her hand, which remained firmly planted on her coffee cup.

"That's the problem."

"What do you mean?" he asked, confused. "I thought you were upset because I haven't been around. I told you that I'm going to remedy that."

"It's not that. I mean, that was it, but not anymore. I'm over that."

"Then what? I'm not understanding."

"I don't know how to say the things that I want to say. It's all trapped in my head. I have so much I want to say to you and I want to say it right."

"Just take your time. Sometimes these types of things—"

"I am taking my time," she insisted.

He sat back, chastened.

She took several deep breaths before proceeding. "I can't see you anymore."

She stopped, letting the words and their implications settle.

"Okay," he said. "I get it." He got up to leave but before he could, she continued.

"I refuse your freedom."

Joe sat back down slowly, his attention completely ensnared by these few words.

"What do you mean, you refuse my freedom?"

"I mean it's a lot of crap, Joe. Everything we talked about, all those things. They sound pretty and I tried. But they're only words. They don't apply to the real world."

"Oh, they don't, do they?" he asked. "And the hell if you tried."

"Don't tell me they do just because they work for you. You're different. Younger. Maybe they do work, I don't know. But only for people like you. People with no responsibilities. And I did try. I moved out. I committed adultery. I signed the papers. If that isn't trying…."

"Just say what you really want to say."

"I am."

"No, say the words that you've been waiting to say all day, all week probably. Go ahead. I'm waiting. You're so weak that you think what you're doing *to me* is a victory for you. And that's the only pleasure you'll ever get because you're too much a coward to say them to Kyle. Go ahead. Have your moment. No? Fine. I'll say them for you. God, you're pathetic. You're going back to your husband. That's what you've been waiting to say. Am I right?" He waited. "Am I?"

"Yes."

"Fucking ridiculous. I don't care, you know," he said bitterly.

"I know," she said.

"You can throw your life…"

Before he could finish, her cell phone rang.

"Hello? I'm at Perkins. Call me back in a minute. I'm doing something. Just call me back." She hung up.

He sat waiting silently, his patience and the words he longed to speak barely held back, his need to say them so great.

"You can throw your life away if you want. What do I care?" he said looking away. "It's not like it's a big surprise. I knew you were incapable of change. Or making an adult decision. You play at life, you don't live it."

"What does that mean?"

"It means—"

It rang again.

"Hello. What? Yes, I'm still here. No. Because. Okay, what? A hot ham and cheese? Fine. Yes, I'll order it right now. Bye. No. Bye."

"It means that you've wasted so much of your life already that you might as well continue. You'd probably have a stroke if you realized how useless your life is. Continue on. It's not hard; inertia will help you out."

"That's very nice, Joe." She waved over the waiter. "Yes; can I get…"

"Well, what am I supposed to say? That I'm real proud of you for turning your back on your life."

"A hot ham and cheese."

"Would you like fries?" asked the waiter.

"Yes. No."

"She'll take the damn fries," Joe barked.

"Please don't make a scene. Is that all you have to say? Yes. To go," she shouted as the waiter walked away. "I know what you're going to say, Joe. I know. Let's just let it go. You go your way and I'll just go away."

"You can't make it on your own, Maggie."

For a moment she felt tears burning her eyes, but she wiped them away defiantly.

"We're destroying a marriage. People's lives are at stake. Doesn't that mean anything to you? I didn't understand until now what a contract meant."

"Even if you're miserable?"

"Some things are more important than personal happiness. This thing I entered into is bigger than me, and you, and everyone involved. I have to stay, even if it's out of some twisted sense of obligation that I don't quite understand yet. I guess it's a moral decision. I can't think about myself all the time. It's selfish and wrong. There's a whole world out there that we are all a part of and I think it deserves our respect. Just think about it later, okay?"

"A decision to be unhappy, that's all it is. Don't bullshit yourself. All this crap about the world and selfishness you're only thinking about yourself. You don't care about Kyle or his kids or your parents. You're just too cowardly to live life on your terms. That is selfish. You're martyring your life. And for no reason. That's the worst kind of selfishness."

"I don't have the options you have, Joe. You're single, you're educated, you don't have kids."

"Neither do you."

"What's his is mine. It's part of the vows."

"Oh," he laughed out loud. "You didn't seem to care about those when you were fucking me."

She pulled back, horrified.

"I'm sorry. I didn't mean that. You don't have to do this," he said tenderly.

"I know."

"I really care about you."

"I know. I just can't do this anymore. I have to go back."

"You don't have to, you want to, right?" he barked. "Is that it?"

"Joe, it's not that easy."

"Sure it is. It's either yes or no. Doesn't seem that hard. Just yes, I want this or no, I don't. I mean, I don't care either way. I just want to have a clear understanding is all. I like to have a clear understanding when people make stupid choices."

"Fine: yes. Yes, it is what I want. Are you happy?"

"Not particularly."

They sat in silence.

"Don't you even care…" he started.

The phone rang again.

"What? Yes. Right away."

"About me?" he finished.

"Yes, I did. I ordered it right away. Soon. Soon. No. I'm coming. It'll only be a second. No, don't come here! I'm coming! Bye." She looked at Joe. "Yes, I care. That's why I am going back."

The waiter set the to-go box on the table.

"I really have to go."

"I know," he said.

"Or else he'll come up here and that's…"

"Bad."

"Bad, yes. But what we had wasn't bad. I'll really treasure it. Always. But I really have to go." Looking into his eyes, she felt a rush of emotion. He felt it, too.

"Just wait two more seconds, okay?" he asked.

"You can't convince me, Joe," she said firmly.

"I know. I don't want that," he said meekly.

"I have to do this. Go back."

"I know. Just stay with me for a second."

"Here take this," she said pushing the book he had given her toward him, throwing a wad of money down. Crying, she threw her bag over her shoulder and left with the grease-stained to-go box.

Pulling the book toward him, he gazed at it sadly. He looked over his shoulder, but she was already gone. He lifted up the book reluctantly, sadly, feeling as if he were taking back a promise.

"Don't go. Please."

"Was there something else you needed?" asked the waiter.

"What? Sorry. I didn't see you. No, no. There's nothing I need. Everything is fine. I have everything I need. Actually, here, take this," he said handing him the book Maggie left behind.

"What do you want me to do with this?" the waiter asked, dropping the book on the table.

"Throw it away, use it as a doorstop, I don't care what you do with it."

Joe pushed the book, and with it the way he had lived for the last few years, into the waiter's hands. The waiter turned and walked away, leaving Joe to his coffee.

HURRICANE LIPMAN

21

Lipman pulled on the gray striped jumpsuit and shut the locker door. He walked out of the boiler room and up the stairs to the main floor of the church where the waxing machine stood, melancholy from its tired habit. Like an industrial-sized candle, it gave off a strong scent. The first time he had used it, he had had to stop every fifteen minutes and step outside, the scent was so strong. Although he was still not used to it, he took on the headaches and watery eyes as a sort of atonement. He looked at his watch and shook his head.

He unfastened the long, gray cord that was wrapped around its base and plugged it in. When he flipped the switch, the loud, dull humming reverberated down the long, empty hallway whose walls were littered with children's watercolors of Jesus hanging on the cross. Grabbing the stiff, unforgiving handle, he felt the vibrations throughout his entire body. This, too, had given him problems when he first waxed the floors. It caused massive, temporarily blinding headaches on top of those that the scent already caused. Shutting it off, he would sit, head in hands, on the cold stairway until the throbbing diminished enough that he could see out of one eye. Then he would continue. His headaches always intensified when he thought of the time he was wasting, his past failures, and all of his wrong turns. A new resolve to defeat his body forced him up. In the beginning, it took him days to wax the floors of the entire church and its adjoining school. It wasn't uncommon for him to stay late into the night to finish his regular duties. But he didn't care. The more his body ached, the happier he was.

Lipman saw Father Campbell approaching from the opposite end of the hallway, his floor-length robe running nervously in front of him. He killed the motor.

"Father."

"How are you doing, Don?"

Lipman leaned on the handle of the waxing machine, then abruptly pulled himself straight. "Fine."

"The windows must have taken you longer than you expected, if you just started waxing."

"Sorry, Father."

"No criticism intended. The windows must be sixty years old."

"Then they should have been replaced thirty years ago," Lipman said with a laugh.

"They let the cold in and the heat out. Probably cost you thousands. They've been painted into place and when you add that to the shifting that the building has done over the last thirty years, they've been epoxyed into place. It should only take another two weeks. Now that I've gotten past the first few, I've encountered all the variables. It's just the work now."

"You're very methodical. And you're right about the windows, they've been costing us money for years and every time we've raised enough money to replace them, something else came up. This time I just insisted. I hate the administrative side to this job. But nevertheless."

"What's your favorite part?" Lipman asked impatiently, trying to see his watch.

"That's an interesting question," the priest said with a hint of reflection. "I spend so much time with the things I don't care for, it's easy to lose track of the things that brought me to the church in the first place. Helping people. Saying it out loud, it sounds kind of simplistic, doesn't it? Not what you'd expect to hear from a man in the autumn of his years."

"I don't think keeping your ideals is a sign of naiveté, no matter what age you are. You've stayed true to yourself. Not a lot of people can say that. There are worse things than wanting to help people."

"I hope you're right, Don," Father Camplbell said, patting him on the shoulder with a smile. "We I appreciate all the things you do around here. Not that I didn't have my doubts. The first time I met you, you showed up with no appointment, no résumé and you weren't a member of our parish or any other. It seemed like you just walked in off the street."

Lipman had just walked in off the street. After leaving Leslie's parent's house on Thanksgiving, Lipman told Leslie that he had to "liquidate his assets," and proceeded to break off their engagement, quit his job, and go on a three-week bender. He was driving down Minnetonka Boulevard when he noticed a police car behind him. Half-drunk, he turned into the next driveway. Finding himself in front of St. Margaret's and with the police car still behind him, Lipman made his way inside quickly. When he first ran into Father Campbell, he had no idea that there was a job opening, but when the Father took him for an applicant, something in his eyes told Lipman that St. Margaret's might be the place for him, at least for a while.

"Dead in the water."

"It was obvious you had never been a janitor, even if you did say you had cleaned offices. Still, I didn't hold it against you."

"No?" Lipman asked surprised, shifting his weight from one leg to the other.

"Not necessarily. There are times when we all bend the truth. Sometimes there isn't any other choice. I figured you were in a bad place. Don't misunderstand; I was suspicious. I was exacting when listening to you, observing your reactions."

"That couldn't have helped," muttered Lipman into his chest. "I was all over the place that day. I don't even really remember it."

"So you don't remember telling me you were from St. Louis? I didn't think so. Of course, you had Minnesota plates. Part of me wanted to laugh. Especially when you said you would join St. Margaret's should you get the job."

"That's embarrassing."

"It kind of softened me, actually. Against my better judgment, but nevertheless. Then you really went into orbit. When I asked you if you had any experience, you said that you had been taught about the letter of the law and the spirit of the law."

"Now it's coming back to me. I said how I was intrigued that there could be two aspects to the law."

"Yes, its essence and the actual words. You thought that people manipulated the spirit of the law in their favor when they sinned, but used the letter of the law when others sinned. No, it's really interesting. I used several variations of this idea in my homilies. Probably why I hired you. You must have senses the old, frustrated writer in me. You conveniently mentioned that you had been a writer."

"Can't blame an egg for trying," said Lipman.

"You told me all sorts of nonsense. That you were a good writer but that you had to stop, not because you were dried up or unable to get published, but because the writer's hands are idle hands. You said that a janitor was like a soldier that sees the results of his work firsthand. After that you got emotionally silent and refused to talk."

"That a dirty floor is cleaned, a burned out light bulb is replaced, a snowy walk shoveled. I remember," said Lipman. Being a janitor gave Lipman a visceral connection to the world he felt he lacked as a teacher or even a salesman. What he hadn't expected was that his creativity was coming back. Since becoming a janitor, he had finished several short stories and had begun a novel titled, *Aristotle's Chicken*.

"That didn't get you hired. No. You were clever, but I wasn't stupid. Did you have any experience?"

"I didn't."

"No, no. That's what I asked you. You said you had been cleaning up after yourself for your entire life. That's why you're standing here today. I better let you get back to work. Don't stay too late."

"I won't."

"Oh," Father Campbell said, peeking his head out from his office at the end of the hall. "I forgot to ask you, do you want the day after Christmas off? No? I don't suppose you do."

Lipman stared at his watch. "Damn." He resumed waxing the floors. Over the last few weeks he had thrown himself into an endless array of projects that didn't need to be finished for months. Making sure that he was constantly busy was his driving motivation. When his hands began to blister, he was comforted. When those same blisters would split from painting, he would draw his hands to his face and be comforted. And when he would leave late at night, insensitive to the sharp winds and snow, his hands so raw that locking the doors caused him to faint, he would squeeze his hands into tight fists and stagger out of the entryway into the street.

Turning off the waxing machine, he wrapped the long gray cord around its base and locked it away. Unzipping his jumpsuit, he stepped out, hung it in his locker, and began to head for his car. He stopped abruptly, went into Father Campbell's office and asked to use the phone.

"Hello. That offer still good? How about we go to Lindee's? Good. What about in a half an hour? Great. See you there." He hung up the receiver and left.

It had been snowing all day so that when Lipman left work, the roads were fully covered with snow. It was hard to tell whether they were slippery. He felt a rush of anxiety when the clock on the dashboard blinked 10:35. Roberts, who had called him at work to say that his car had broken down, had been waiting for him for over two hours. He told Lipman not to rush, that there was a small bar a mile or so from where his car had broken down, jokingly telling him that the longer he took, the better his odds at having his car stolen and collecting on the insurance. Lipman felt a second rush of anxiety knowing that it would take him longer than a half an hour to pick Roberts up and take him home. He accelerated harshly.

Pulling into a parking lot that really was a large, unpaved plot of land, cars strewn about as if they were toys that had been dropped by a bored child, he saw Roberts emerging from the bar. He flashed his lights and pulled up to the entrance of the bar.

Opening the door, Roberts yelled, "Thanks. I was just getting some air. Damn places get so smoky. I don't know what I would have done without you. Kilzer's out of town and you're the only person I know." He laughed loudly. "Fun little place. I've passed it a hundred times without even going in."

"Sorry I took so long."

"Not a problem," Roberts said, finally adjusting his voice to his surroundings.

"Windows kept you late?"

"Snow."

"Good to see you. It's been a while."

Lipman smiled meekly. Each was tired for different reasons. They drove for several miles without speaking, Lipman alternating his glance from the road to the clock, Roberts shifting nervously, having absorbed the energy of the bar. Lipman realized that he was driving toward Roberts's home and not in the direction of the stalled car. He swore to himself and began to slow the car.

"Don't worry about it. I'm pretty sure it's the alternator. Nothing either of us can fix it. Anyway, I called a tow truck and had it towed."

The car sped up again.

As they continued, Roberts noticed that Lipman had taken a few of the curves in the road loosely, nearly jerking them into a ditch when the wheel actually slipped from his hands. Inspecting Lipman, he saw the heels of his hands resting on the wheel, his fingers arched into the air. Blisters. Roberts felt there was something about those hands, something tragic or sad.

"I met a girl tonight. Sheila. I think we're going out this weekend. I was thinking of taking her to Albany. We'll have to go up north next weekend, if you don't mind."

"Huh? Oh. Yeah, no problem," Lipman said slowly, with effort. After a long minute he added, "I'm supposed too see someone too."

Roberts made sure not to act too surprised. "Yeah? That's cool. When?"

Lipman glanced at the dashboard. "Now."

"Oh shit, I'm sorry. I could have taken a cab."

"Don't be ridiculous. Truth is, I have no idea what I'm doing. It's all such an enormous waste. When I think about all the women I've seen, and all the energy I've spent on them, it's amazing because I never could stand any of them. *"I did love Caroline and Leslie and even Maggie, he thought to himself."* And this woman will be no different. Hell, maybe I can't stand myself."

"You'll be singing a different tune after you've been with this girl."

"I don't know. I have no need of fire anymore."

"Eh, that's just how you want it to be," Roberts said, shifting in his seat. "How you believe yourself to be now. I've seen you smash a full-length mirror because of a woman. I was there when you chased Teri down the hall of your apartment after you proposed. And I was there when you moved out, when it was finally over with Mandy. We met at that liquor store by your place and collected as many boxes as we could. We didn't stop moving up and down those stairs for three and a half hours. You didn't say one word. Then when we got to that little motel you couldn't stop crying. So don't tell me about fire. It's in your blood."

"I'm not lying. Or deceiving myself like you think I am. I'm different now. Different from all the different Lipmans of before. It's hard to explain and I know you think I'm full of shit."

"Call me in the morning and then we'll see."

"I don't miss being in love and I'm not going to fall in love with this girl."

"You were never in love."

"With every one of them," Lipman exclaimed with an alarmed turn of the head.

"You needed to believe that to write is all. You would fall for some girl and then it wouldn't work and then you'd write.

That was the payoff, not the women. And it did pay off. I've read your stuff. Or else you just feel guilty now."

"That's bullshit. And way too easy."

"Maybe, but I've had longer—monogamous—relationships than you have."

"I haven't met Mrs. Roberts yet."

"You know what I mean. If I was with someone longer than six months, you'd tell me that I was getting complacent. That I was living a life of exemplary mediocrity."

"I still would."

"At least that's how you were until you met Leslie. Then there was no chaos and no writing. I know that's why you left her."

"I didn't leave Leslie because of that. Do you really think I don't want a wife and a family? I do. At least I think I do but it has to be on my terms. I bailed on Leslie because I was settling. I was doing what a guy is supposed to at that age. It wasn't an authentic choice. Nothing bad can happen to you if the choices you make are authentic. When I'm ready for that life it will happen and I'll be able to write and work wherever I chose, whether that means being a janitor or an executive." Looking to the right, he knew they were approaching Roberts's house.

"You see that?" asked Roberts.

"What?"

"Over there, in the fields."

In the fields and ditches to the left, Lipman saw the occasional flashing of lights.

"Oh, the snowmobiles?" he asked. "What about them?" He continued to watch the ditches and fields, his eyes darting back to the road only long enough to ensure their place on it. The snowmobiles tore over the uneven paths, their headlights disappearing and reappearing.

"They look pretty," offered Roberts. "Like twinkling Christmas tree lights."

Lipman thought about Roberts's description and looked to the fields again: he was right. Without realizing it, Lipman made a decision not to forget this image. "They're really going."

"They're overdriving their headlights."

"They're what?" asked Lipman, his eyes glues to the darkness and fleeting flashes of light.

"Overdriving."

Lipman gave a confused, questioning look, although Roberts didn't see it.

"They're going too fast for their headlights to keep up. They're going so fast that by the time their lights shine on something of potential danger, like a tree, it will be too late. They've hit it before they can react." Roberts paused, looking back to the rising and falling lights. "It's the equivalent of driving into complete darkness."

"That kind of defeats the purpose of the lights, doesn't it?"

Turning back to the road, both men reflected on the tiny dots of light dashing beside them and on the headlights ahead of them.

"Overdriving?" mused Lipman, easing back into his seat.

"Yeah."

The car continued on.

Leaving Roberts's, Lipman made his way up to Huron Avenue. Turning onto it, he approached the bar that bar faced Huron, its front all windows. He slowed his car dramatically so he would be able to see everyone at the bar, even those sitting toward the back, farthest away from the street. But he needn't have done so. There she sat, at a table only a few feet from the bar, near the entrance, her hands wrapped tightly around a beer. Pulling his face away from the bar and the windows, he looked at the dashboard: 11:45.

Pulling into the parking lot, he sat for a long time watching her sip her beer and look around occasionally, at the front door. When the clock on his dashboard read 11:58, he went in.

"Hey," he said enthusiastically, still behind her, rubbing her back. "I'm sorry I am so late. I got way behind at work. Then my friend's car broke down and I had to give him a ride. Needless to say, I am finally here."

"I was beginning to think you got cold feet."

"Me?" he asked playfully. "Never."

"I want to know more about your writing. You don't remember that, do you? It was a long time ago and you were drunk, but yes, you did tell me that you were a writer."

"*Was* a writer," he said with emphasis.

"Well, when you were a writer what did you write about?"

"Women."

"Sounds interesting."

"Not really."

"Will you ever write about me?"

"Do you think that you've been memorable enough for me to immortalize? Because immortality is quite a burden," he teased.

"If not, I guarantee that will change."

"Really? Well, I better get some paper," Lipman said, slowly pulling the napkin from under his beer.

"So, when do I get to read something?"

"When you've earned it. My fiancée—ex-fiancée—was always asking me that," he said, replacing the napkin.

"A fiancée? I knew there was more to you than meets the eye. What else don't I know about you?"

"Let's see. I worked at a temp service and traveled through Europe visiting the graves of many literary heroes. I got my teaching license and began student teaching creative writing, and eventually going for my Master's degree. I did odd jobs for a while and then I started teaching as a professor. After that, I went into admissions, met Leslie, got engaged, nearly bought a house and now I've ended up at St. Margaret's as a janitor. I think that about does it."

"How did you go from aspiring writer to a janitor? No criticism of manual labor; I'm just curious."

"You cannot be a writer and have a career. They are antithetical to one another," he said, drawing the syllables out. "For one thing, the hours are never in sync. As a career man, you work nine-to-five. Writer's hours aren't hours at all. You write when you have to. And getting up at three in the morning to polish off a paragraph and then leaving for work a few hours later never helped either one. They always end up undermining one another."

"So you're a romantic? Why didn't you say so? No wonder you became a janitor. No one can be a romantic and live in the real world. That is, unless you're independently wealthy, which I am guessing you're not. I think it's cute. I can just see you writing on lunch breaks, before work, after work, on the weekends. I see why you don't have a fiancée."

"Writing is a full-time job and a spoiled child."

"Does that go for the writer as well?"

He laughed despite himself.

"You give your entire life to writing, not a certain amount of hours," he responded.

"Or else what? It will destroy you? That would be the romantic logic, right? So you had to give up a career so you could write. Yet you don't write anymore."

"Shit, I gave up a promotion, a fiancée, a house, a literary agent."

"That's a lot to just throw away."

"Not as hard as you'd think, Tina. It's like ripping off a band aid—the quicker you do it, the better."

"I'm impressed, Mr. Lipman. Everyone's thought about ditching everything, starting a completely different life. But usually it's just wishful thinking. But why give up writing? Isn't the point of romantic exile that you can pursue your dreams? Find truth through your art?"

He thought a long time about what she said before answering.

"Do you know what the real cause of suffering is? I do. Desire and denial."

"I like the first part of that equation," she said, looking him in the eye.

"Do you know who Rimbaud is?"

She shook her head no, her eyes filled with desire.

"He's a poet who revolutionized poetry. Then, one day he stopped and never wrote again. He left his home and family, lovers, literature, everything."

"Everything?" she repeated, her lips pouting.

"Absolutely," he declared.

"Rimbaud might be able to run away from life, and you can try, but you'll never be able to run away from me," she said, leaning in and taking his hand. He pulled away.

"That's just what Verlaine believed and he tracked him down. He wanted him to keep writing and he wanted him back."

"Probably just missed his lover."

"You know what Rimbaud said to him? Fous-moi la paix," said Lipman in a horribly fractured French.

"Is that what you're doing? Telling the world to fuck off and die?"

"I was when I became a janitor. I don't know anymore."

"Well, as long as you don't tell me to fuck off and die. I'll be right back. Don't you go anywhere," she said, excusing herself to the restroom.

While she was gone, Father Campbell burst into the bar, briskly approaching him.

"Is everything all right, Father?" asked Lipman beginning to stand up.

"I'm sorry to bother you, but this just came for you," he said handing him a large unmarked manila envelope. "I wouldn't have come, especially this late, but you've never received anything before. I figured it was important and this place isn't far from the church. I just walked over, hoping to find you."

"Where did it come from?" asked Lipman, indicating its lack of postage.

"A woman brought it. She wouldn't tell me her name. She said to tell you that it was something you had left behind."

"Thank you, Father," whispered Lipman.

"You enjoy yourselves then and don't stay out too late," said Father Campbell before excusing himself.

"Holy shit, that was close," Tina said, coming back to the table. "What's this?"

"I don't know."

"I guess you have more than one admirer."

Lipman opened the envelope and pulled out his worn out yellow and green copy of *Death in Venice*. He knew immediately that it had been his, the one he had given Leslie years ago.

Tina took the book from him and began examining it.

With a wave of nausea, his former life rushed back: Leslie, the abandoned house, the broken engagement, the promotion he passed by, his first unpublished novel, his entire unlived future. Regret and anger and sadness swirled around him until he was nearly blinded. The sound of Tina's voice brought him back. "I've never read this. Is it good?"

"What?" he asked.

"This book, is it any good?"

"Yeah, it's not too bad."

"What's it about?" she asked.

"An old man who falls in love with a little boy."

"So you like the kinky stuff?" she asked, running her hand over his thigh.

"I guess I must. It's more than that, though. It says a lot about inspiration and how important it is to stick to those tasks that make your life worth living. Too many people abandon those things that give life meaning."

"That sounds pretty good. Do you think I could borrow this? My life could use some inspiration."

"How 'bout we go to the bookstore in the morning and I buy you a copy?" Lipman suggested. "This one's old and deserves to be thrown away."

"So I'll be seeing you in the morning?"

Looking at Tina, Lipman felt like an addict who had decided not to use anymore and who, when offered the drug saw all his resolutions melt away. There she sat, like an apple on a tree just waiting to be plucked and devoured. He searched her face and body for any deficiency that should spoil her appeal, but he could find none. *He wanted her.* He didn't know why, but he felt an undeniable lust for this woman. But for once, he wasn't going to analyze his feelings, he was going to act on them. Leaning over, he kissed Tina passionately.

"I'll take that as a yes," she said.

"Let's get out of here." Lipman was sick of guilt. He wasn't going to let his feelings about Leslie and his former life get in the way of a great time.

"We got lucky," she said, picking up her purse and dropping a ten-dollar bill on the table. "Some day your recklessness is going to catch up with you. Taking me to this place. It's just down the road from the church. If I hadn't gone the bathroom, we'd both be unemployed."

Lipman stopped. His head fell into his hands. Was he interested in this woman because it was against church policy to date coworkers? Did he really want her or was he simply lonely? He didn't know.

"I am glad you finally took me up on my offer. I thought I was going to have to do something crazy," she said. "I knew eventually you'd ask me out."

"How could you know that?" asked Lipman, giving her what would have been the most helpless look she had ever seen, if she had been paying attention.

"It was just a matter of time."

"Time until what?" he asked.

"Until you let go of the guilt or whatever it is that's made you turn your back on everything. I can sense these things. I know who a man is no matter what he pretends to be like in his daily life. I knew that behind that quiet, hard-working janitor there was a dormant animal just waiting to be unleashed. Now, let's get home so I can unleash you," she said, kissing him.

"You are sexy, but there's no way you could possibly know that," he said condescendingly.

"I don't have scruples and you don't have to pretend you do."

"You're right. I used to be the person you're describing and I did stop out of guilt. I even became a devotee of Kant and tried to live right. God knows I wasn't cut out for that, so I became a janitor and told the world to fuck off and die. But I've had plenty of opportunities to have women and I've felt nothing. No urges. Then I come here with you and it all comes back. It took me a long time to get away from the person I used to be. Why is it all coming back now?"

"Because I'm something special, that's why."

Sensing that she was getting annoyed, Lipman caressed her cheek and, as he was leading her to the door, said, "I know you are. Let's stop all this talking and get to it."

"Wait, don't forget your book," Tina said going back to the table and bringing it to him.

"Leave it."

Pulling the cover of the book open, Tina looked at the inside flap and at the carefully printed name. "Are you sure? Was this your brother's."

"What?" asked Lipman.

"Here, look," Tina said, holding up the book, showing him the inside flap. "Joe Lipman. You never told me that you had a brother."

"Didn't I?" he asked. Lipman dropped the book on the table and attempted to keep at bay the questions that were still haunting him. Who was the real Don Lipman? Was there a real Don Lipman? Or was everything in the world, including who he was, only based on random, contingent choices?

He held these questions in his mind. Although frightening and overwhelming, they were not wholly unrecognizable. Maybe, at some point, they would be beautiful. But right now, he was with a beautiful woman who wanted him. These questions would have to wait. What he had taken as the end of a storm had only been his penetration deeper into it; as his lives circled around him, he now knew that he sat in this storm's eye. The quiet and the calm and the peace of his current life were illusions. In truth, he was surrounded.

Donald Joseph Lipman had no siblings.

22

Pulling into her driveway, Caroline shut off and exited her car. She was exhausted. She looked at her unlit trailer, which looked back at her with the same dark, mournful expression. Taking a step toward it, she stopped, glancing sideways from her car and to the trailer again. There wasn't anywhere to go. Turning around, she walked to her driveway's end. The pavement was uneven. Her shuffling step was the only sound she heard. It was as if all the sound in the world had been swept beneath her two tiny feet. Sitting herself down on the curb, she finished her cigarette and quickly began another.

The smoke rose from her mouth toward the sky. It was cloudy. She set the cigarette on the edge of the curb and watched the clouds in the sky. From her purse she pulled the piece of paper with the start of Joe's short story, reading the title: *Hate, or how a typewriter is better than a wife.* Placing it in on the ground she laid her cigarette on the paper until every word was burned away and there was nothing left but a gigantic hole.

Putting her cigarette out on the ground, Caroline went inside her trailer. It was suffocatingly small, the living room furnished only with a torn brown couch and an upside-down cardboard box. An open razor and a pear sat on the cardboard coffee table. Next to it rested a rolled-up sleeping bag. She had come home to die.

An open razor is the perfect lover. She reached for it. In her hands, it was cool and pleasing. It danced along her arm, wiping away the tiny blond hairs. They fell like snow to the matted carpet. Already she felt relief. She made a tight fist with her left hand. With the pinky of her right she caressed the veins that rose like hungry mouths. It will only be a moment now, she thought. The blade will cross my wrist and death will inhabit the space left by my rushing blood; happiness and death interceding, one born at the time of the other's departure. It was what her life had been leading up to. Looking at the sleeping bag and pear checked her hand and forced her to drop the blade.

These two objects seemed to offer her a rationale to live. In the pear she knew was sustenance, and in the sleeping bag, warmth to survive the cold night. Even the open razor seemed potentially life-giving. She knew its sharp edge could cut off slices of bite-sized pear pieces. She sat back on the couch, disgusted with herself and, without realizing it, fell into a hard sleep.

In her dream, the simple contents of her trailer revolted her and she exited through the rusty door, its creaks begging her to come back. Cutting through the yard of abandoned trailers, past rusty yard ornaments and add-on decks, she headed toward a dilapidated farm in the distance. If she couldn't kill herself in the trailer, she would find an adequate place and means elsewhere.

She walked. Eventually the farm and barbed wire fence rose on the horizon as if on a steep hill. Her stride quickened. It would take minimal effort to slit her wrists on the barbed wire fence. There was no ambivalence here. She moved faster.

It was the sound of thousands of feet pounding on the ground that made her look. Raising her head, she found herself in the middle of an ice storm. This caused her no alarm. With her narrow stride and beleaguered pace, she pushed forward. Soon she was there.

She closed her eyes and reached out with both hands, grabbing the barbed wire fence as tightly as her hands could. Her hands felt a shock. No amount of bloodshed would be too little, she thought. She opened her eyes. Nothing had happened. She looked at her hands in disbelief and back to the fence. The ice had beaten her. An inch of ice coated the barbed wire, as smooth and solid and cold as God. She gripped it again, more desperately than before, trying to melt the ice with the warmth of her body. Nothing. She looked to the sky, a fierce light in her eyes.

She would not be beaten. She walked back toward the trailer, veering off to the perimeter, entering at the road entrance. Pushing aside the large steel gate, which slammed behind her with the clang of a bell, she walked to the middle of the trailer park. The ice storm had not ceased. Coming to another smaller gate, she entered, pleased. She saw the empty cavity of a swimming pool: the pool had been drained. She stepped cautiously onto the icy diving board, making her way to the end. She looked past the edge of the diving board. The void was immense. She looked at the pool's bottom nine feet below. It was filled with a foot of ice as clear as a mirror. Her blurry reflection looked up at her. Pulling her arms back to her side, she leaned forward as if skiing, and watched herself on the pool floor. She stood in this position just a moment before leaning forward little by little until her body was bait that gravity could no longer resist. As she was pulled downward and inward her reflection was replaced by Joe, smiling, welcoming her with open arms. She flailed her arms and her voice failed her as she attempted to say, "No."

She awoke more terrified and confused than she had ever been in her life. Why Joe had appeared to her at the bottom of the frozen pool, she didn't know. She had a vague sense of relief at being alive, yet her inability to kill herself, in her dream and in real life, left her empty. She staggered to her feet and made her way down the darkened hall, her arms stretched out to either side to steady herself. She came to the bathroom, the urge to vomit overwhelming, her face moist. She stood before the closed door only a moment before grabbing the doorknob and throwing it open. The smell of old air greeted her. In front of her was her uninhabited bathroom. The window was painted shut. The curtain hung without moving. It was absolutely still. Turning to the right, she caught a glimpse in the mirror of the image of her own face, as if for the first time. She thought of the line by Rilke that she used to recite to Joe: "Standing on my breasts' hills my feeling screams for wings or an end." Glancing at the sealed window and gasping in the stale air, Caroline turned and walked once again down the dark hall, her arms stretched out to either side to steady herself.

BLUE MOONS

BY

DONALD LIPMAN

*C*harles' *life had been awful recently. For whatever
reason, things were falling apart. Sitting in a dark bar,
alone, a random memory asserted itself: the image of his
lover entering the house where they lived. This image was all that
came to him; it represented relief. The rest of the memory, or rather
it's beginning, was too raw to recall but it forced itself on him. As
he was driving away (they had had one of their very short, very
intense, and as of late very frequent arguments; they had left the
restaurant early and he went off to the bar) and when he pulled up
to the house, she got out of the car, stormed toward the front door,
and, the instant before entering, turned, flipped him off, and went
in. A million impulses coursed through him: to reciprocate the
action, to speed away, indifferent, to scream from the window how
immature she had been, to jump out of the car and chase her down.
This last impulse had been the strongest and the hardest to resist.
Of course, it was academic; by the time he considered all of his
options, she would have already gone up the stairs and into their
room. Instead, he turned, with every ounce of anger gripping the
steering wheel, and drove off. Once at the bar, he made sure not to
drink for at least an hour; it had still been early. And, in his usual
way, when feelings threatened to overturn him, he channeled them
into furious intellectual activity. After this fight with his lover, and*

the image of her flipping him off, he sat, alone, in a small, dark bar, thinking of Descartes.

In the Second Meditation, *Descartes discusses a piece of wax. He describes it as hard, cold, tasting of honey, and having a particular odor. He moves it near a flame: the taste of honey leaves, its odor disappears, its color and shape changes, it becomes liquid and hot. Yet, he asserts, the wax as wax remains. In the same way his life had changed, significantly, and not so significantly. The outer things—jobs, cars, residences, clothes, weight, even the very cells of his skin—these changed frequently and without much consequence. Then there were the things that were somehow more a part of him that changed as well: pets, friendships, teachers, bosses, even family members at death. What he found the most shocking was that the most inner things, the things that identified him most as Charles, transformed as well, became liquid and hot: feelings, ideologies, faith, humor, worldviews. It was frightening. If it were possible to view the loss of cherished things without sentimentality, if his very person could be heated in the fires and reshaped beyond recognition only to harden into some new unrecognizable shape, what then was left? How was the wax still wax?*

Yet, what did persist was the writing. Even in the midst of continual upheaval and transformation, he worked at this. The realization of its place of permanence relieved him. Never did he look upon his work with betrayal. Despite all the roles he had assumed in his life, he had responded in his work honestly. It was a privilege to be a writer. In the light of the many "final" estimations he had made about his life, his place in it, those he loved, once loved, or wished to love, this was nothing short of extraordinary.

When he had arrived at the bar, he separated himself at a corner table. A group of people whom he recognized then entered. They approached him. They explained that they usually sat in this same corner and asked if he wouldn't mind moving. He apologized but stubbornly refused, delighting in insisting that he was waiting for friends. It was a petty thing to do. He was petty when he was mad.

And when upset, he had no problem using these upset feelings as an excuse to manipulate others: free drinks, sympathy, attention, any opportunity to rhapsodize. Or in this case, to lay claim to a table he cared nothing for.

His pettiness continued when he approached the bar several minutes later.

"I'll have a Coke."

The bartender grabbed a glass and began filling it. "That's a buck twenty."

He pulled a dollar out of his wallet. Looking at the other bills, he searched his pockets in vain, raised his hands into the air with a sigh of futility. "I don't have it," he said, pushing the Coke toward the bartender. "Forget it. Sorry."

The bartender looked at him blankly.

"Just one of those days, you know? I got in a fight with my god damn girlfriend, my car's making some awful noise, and I got fired today."

The bartender's face relaxed immediately. He pushed the dollar back to Charles. With a confused expression and a shrug of his shoulders, Charles asked, "Are you sure?"

"Don't worry about it."

Charles walked away and looked humbled and thankful. Sitting in the back corner, he was neither. He just sucked on the Coke and the bittersweet acid of pettiness. He knew it had been petty and he didn't care. He wasn't a small person who cared about insignificant things, but at times, at most times, the insignificant things were the only things you could control.

He remembered being caught in traffic on the way to the bar. After a half an hour, his car had approached the nucleus of the slowdown: on the opposite side of the highway, a deer was trapped on an overpass. It looked around frantically, trying in desperation to identify any means of escape. And so its head twisted and turned, its legs started and stopped. Finally, when it had too much, it turned, looked for only a moment, and then leapt into the darkness, down into the waiting arms of the other highway beneath. The traffic was stunned and seemed to stay immobile for minutes and minutes. Now, thinking of his girlfriend, Charles knew she was in their apartment, placid as a winter evening, but that beneath her calm exterior she fought a silent battle to hold onto that calm. He knew that, when she no longer could maintain it, her life, too, would end brutally.

But that was back at their apartment and he wasn't there. Nor did he want to be. Instead, he focused on the bar. He caught sight of a waitress rolling silverware at a table. At first his eyes, jumping from thing to thing, person to person, simply landed on her without recognition. Yet something stopped his eyes from moving on. It was nothing dramatic, just a subtle movement of her lips. It was barely noticeable; they opened just wide enough for her to communicate with herself. He thought she was talking to herself but, as he watched, he knew this wasn't so. When he watched long enough, carefully enough, he could see rhythm in their movements, melody filled with pauses and emotion: he could see that she was singing. The sounds of the bar overwhelmed him. He hadn't noticed that his intense observations had cut out all the sounds around him. Background music made its way brazenly to his consciousness, nearly startling him. Yet with undeterred attention, he finally made out that she was singing along to this same background music. It was Blue Moon.

He watched as the syllables formed on her mouth. In the thin space between her lips, the consonants, stretching the whole of her mouth, passed, her tongue wet and rhythmic. Yet it was the vowels that sat him up straight; she looked as if she were accepting communion. When an "O" appeared, her mouth contracted, pulling itself tightly yet delicately around it, making it nearly tangible in the darkness between her faded pink lips. When flagged down by a customer, she would interrupt herself, pulling out her pad and pen, listening attentively, nodding and writing. Once finished taking the order, she would resume singing. He watched as she turned away, the syllables forming effortlessly on her lips. Giving the bartender her order, she would stop. Heading back with the glass of beer, she would begin again.

She had no idea that she was singing Rodgers and Hart. And, looking at her, he knew that she had no idea of the song's or the songwriters' history. But it didn't matter. There she was, neither beautiful nor exceptional, rolling silverware, being comforted by a song older than she. It was unconscious and it was perfect. He was transfixed even if it was mediocre Rodgers and Hart. He considered ordering from her but he couldn't stand being the cause of those wonderful lips stopping. Instead, he watched her long after the song had ended and long past when he needed a new drink.

Finishing his third Coke, he knew that this fascination had turned her into metaphor even if her name, as her nametag indicated, was Norah. That in watching this woman singing Blue Moon, he concluded that she represented all the things he thought he loved about women: passivity, silence, and servitude—things he desired only when Tina disappointed him. And what's more, when he disappointed himself.

"Are you Charles? There's a call for you at the bar."

"Thanks," he said, rising in shock and following a waitress to the bar where the bartender handed him a phone. "Hello?"

"Hey, Dude, it's me, I thought you might be there."

"Hey, Todd. I got in a fight with Tina."

"Again? Sorry. I was just making sure you'd still be there when I get there."

"I'll be here."

"I won't be till nine."

"I'll see you then," he said, hanging up the phone. He handed the bartender back the phone and looked at the clock above the bar:

5:15. Pulling a dollar from his wallet, he handed it to the bartender, "Can I get some change? Didn't know I had it."

Walking to a small hallway, he picked up the receiver and placed a quarter and a dime in the pay phone.

"Hi, it's me," he said when, after the fifth ring, he heard the flat sound of his recorded voice and the inevitable beep, "I thought you'd be there. I'm at MT Bears ... um ... if you get this message, I wish you'd come here. I'll be here. I'm sorry about everything. Love you." He hung up the phone and headed back to the dark corner table.

Later that evening, she came into the bar, shy, reserved, like a frightened animal. He walked to her slowly and hugged her. Neither could explain why all the anger, sadness, loneliness, and resentment that they caused each other and would continue to cause one another transformed themselves into "I'm glad you came," and nothing more.

ABOUT THE AUTHOR

David Haight was born in Minneapolis and educated at Hamline University, where he received a degree in English and philosophy and later, an MFA in writing, where he was distinguished by the Guay W. Grigg Award for Excellence in Literary Study. He has been a teacher, a salesman, a car wash attendant, a terribly off-key singer in a local band, and can be seen for a total of two seconds at the end of A&E's *Biography* about F. Scott Fitzgerald. He travels to Europe semiannually and lives in Maple Grove with his fiancée, Ronica and his cat, Grapefruit.